Fremont's Promise

Faith, prospects, and dreams
in the early 1940s

Book 3

Kathryn Spurgeon

with Margaret Pope Akin

MEMORY HOUSE
PUBLISHING

Published by Memory House Publishing, LLC
Edmond, Oklahoma, U.S.A. 73034
www.memoryhousepublishing.net

Published in the United States of America

ISBN 978-1-946887-12-2 (Paperback) Christian historical fiction

Book cover design by Seedlings
First cover by Krystal Harlow
Photo Credits: Margaret Pope Akin and
Pottawatomie County Oklahoma Historical Society

Promise Series Books

by Kathryn Spurgeon
with Margaret Pope Akin

A Promise to Break
A Promise Child
Fremont's Promise
A Promise of Home

Winner of **Illumination Book Award**

Reviews for the Promise Series

"Exceptionally well-written, making it a consistently
compelling read from beginning to end…
One of those rare stories that will linger in the
mind and memory of the reader long after
the book itself has been finished."
James A. Cox, Editor-in-Chief
Midwest Book Review of *A Promise to Break*

*"You really made the book vivid
and emotional. I cried."*
Jeri William, English teacher

Fremont Pope as a boy

1939
Chapter One
April 1939

Sibyl

Music blasted through the post oak trees in the front yard, rumbling down Beard Street to Highland. A familiar Benny Goodman jazz song boomed through the air, shaking leaves to the ground while voices yelled over the noise—voices laced with laughter.

I stood under the hazy streetlight, puzzled, and glanced to the right and left. This was my mother's home all right. I tiptoed toward the side window and peeked into the large two-story house where lamps illuminated the festivities. People milled around, women dressed in finery with swanky coiffured hair and men in vests or suspenders. Dancing. A Saturday night shindig? At my mama's?

Stepping back from the window, I looked down at my dungarees, stained and torn. One of Fremont's old shirts hung on me like a feed sack. Newspaper lined the bottoms of my brogue shoes. My hair lay tight, pulled back out of my face, even though curly wisps fell all around. No makeup. No lipstick. I had spent most of the day planting irises and tending children.

My husband, Fremont, would be leaving soon for his nighttime job at Norton's. I'd driven down Shawnee's quiet, cobblestoned Main Street to

Mama's for a cup of sugar for our oatmeal in the morning. We had no eggs or bacon, but we had oatmeal, and Mama always managed to have sugar on hand.

Tears formed in my eyes, and my bottom lip quivered. My family was having a bash, and I hadn't been invited. How could they? Worse, they were having fun while I mourned my baby, Keith. He'd died just a little over a week before, and depression surrounded my heart as dank as the air around me, damp and disconnected.

I blinked back tears and turned to leave.

As I rounded the bushes toward the dark front yard, I saw a movement to my right and came to a sudden halt.

A silhouette of a man swayed and shuffled toward me making my heart thump louder than the music. He could be a criminal for all I knew, tipsy, a drunkard lost from the party. I was a small woman and wouldn't be able to defend myself.

The man took a step toward me and tripped. I jumped back, crouching behind the bushes, and then leaned forward to see better. Still in the shadows, he looked like a hobo with long, unkempt gray hair, a ragged coat, and old boots. Many jobless, penniless fellows wandered the streets.

My body tensed and I backed away. Should I run back to Mama's? Back to the bright lights and shouting people?

The man took another lunge, this time into the pale glow of the streetlight. I gasped and then sighed with relief. It was Grandpa Bennett.

I moved toward him. "Gramps! It's me, Sibyl."

Startled, he opened his eyes wide and raised his hands. "Don't hurt me. I didn't do nothing."

"It's Sibyl Pope. Your granddaughter."

"Who?" Grandpa stopped and tilted his head as if trying to understand. "Oh dearie, I'm lost as a goose. Can you help me get home?"

Grandpa's mind wandered so much these days that he often ended up a few blocks away at Richard's Drugstore or the Cozy Barbershop or Brown's Grocery. Every time, someone in the family had to find him and bring him back home.

I took Grandpa by the arm, squeezed it gently, and led him toward Mama's house where he lived. Without knocking, I barged through the front door, pulling Grandpa behind me.

No one noticed. The Persian rug Papa had bought was rolled back to reveal a wooden floor, waxed, and shined. The place smelled of liquor and cheap perfume. My sister, Marjorie, with fancy finger-wave curls and dressed in a low-cut dress with a full skirt, swirled to a lively swing dance with a partner I didn't recognize. She had returned from Phoenix a few days earlier and already found a fellow? Marjorie and her beau flirted openly, twisting together in an embrace.

Another sister, Blanche, stood nearby with a bottle held to her lips. Tall and lanky, she would soon graduate from high school. The phonograph box player stood by the north wall, spinning around and around, screeching out the tinny music while a few of Mama's boarders and neighbors stood around it, arguing about which record to play next.

"Where's Mama?" I yelled above the din of Lombardo. No one heard me, so I yelled again. "I found Grandpa wandering around outside!"

Tapping Blanche on the shoulder, I shouted into her ear, "Why is no one watching Grandpa?"

Blanche shrugged as if she couldn't hear, so I walked over and jerked the needle off the record.

Sudden silence, and then everyone turned to see what happened.

"Why'd you do that?"

"What's wrong?"

"It's Sibyl," said someone in the crowd. "You shouldn't be here! Go home!"

I stood still until quiet reigned, anger running through me. "Why was Grandpa outside this late at night?"

No one spoke.

Mama appeared from the kitchen. "What's the problem?"

My youngest sister, Frances, followed her. Surely, Mama didn't let the twelve-year-old attend a grown-up party and drink alcohol.

"Sibyl, what are you doing here?" Mama's long hair, pulled back into a loose bun, accentuated short, curly bangs. Her face showed an ageless beauty not completely passed on to her daughters.

Everyone wore fancy clothes. The women were decked out with beads and lace, while the men sported ties, vests, and high-waisted trousers as if they were dressed for a nightclub or the Blue Bird, one of the speakeasies Marjorie and I had snuck out to several years ago, long before Fremont and marriage and babies had changed everything.

I looked down at my clothes and felt the heat of shame and embarrassment spread through me. "Well, obviously, no one notified me of a get-together." My words sounded more like pity-me-whining than anger, even if both feelings jumbled inside me.

Blanche spoke up, disdain dripping from her words. "Everyone knows you don't dance or drink anymore since you became 'Little Miss Goody Two Shoes'. Of course, we didn't invite you. You should be home with your family."

The rejection stabbed me like a broken glass—sharp and painful. I stepped back. My sister's words struck their mark because according to my family, I married beneath myself. My papa, a wealthy Oklahoma bank examiner, disapproved of my husband, Fremont Pope. Papa—Malcolm Calvis Trimble, Senior—smoked Havanas, wore tailored suits, and donned expensive trilby hats.

Fremont came from different stock, growing up on the south side of Shawnee, poor as the many farmers migrating to California. My in-laws were strict Christians who didn't believe in dancing, drinking, or card playing. Hence, I had given up those activities for Fremont and the Lord, a decision that drew me closer to God, even though, when my feet tapped to the music, I sometimes missed it and wished to boogie along with the rest, but I doubted if I'd ever enjoy that kind of gaiety again.

Grandpa Bennett wandered away from my grasp. A natural-born musician, he picked up his fiddle and began to play an old Yankee Doodle song, dancing a little jig while he played. Tall and good-looking when young, he still had dark blue eyes and a head full of hair that glowed white as cotton. Once nearly six feet tall, he now bent over with age.

After a few chords on the fiddle, he grew tired and tripped over the notes. The groans from the dancing group could be heard above Grandpa's playing because, evidently, the merrymakers preferred Glenn Miller or Bing Crosby, anything but fiddle-playing. Grandpa dropped his violin and leaned against the wall, as unwelcome and out-of-place as I was.

I turned away, feeling awkward around my family, unaccepted and unwanted. Why were close relationships so difficult? Why did they hurt so much? My emotions flared and hot tears sprang to my eyes as I stumbled toward the door.

"Take Grandpa to bed," Mama told Blanche as she ushered me out to the front porch.

I heard my sisters' words behind us before the loud music began again, "Never mind her. She's just a crybaby. She'll get over it."

Did she know the hurt in those words?

Mama put her hand on my shoulder. "Dear, we're just celebrating Marjorie's return from Phoenix. You're still grieving and don't belong here. Go home to your sweet little family." She shrugged and clenched her mouth tight. "Life must go on, no matter what. Do what I've done since your papa left me—pretend life is bearable."

She paused, then spit out her next words as if they'd been seasoned with bitter herbs. "I'll always hate that man."

I cringed and tears scorched my face. My broken heart wouldn't find any understanding here..

Chapter Two

Fremont

Margaret, my five-and-a-half-year-old, balanced on a stool and rinsed potatoes under running water while I stood beside her and cut them into sections. "You're doing a great job, Little Miss Daddy's Helper."

The grin that spread across her face was worth a million gold nuggets.

I placed the potatoes in a pan over a low fire for our later-than-usual supper. Judson, the most rambunctious five-year-old in Pottawatomie County, jumped around the living room like popcorn in a skillet, spreading kernels all the way to the North Canadian River and back.

Sibyl had driven across town to her mother's house and promised to be back before I needed the Chevy to get to my night job at Norton's Motor Sales, but, as often happened, she was running late. Knowing she'd struggled with Keith's death all day and needed a few minutes to herself, I had agreed to finish supper.

"Go get your pajamas on," I told Judson for the umpteenth time. "Or you'll be slathered with slippery kisses."

He rabbit-hopped into the bedroom, chased by his big sister.

I turned back to the cabinet to see what else I could offer and found a tin of Spam, mushy meat I hated but the rest of the family would devour. As I slashed it into slices, I nicked my finger, and blood leaked out. I hurried and washed my finger and wrapped it with a clean cloth. When I finished, I resumed cooking, laying the thick Spam slices into the skillet to fry.

7

The children returned and I noticed Margaret's hair was a tangled mess and Judson's pajamas were buttoned wrong. When Margaret walked past me, I leaned down and looked into her eyes—sky blue eyes identical to mine. "Child, you dressed too hurriedly because your gown is wrong side out. Do you want me to help you fix it?"

She nodded and I followed her into the bedroom and turned her pajama gown right side out before pulling it back over her head, tickling her as I did so. We slipped back into the kitchen.

Wearing his plaid pajamas, Judson came over to me, and I fixed his buttons and ruffled the mop of hair that fell around his face. "I'm hungry," he said. Our overactive kid, who had a bottomless pit for a stomach, bounced like the last few kernels of popcorn.

"Here, son. I'll get you some milk." I guided him to a chair and poured from the jar of milk my mother gave us.

After I put the food on the table, I slid into the seat and blessed the spread with a short prayer of thanksgiving. For a few minutes, we ate in silence.

"When's mommy coming home? I want to show her my new dolly dress."

"Soon. She'll be back soon." I had hoped she'd be back by now.

Judson jumped down and loped past me.

"Son, come here and finish your meal." I snagged the boy and wiggled his nose before plopping him back down in his chair. "Slow down, child. Life's too short to rush it." Although he tried to be obedient, he couldn't contain his bursting energy, and my scolding would only slow him down for a few minutes.

After the meal, I took Margaret and Judson into the bathroom to brush their hair and teeth before tucking them into bed and listening to their prayers. Needing reassurance because of the empty baby crib, their hugs lasted longer than usual. Margaret snuggled in my arms, her bouncy dark curls brushing my skin. My heart lurched at the emptiness in the room and I held her tight.

I kissed them goodnight and left the room to put the dirty dishes in the sink. When the whispers from their bedroom quieted, I heaved a sigh, slid onto the worn-out couch, and plunked my stocking feet onto the cheap coffee table. My eyelids drooped more every minute, so heavy with tiredness I could hardly keep them open.

***

Sibyl stomped into the quiet room as if to make a statement.

I sprang to my feet, stretched, and walked over to kiss her on the cheek. She turned away, likely assuming I had spent the last half hour lounging like a sleepy cat—which I had. Her reaction gave a good indication of her mood.

"Honey, what happened? Is something wrong?" I followed her into the children's bedroom where she kissed the sleeping children.

Sibyl didn't answer as we returned to the kitchen, and that was when I noticed she looked downright unkempt and exhausted, so unlike the dapper lady of a few months ago. The dollar and a half I earned for eight hours of night duty barely covered rent, food, and utility bills. I was doing all I possibly could, but guilt weighed as heavy as a yoke on my shoulders, knowing I couldn't keep my family looking presentable. I wasn't able to make everything right, even though my greatest desire was to keep my little family wrapped in a safe cocoon.

She glanced down at the cold plate of food before she muttered, "Oh. I forgot the sugar."

"We can eat toast for breakfast." I winked, trying to cheer her up.

Even though we'd been married for six years, I still could *not* decipher this woman. When I met Sibyl, I was a penniless hobo in ragged clothes, lying on the ground at the Santa Fe Train Depot, beaten to a pulp. She was a banker's daughter waiting for her well-to-do father to come home from a business trip. Like a lovely, compassionate angel, she appeared out of the cloudy locomotive steam, looking down at my bloody face with concern in her eyes, her empathy a rarity in the days of every-man-for-himself.

Sibyl still claimed my handsome face and piercing blue eyes made her heart flutter, while her sad eyes reminded me of the softness of sweet black-eyed Susans. I was glad we loved each other so much or our marriage might not have survived all we'd gone through.

"You're upset because you forgot the sugar?"

Chopping her Spam into small pieces made me think she might not like it any more than I did. "No. Mama's having a party. After Keith's horrible death, she's throwing a shindig." I could hear the hurt in her voice, whiny like a cat crying in the dark when it's afraid, but I didn't let on I'd heard it.

"Why would she do that?"

Sibyl put her fork down. "To celebrate Marjorie coming home. But the problem isn't *why* she's partying. The problem is that she doesn't care what we're going through."

"Would you have gone if she'd asked you?" Neither of us would have been comfortable at one of Mrs. Mable Trimble's parties, and not just because of our baby's recent death, but also because of our beliefs. I'd often felt her family's jabs, snide remarks, and accusations, and the thought of Sibyl's distress weighed as heavily on me as a bowl of day-old mush, a distasteful thought if I ever had one.

"You don't understand. They're rejecting me. It's like I don't exist in their world." Sibyl mumbled to herself, pushing her supper around on her plate.

I had only a short time before skedaddling off to work and would've preferred a quiet evening without all the hubbub, but it didn't happen. I poured myself another cup of coffee and sat down again. "Your mama's shindig may have been hurtful, especially so soon after burying her grandchild," I said, "but you can't fix her. Maybe you should let it go."

"Let it go? I can't let it go. She's my mother! She should know better."

"Honey, being upset doesn't do any good, not for you, not for us," I said gently. "Stay calm and put it behind you. It'll blow over like it usually does." I wished that were true, but I'd seen my wife's feelings get hurt too many times.

She rose and looked over her shoulder, throwing me a vexed look. "You're not listening. It isn't just about tonight. They disapprove of everything I do. They don't want me around." She turned to face me and placed her hands on her hips, an adorable stance if I must say so. "Now, why are you looking at me like that?"

I wasn't sure how I was looking at her, but I knew she didn't like it.

Understanding my wife's relationship with her family was difficult because her parents were impulsive and volatile. She found their behavior—divorce and abandonment, bickering and bitterness—embarrassing. At the same time, she sought their approval and didn't want me to think less of them. As for me, I resented their treatment of my wife, though I kept my feelings hidden—staying strong for my lady.

"Did I tell you Marjorie was there? Partying along with the rest of them? She's been home from Phoenix for two days and already made up with Mama but couldn't find time to come see us. I can forgive her for not making it back for Keith's funeral, but she's married and trifling with other men. Why can't she settle down and pay attention to her son instead of gallivanting around? Doesn't she know how important children are?"

The image of our lost baby hovered between us. Not that he ever went far.

"Maybe you should talk to her and explain how you feel." I rose from the small metal breakfast table to put the plates in the sink. I needed to leave for work soon, and tomorrow I would sleep until late in the afternoon. We had little time together, and I hated wasting it on complaints. "Your sister might need a little direction."

"For a quiet man, you're suggesting I talk to Marjorie?" Sibyl shook her head and stood to put away the milk. "I doubt if she'd listen to me."

Sometimes my answers to Sibyl's problems irritated her and made matters worse.

Today had not ended well, and it was time to leave for work. While Sibyl finished cleaning the kitchen, I shaved with Burma-Shave and put Brylcreem on my hair, combing the dark curls back away from my face. Liking to look neat, I changed into clean khakis and tied my freshly shined boots before trekking into the living room where I sat in my favorite wing back chair, trying to collect myself. Sibyl appeared in the doorway.

"Honey, come here," I said and pulled her to my lap. She felt vulnerable beside a husky, barrel-chested man like me. "You're a beautiful lady, and you still make my heart flutter." Naturally, she'd been sensitive this week after Keith's death, and I didn't expect her pain to go away instantly, but the Trimble's party convinced me that we needed to get away. Their lack of concern for my wife irked me, and we had to escape the heartaches.

I let her tears soak my shirt, patted her hair, and wiped her wet face. So much for my clean shirt. I could feel her relax in my arms and a few minutes later, she leaned away from me, her large brown eyes looking grateful for the relief.

After a few minutes, she said softly, her voice holding more pain than I wanted to hear. "I don't know if I can handle these disappointments. I thought my family would understand I needed them after losing Keith. Appeasing my mother takes all my effort, and there're so many things I want to do with my life." She paused, shaking her head in despair. "Someday, I hope to follow the Lord without worry of being hurt."

I grieved as much as Sibyl did but in my own way, mulling over why the Lord had taken our baby. Ignoring the open wound and pushing the ache inside, I sucked in a deep breath to remain calm. "I promised when we married that I'd take care of you, and I will. Even if that means moving all the way to California."

"You promise?"

I ran my fingers through the curls around her shoulders and then cupped her chin. My dear sweet wife. "You better believe it. I promise we'll leave this chaotic life and get away from people who hurt us. We've put up with this for six long years now. Your family makes you cry every time you see them, and we can't live like this anymore. We have to move. We have to move soon."

She shook her finger at me. "I'm going to hold you to that."

"We *will* move. I promise."

After a lingering hug, I told her goodbye and walked slowly through the front door and down the concrete porch steps. After opening the door of my Chevrolet, I climbed into the driver's seat where I leaned my head against the steering wheel, dazed. Overwhelmed. Would our faith be enough to get us through? I desperately wanted to protect my wife from the despondency that pulled her down like quicksand.

I prayed. I prayed that grief would not destroy us. And I determined, then and there, it was the right time for a move away from Shawnee.

In the meantime, I had to find another job before Sibyl changed her mind about leaving.

Chapter Three
May 1939

Sibyl

My sister Blanche went ahead with graduation plans as if nothing had happened, as if her nephew Keith, my sweet baby, had not just left this earth. My heart might have been broken into slivers of crystal, but I couldn't blame Blanche, even if she was a rude sort of person. She was an eighteen-year-old senior with her whole life before her, and high school graduation happens only once.

Blanche needed an evening dress to wear to her prom. After her divorce, Mama had converted her home into a boarding house to provide enough funds to pay the bills, which left no room to open the sewing machine and spread out fabric. Therefore, Blanche and her ideas came to my house. I didn't mind because it would help me forget the sadness and allow a chance to build a closer relationship with her, which had been strained lately.

Most of my younger sisters' clothing were hand-me-downs or re-sewn, second-hand purchases. Since neither of us had money to buy yards of new material, and I hadn't been out in public since Keith's death, I encouraged Blanche to walk through the aisles at Sears & Roebucks, noting new trends without purchasing anything. She came back, exuberant, describing the latest styles and dressed-up mannequins, commenting on the silky material and padded shoulders and new millinery.

We needed money for a castoff dress to re-make. Fremont and I kept a wooden Havana cigar box on top of our cabinet where we saved nickels and dimes for the future, but I didn't want to touch that, so Blanche and I plotted a way to earn money.

Several neighborhood women wanted their hair pin-curled to cover the bald spots on top of their heads. Over the next week, Blanche curled several ladies' hair for a quarter each. With that money, she purchased a dress from a second-hand clothing store. We discussed how to redesign it and use the remaining money for thread and buttons.

Mother Pope, Fremont's big-hearted mom, offered to watch Margaret and Judson while Blanche and I sewed. The brisk walk to take them to my in-laws' house brought back memories, and when I arrived home, I burst in the front door ready to do anything, even tackle a runaway horse to get my thoughts off my sorrows.

Blanche lounged on the sofa as if she planned to stay there all day. "Thanks for offering to make me a prom dress."

"Oh, no you don't. You took fashion designer classes at high school, so *you* will do the work." I set my sewing basket on the counter and scrambled through the corn pincushion, wooden spools of thread, and packages of needles before I pulled out a pair of scissors and a seam ripper. "You need to learn how to stitch a dress."

Blanche roused, and we shoved the coffee table back and sat in the middle of the floor, where we ripped out every seam of the castoff dress and laid the material flat.

That part of the project complete, I leaned back against the sofa and stretched my arms overhead. "It'd be quicker with Mama's help. She's a good seamstress, you know. She's made more than a few dresses over the years."

Blanche's face lit up. "Remember that checkered dress she made me? I loved it. I wore it twice, washed it, and hung it out to dry where you used to hang your stockings."

"Over the stove?" I raised my eyes, guessing what might have happened.

"Yeah. It fell off the line into the embers and caught fire just like your stockings did. I had to throw it away."

We laughed together at the disaster and had more fun than I'd anticipated. I was glad to relax and ignore the heartache that wouldn't let up. The dress project also helped me forget Mama's party, which neither of us mentioned.

After cutting a new pattern, I began sewing, peddling the treadle sewing machine at the speed of Fremont's Chevrolet. The clickity-clack sound kept us from talking until the dress was almost complete. Blanche tried on the formal and, since she was taller than most women, I had barely enough material to lengthen it. I pinned it with pins from the ear of corn pincushion I had crocheted using Grandma Bennett's sample. With a black velvet fitted waist, puff sleeves, and a white taffeta A-line skirt, the gown turned out prettier than I'd expected. It looked like a dream on her.

Blanche pranced around like a fashion model, swirling in a circle. "I look like Greta Garbo," she said. "That starlet makes sexy pictures and saves the day. She's dazzling. I dream about her when I see her picture in the paper."

"Blanche Harriet!" I said, "Don't even say it."

"I could have been a famous movie star if only I'd had a more assertive mother." Blanche wiggled her skinny hips while looking at herself in the wall mirror. "Honestly, Mama should have pushed me into it."

"Pushed you?" I couldn't imagine anyone pushing Blanche to do anything. Even though tall, thin, and dramatic, I didn't think she was actress material—not what the public would call attractive or endearing. But she did obsess over movies, saving pennies to walk downtown to see the same flick a dozen times, memorizing every line and facial expression, and re-hashing the scene to the annoyance of us all. "How are the graduation plans? Is Mama buying you a senior class ring?"

"She says we can't afford it." There was a catch in Blanche's voice as she stepped out of the beautiful prom dress. "Mama wouldn't buy me a Caldron yearbook either. I think she resents having to take care of us by herself, but don't worry. I gave her the cold shoulder."

"As Fremont's mother says, 'Worry often gives a small thing a big shadow.'" I was proud of Blanche. She'd worked extra hard to make good grades, so I pulled out my black pocketbook and counted a dollar in change. Not enough. Should I use our savings for Blanche? I hesitated. Would Fremont understand how much I needed to help my sister? I pulled down our cigar box from the kitchen shelf and poured out the nickels and dimes we'd saved. I methodically counted two dollars from the funds and handed the total three dollars to Blanche. "I can't afford a class ring, but this should be enough for a yearbook."

Blanche's eyes widened, and her bitter voice softened. "That's the nicest thing anyone's ever done for me. No one really cares."

She grabbed me into an awkward hug and ran out the door.

I wanted to help Mama and my sisters, as well as the dozens of children begging on the street. If I had the money, I'd feed every starving vagabond, but unfortunately, we had only enough to survive ourselves. Our box of savings didn't hold enough to purchase Margaret a new dress, much less move away from Shawnee, and at this rate, it might be years. My sanity couldn't wait that long.

I shook myself to reality.

Right now, I couldn't think about helping people or moving. I had to pick up the remnants of material and thread scattered throughout the house before the children returned home.

Before my *two* children returned. How was I going to live without my third?

***

Blanche came by the following week to tell me about the prom.

I lay on the sofa, depression a factor in my day-to-day life. Reading the classified note about Keith in the morning newspaper had brought me further down. "*We wish to thank our friends and neighbors for their kindness shown us during the illness and death of our beloved son and grandson. We especially thank the Norton Motor Co., the members of the First Baptist Church, the Calvary Baptist Church, and the Murrow Chapter of the Eastern Star.*" It was signed: Mr. and Mrs. Fremont Pope,

Mr. and Mrs. W.O. Pope, Mrs. Mable Trimble. Papa was left out, though he'd been included in the newspaper's death announcement.

Would this heartache ever end?

"Are you sorry you didn't have a date?" I set down the newspaper and shook the gloom out of my head.

"Nah. I'm too tall for most guys."

"How was your ride with Mr. Collins?" Their next-door neighbor had offered to drive Blanche and a girlfriend to the prom.

"Don't ask. The car was as filthy as a cow pen."

"He works out of his car, dear."

"No, Sibyl. You don't understand. He spread newspaper in the back seat to cover the chicken poop. It was no Cinderella carriage, I assure you. Oh, by the way, Irene was there."

I raised my eyebrows hoping she'd continue. Fremont's sister, the same age as Blanche, was also graduating from Shawnee High. I had encouraged them for several years to become friends—to no avail.

"Irene's gone batty over chaps. That girl was a dancing fool to Callaway's jitterbug, buzzing like a bee from guy to guy. Dressed to the hilt. She wouldn't speak to me, especially with all the eligible males in the room."

I almost smiled, suspecting Blanche envied Irene and the men she attracted. "Did you enjoy the dance?"

"I did. And my dress was perfect, and you won't believe this. Mama took us to Mammoth's Department Store yesterday." A broad grin spread across her face. "We bought new clothes. I got the nicest Sunday dress I've ever had, and Frances got more clothes than I did, like always, of course."

"How did Mama pay for them?" I moved to the edge of the couch, alarmed. Mama didn't have that kind of money. Had she lost her mind?

"She charged it all to Papa. Can you imagine the look on his face when he finds out?"

Frances, I knew, did not have enough school clothes. She attended Jefferson Elementary, the one-story building on Kickapoo, replacing the massive two-story school destroyed by a tornado in '24. Since Frances got by with hand-me-down frocks and worn-out oxfords, I hoped Mama bought her some decent apparel. "Why did Mama do that?"

"He got behind on child support, and her lawyer advised her to go shopping." Blanche raised her eyebrows as if they'd played a joke on Papa.

"Behind on payments again?" Surely, Mama wouldn't have to file another lawsuit.

"Yep. She's worried she might have to pay the clothing bill, but so far, no complaints from the store. Papa will have a fit when he finds out."

"And after all that scrambling around to make you a prom dress." I smiled, knowing they couldn't have afforded an expensive formal even if she'd charged it to Papa.

Blanche shrugged as if nothing mattered, but I knew it did. She needed acceptance and love the same way my children needed it. The same way I did. I yearned to give my family limitless adoration, but how could I teach anyone to be loving if I had never seen it exemplified between my parents?

Mama nagged Papa every time she saw him. She needed more child support. He hadn't come by to see his daughters in months. He was an unfit father. He'd cheated on her. My divorced parents despised each other, and havoc ruled whenever they happened to be in the same vicinity. Tension infused every encounter, every happenchance meeting between them, and neither seemed to realize what was important.

Losing a child had certainly narrowed my focus onto what was important. I yearned to move our little family away from this dysfunctional family and give them a better life. I wanted to teach them about real love, which I couldn't do when my parents' issues kept me upset all the time.

For me, showing love would be more challenging than making a princess dress out of someone's castoff clothing.

Chapter Four

Fremont

Malcolm Calvis Trimble, Senior, occasionally dropped by our house without warning. My father-in-law's visits made Sibyl as jittery as Dad's clackity pickup, the noisy clunk getting worse every time he hit a pothole.

Mr. Trimble's behavior after Keith died stung us at our weakest, but we decided forgiveness would be better than retribution, and we kept him in our lives. As for me, I prayed godly love would burst his balloon of arrogance and reconcile him to the Lord—mostly for Sibyl's sake.

I was relaxed in my favorite cushioned chair with my feet up when Mr. Trimble entered with his usual pomp and intimidation, fancy dressed as always. I leaped up and caught myself envying his slick pin-striped suit, trilby hat, and glowing white shoes.

"Just came from Blanche's graduation at the auditorium," he said. The Shawnee High School, a three-story red brick building on the corner of Union and Highland Streets, was not large enough to hold everyone. Therefore, the graduation had been moved to the new gym-like Shawnee Municipal Auditorium, which had concrete bleachers along three sides and a stage on the north end, large enough to hold a crowd.

The town of Shawnee was settled from surplus Indian land during the land run of 1891. The area boomed until the depression hit hard in the mid-30s. Townspeople claimed the worst was now over and the county would begin to grow again, but I wasn't so sure.

Mr. Trimble ignored me and turned to Sibyl, who rose to face him. "I didn't see *you* at the graduation," he said. "Surely, you can manage to do your duty."

Going to our sisters' graduation had been out of the question. After losing our baby, Sibyl and I were not ready to sit in a crowded room of strangers clapping every two minutes as someone crossed the stage. Grief still engulfed us. Losing a child can change a person, push them to withdraw inside themselves.

Tension filled the room, and Sibyl looked at me before answering. "It's been hard, Papa." She dropped back into a chair, looking defeated.

I heaved out loud. I had heard Mr. Trimble's stern voice for years and could do nothing about it. Weariness penetrated my body from frustration with him. Growing up in a fun-loving, casual environment, I didn't understand his sternness with his daughter. This man showed no empathy whatsoever, and I resolved to move Sibyl away from his imposing presence.

During the early 30s, Mr. Trimble had traveled across Oklahoma auditing banks. He'd had a hand in closing dozens of them and putting people out of work, and I couldn't think he showed much sympathy. I could take or leave the man, except I believed even someone like him needed the peace Jesus offers.

No one could explain grief to a man so callous as Mr. Trimble, so instead, I said, "My sister Irene also graduated. Since my parents went to the ceremony, they couldn't babysit Margaret and Judson, so we stayed home."

"Where are the rascals anyway?" Mr. Trimble looked around the room for our children.

"They're napping."

I jiggled the coins in my pocket and looked out the window at Mr. Trimble's shiny new vehicle parked on the street. Gladys—Mr. Trimble's wife, Sibyl's stepmother—sat in the front seat looking straight ahead. The outline of her wavy hairdo looked stiff as steel.

Mr. Trimble came and stood beside me. "How do you like my new car?" He bought a Lincoln Continental—but Sibyl said he hadn't paid child support?

I threw my chin back and examined the fancy machine closer. Mr. Trimble knew my passion for vehicles. I loved mechanical work and admired any shiny slick frame that promised an industrial future while the dust howled around us. But automobiles were not my first thoughts that day. Had not been for weeks. Keeping my family from drowning was foremost. "Gladys is welcome to come in and sit a spell."

"Oh, she's tired and wants to rest in the car. We can't stay long." As usual, he didn't care to sit down when I asked.

This nicely dressed man put me on edge. I didn't want to think badly about my father-in-law, but I couldn't be myself with him or joke around because of the strain between him and Sibyl. I wanted to give him the benefit of the doubt, however, he had not only abandoned his wife and daughters during this awful depression, but he'd married again as quickly as possible and refused to support his youngest children. Any of those situations would be enough to make me wary of him.

My family and Sibyl's family were so different. My parents were relaxed, warm, and God-fearing. The Trimbles pretended to be jovial while harboring bitterness like a two-edged sword. I had never known bitterness until I met them, except maybe the brunt of someone's bitterness when I got beat up by the railroad tracks as a hobo. I was torn between love for my relatives and loyalty to hers. Such opposites.

Mr. Trimble's voice grated as he continued. "I was pleased Blanche received so many awards. And third highest in her class. Can you imagine? Third. And a college scholarship. That's my girl." He paused as if thinking over the graduation. "Like Gladys told me, I should have expected her to get awards because she has the brilliant Trimble mind, taking after my side of the family." Not usually free with compliments, he pulled his shoulders back as if to congratulate himself instead of Blanche.

Papa acted like he believed Blanche, the daughter who spoke back to him, sassed him, and insulted him, to be more intelligent and wittier than the rest of his children. Years earlier, Sibyl graduated a year early from high school with high honors and went to Cheatham Business School, inheriting her father's analytical mind. I didn't recall him praising her.

"The keynote speaker wasn't as good as the one at OBU last year. I heard FBI Director Hoover's speech. He and OBU's President Raley are in cahoots, I warrant." Mr. Trimble turned toward Sibyl. "Your mindless mother was sitting on the highest tier in the auditorium by a propped-open window when Blanche Harriett's name was called. And that nincompoop almost fell backward out the window when they announced the honors."

Sibyl gasped. "Mama almost fell out of the window?"

"Thankfully, someone caught your daft mother before she fell."

His swagger almost choked me, and I pulled in a deep breath to stay composed. No other person incited my nerves as he did and I turned to leave the room and let Sibyl deal with her father.

Mr. Trimble shouted over my shoulder. "Son, did you see the Kodak folding camera I gave Blanche for graduation?"

I turned around but didn't respond. I couldn't offend my wife, didn't want to be unkind, so I nodded.

Still standing, Mr. Trimble reared back with his arms crossed over his chest. "To my knowledge, it's superior to the Brownie box camera. Exposure is made by a shutter-release button on the top, and it uses a bellow to fold up."

Neither Sibyl nor I repeated Blanche's statement when she opened the gift. She had complained loudly. "What he's doing is flat-out wrong. I don't need anything from him. However, I suppose I can keep the camera."

Mr. Trimble scanned our house—the worn floor, the second-hand furniture, the toys strewn about. Our low income was evident, and I felt my face turn red in shame.

"At least I'm able to give her a decent gift," Mr. Trimble said. "I hope she values the camera because I purchased it used from a banker friend and paid good money for it too."

"I'm sure she'll appreciate it." I took a deep breath and pulled Sibyl to my side.

Mr. Trimble looked at me with his beady little eyes. Never mistaken for a nice person, he'd purchased a used camera and congratulated himself on the money he'd saved. That man needed to leave us alone to our grief. I regretted my awful thoughts the moment they came and prayed for forgiveness. I was no better than he was.

He stepped toward the door. "I doubt she appreciated it. My children have never appreciated my views of this world. They don't see that Utopia is coming as soon as we get rid of the bad people."

Sibyl's whole body seemed to collapse, to shrink in size. Did Mr. Trimble think we were bad people?

As I worked to remain composed, I realized my father-in-law's rude behavior ran deeper than I would ever understand. And though I ignored his cutting words, I could see their sharp edges cut Sibyl worse than a hunting knife, withering her essence, and I felt the sudden urge to protect her from his insensitive visits. She needed me, especially during this time of grieving.

Most of the Trimbles were bold and smart. An adventurous lady, Mr. Trimble's mother, Lavelet Blanche Andruss, was known to be much smarter than she looked, the same as Sibyl's sister, who was named after her. Blanche was brilliant, but no looker. On the other hand, my Sibyl was smart *and* a beauty queen, carrying herself with the dignity of a princess.

My princess needed me. She needed to move away from a father who had never supported her, disregarded her, and whose past behavior had caused the family so much heartache. My compulsion to move grew stronger.

I put my arms around Sibyl's slim shoulder to shield her. Looking at me, her face a picture of stress, she whispered, "I'm all right." Then she turned to her papa, and fibbed, lying to appease him. "Blanche liked the camera. Said it was the best gift she's ever received."

Mr. Trimble almost smiled at the words. Appreciation from Blanche was unlikely, and we all knew it. Sibyl couldn't help trying to please her father, but the effort drew her spirit into a depressing hole, and I couldn't let her stay there.

Mr. Trimble might never be a loving man, even if I prayed for a thousand years. Prayers. He needed more prayers. Like we all did.

Chapter Five

July 1939

Sibyl

I'd put off gathering the last belongings of my precious little boy long enough. It had only been five weeks, but it seemed like forever since we'd lost him. Today, July the third, Keith would have been two years old.

A jubilant and clever child, he'd been a spirited boy loved by all who knew him. He accepted every individual he met, jabbered to old ladies, snickered with his siblings, and hugged our pastor. And to me, he was all things beautiful. Keith would forever carry a big part of me. His sickness and death had ripped my heart as if it were made of paper and left it lying on the floor to be trampled on.

I went through the house and gathered Keith's belongings. They went into two piles: one to keep and one to throw away. I pulled his clothes from the bottom drawer, the remaining items after the church ladies had come through and disposed of what they could. I found a pair of shoes under the bed. A teddy bear in the closet. A red toy truck. Warm flannel pajamas. A blanket I held to my nose and breathed in, tears forming in my eyes.

I pulled his metal sippy cup with a handle out of the kitchen cabinet. It wasn't just any sippy cup, but the one I received when he was born. It had *Skippy* written on the outside and a picture of the cartoon character of the same name. Keith also had a special little yellow bowl from which he loved to eat fresh berries and drink milk until he found the kitten picture

25

on the bottom. I held that bowl to my bosom before putting it in the 'keep' stack.

The white, heart-designed tiny baby shoes he wore his first few months, the same ones worn by Margaret and Judson when they were small, I would keep forever. Maybe someday I'd have another child who could wear them. Then there were pictures of Keith, some with Margaret and Judson, some with Fremont, and some with the whole family. Where could I keep them safe?

I dragged my steamer trunk out of the closet—the one Mama had given us for a wedding present six years ago. The treasured brown leather trunk with brass trim held our family's heirlooms and I was certain that, if I searched long enough, I'd find a dark pit at the bottom hiding family secrets.

I yearned to run to Mama and unload my heartaches, cry on her shoulder, and reminisce about the good ole days, but she was too busy to approach. She didn't understand why I still grieved. What would it take to get her attention?

I opened the trunk gingerly, cautious as if a trap had been set to catch me unaware. I organized the belongings lying inside. Heirlooms. Tintype pictures. Embroidered linens. Grandma Cordelia Clay's Bible.

Judson played outside, as usual, while Margaret sat on the floor beside me, her ankle socks and oxfords tucked under her dress, her face stoic, and her grief locked inside.

"Do you miss Keith?"

She nodded yes. As a big sister, she had probably felt helpless, sitting beside his sickbed during his last days. Oh, the memories. I recalled Keith's funeral, Margaret wearing her turquoise silk pleated full skirt, her large blue eyes holding tears.

I hugged her and wiped her wet face.

Devastating pain for our little family.

I placed Keith's keepsakes on top of the other items, and my tears splattered onto the lid as I closed it. Closing that trunk felt like closing a part of my soul. My baby. My little one—gone. I could not whisper his name without wondering where he had vanished to and when I'd see him again. *Keith.*

Fremont

Thinking of Keith could send Sibyl into a tailspin quicker than a lightning bolt. While I held my sorrow inside, her grief flowed outward. One day she appeared quiet and withdrawn, and the next she would burst into tears, sobbing until her body shook. My wife's emotions were up and down like a wind-blown seesaw, so much that even church activities held no appeal for her. Blazes. Until her grief lessened, she could hardly leave the house, much less move away from Shawnee. What was I thinking—wanting to move so quickly?

The whole week that would have marked Keith's second birthday, Sibyl had been despondent. Her preoccupation with helping Blanche had aided her through the first month after the baby's death, but now she fell into a chasm of memories. She couldn't seem to focus on daily tasks such as cooking, giving the children baths, or even washing her hair and rolling it in rags. I took notice but couldn't reassure her to get up and go on.

Depression is a hard taskmaster.

I enjoyed my job at Norton Motors, helping the mechanics when they couldn't solve a problem and doing mechanical jobs on the side for extra cash. Wrestling with tin cars like they were cardboard puzzles could keep me focused for hours. Recently, though, I'd had to cut back the hours and rush home early from work to tend the house and kids, not sure what I'd find each day.

That morning after getting home from a long night's work, I found Sibyl standing at the kitchen sink wearing a ragged robe and staring out the window. It might not be a good day. "It's not fair to make you and the kids go through this," she said without turning around. "I wish I were a better wife and mother."

I plopped into a metal chair and began untying my brogans without looking around at the disastrous room, the stack of dirty dishes, the trail of dirt on the floor. "Honey, you don't have to apologize. You're a good woman."

Sibyl turned to face me—her eyes full of sadness. "I feel guilty about wanting your attention when you come home. You listen to me for hours." Tears rushed down her face.

"Where are Margaret and Judson?" Sibyl didn't need to answer because I heard squeals from their bedroom, sounds of giggles and mirth, the normal sounds of children playing. At least they were recovering.

I stood, set my boots by the back door, then turned to Sibyl and wiped the tears from her face, "Looks like a ton of bricks sits on your shoulders. I wish I knew what you needed."

I assumed she didn't need to know about my struggles or that my heart also had a massive hole inside since Keith died. She needed for me to stay unruffled, strong against her weakness. I couldn't let her see my pain.

Sibyl followed me into the living room, and I dropped into my favorite wingback chair. My shoulders sagged, my weariness matching hers. Our only hope was to trust God to heal our hearts. Somehow, Keith's death had brought my focus back to Christ and my need for him. The Lord could help us both. "Honey let's go back to our old church—to Calvary. We haven't been to a service in weeks, and there's no reason not to go."

"I can't work for God right now." Sibyl shook her head vigorously before she slid onto the edge of the sofa. Her voice sounded like an angry animal defending itself, gritty with underlying tones of threat. "I don't have a drop to give—not after all we've gone through. What can I do for Jesus? I'm in no shape to help others. Why, I can't even help myself."

I moved to the sofa and scooted next to her. "The good Lord will take care of us." Even though I believed those words, maintaining balance seemed impossible, and the more I thought about continuing as before, the less strength I had to cope.

Sibyl leaned away and looked at me, her brows furrowed. "I'm torn. Sometimes I want to leave this town and begin a new life, and other times I want to bury my head and never come up for breath. You probably don't understand."

"I feel a tug too. It's difficult to know what God wants from us right now, but I trust him. He'll show us the right time to leave." I caressed her soft hair. "We can't quit listening to him."

"Where's the faith that carried me through the last few years?" Her voice rose, and, if honest, I would ask the same question of myself if I had the courage. My faith went as deep as Grandpa's well, but circumstances pulled doubt to the top.

"We have to keep trusting God is in the middle of this."

My wife seemed close to blowing over in the wind, so I pulled back my feelings, wanting to be the one who stood steady against life's unpredictable storms.

"I'm not ready to attend any women's meetings or go to any covered dish luncheons," she confessed, "or sing in the choir—in case that's what you're thinking." She put her head on my chest. "I can't even help my family—how can I help others?"

Pulling her close, I rocked her back and forth. "Honey, you don't have to do anything. It's not about what we can do for God. Church is a healing place, and we both need encouragement right now."

***

I was right, at least this time. I knew where we needed to go—Calvary Baptist Church, the southside church on Farrell Street where my family had attended for years.

We walked through the big wide double doors and passed the stairs at the right going up to the unused balcony. We crowded onto the hardwood back pew for the Sunday night service and my heart swelled with gratitude. It may have been difficult to go back after our tragic spring, but it felt right.

I squeezed Margaret's hand and pulled Judson toward me to keep him quiet. It was a song service, no preaching. Many of my favorite hymns lulled me into a peaceful contentment and reminded me of the truth. *Amazing Grace. Rock of Ages. Love Lifted Me.* Hymns I'd heard over and over since I was a tot.

After the service finished, I stood and shook hands with my good buddy, Doug Douglas, but before we could discuss anything, Dad stepped to my side and slapped me on the back. "You doin' okay, kid?"

Those words made me want to cry, but I nodded. I'd make it. I'd be strong like him.

Before I could say much of anything, church people surrounded us. Kind words from family and friends lifted my spirit, and I knew we weren't alone through our sorrow.

Across the small auditorium, I spotted my mother, a buxom, white-headed woman dressed neatly. Maybe she was the reason I liked to dress with care. She stood stately, her shoulders back. She turned, saw our family, and began to make her way toward us between the pews, nodding to folks or stopping to say a word to friends, the light in her eyes evident even from where we stood gathering our belongings.

Mother stopped in front of Sibyl and held her arms out for a hug as I stood close enough to hear their conversation. "Glad to see you in church, dear," Mother said. "Glad you came back."

Sibyl's voice was quiet, and I strained to hear. "I've been so busy. House, kids, family upheavals. I can't think about anything except surviving."

"And you're grieving too." Mother's voice held sympathy like a solemn bell tolling far off in the distance. "At some point, dear, you must let God show you His plans for your life. Tragedy doesn't have to define you. Don't sit on the sidelines. You're too spunky for that."

"I feel the opposite of spunky these days." Her laughter sounded like a cry. "But I'll think about it."

"Good. And consider praying about it, too. He'll show you the way."

I was glad Mother took an interest in Sibyl, wanting the two most important women in my life to care about each other. I had not told her of our impending move. She would be heartbroken. I had seen the pain after the loss of her grandchild.

I might never understand the good Lord's ways, but his presence in my family and this small church could lift a rock wall out of a sinkhole. I prayed we were strong enough to pull through and follow wherever he might lead, even if that meant leaving the caring people in this town.

Mother Pope leaned down and spoke to Margaret and Judson and then turned and gave me a big hug. Mother's hug felt like a warm quilt draped around my shoulders, like coming home. This wonderful, godly woman, the one who brought me into the world and taught me to stay calm in crises and laugh at unexpected calamities, brought harmony to every situation.

At the least, she brought a love and normalcy we all needed.

Chapter Six

Sibyl

Margaret staggered into the house from playing in the back yard. "Mommy, I don't feel good." Normally a sturdy girl, she looked faint, her eyes half closed.

I rushed to her as she slumped down into Fremont's chair, her cheeks flushed.

"Maybe you've been playing too hard." Her forehead felt hot. "I told you to slow down. I hope you didn't catch something at school."

I led Margaret into the children's bedroom and told her to lie on her twin bed. Her dark curly hair settled about the pillow, and her cheeks glistened bright pink.

Judson stood near the doorway with a befuddled look on his face. Only a year younger, he was half her size and as temperamental as a wild goose, always into some shenanigan. As a big sister, Margaret watched over him like a mama bird after her fledgling, making sure he stayed out of trouble and the older kids left him alone. Now, he looked helpless, watching her.

"Run and get a glass of water," I said.

Judson returned carrying a glass too full, splashing water as he walked. He handed the glass to me and slipped back out the door.

I lifted the water to Margaret's lips, and she took a few sips. Her big blue eyes, as tender as Fremont's, were clouded over with misery.

Soon after I put her to bed, I checked her again. Two blisters appeared on her face. I examined her closer—several spots on her stomach.

Chickenpox? My heart ached for the poor child. I remembered how she'd cried the first few months of her life, hungry because I didn't have enough breast milk. Helplessness attacked me, and I despaired of ever being a decent mother.

The rest of the afternoon, I kept Margaret in bed, wiping her body with a cool cloth. The eruptions got worse and more blisters appeared. Red spots splashed over her body. My sweet girl looked miserable, and there was not much I could do.

Fremont came home from working on someone's jalopy, and as soon as he entered the front door, I ran to him. "Margaret's sick. Terribly sick. It may be the chickenpox, but I don't know. She has a high fever and could die and…" Fear rose in me like steam, hot as Margaret's forehead. My body tensed, and I held back tears.

Fremont slipped his arm around my shoulder and squeezed. "A lot of kids get chickenpox, honey. It's a simple childhood disease."

"But it can get bad. I mean, horribly bad. Kids die from this. We can't lose another child. We can't!"

"Take it easy. We'll wait another day or two, and if she's still sick, we'll call the doctor."

I tried to hide my fear while I worked to make Margaret as comfortable as possible.

Sitting beside Margaret, I recalled when I was her age—seven years old. In 1918, the flu blew through town like a raging wind. The Spanish flu they called it. Many died. Many neighbors and friends. Marjorie and I lay ill and feverish in bed for several days, but my darkest memory was of Mama. It was too dangerous for Mama to come into our room because of our new baby brother Calvis, so Papa brought us food and water and tended to our immediate needs. But Papa's duty lay with Mama, and he spent most of his time with her, leaving us to feel abandoned, yearning for a mother's touch.

I rose from the chair and lay my hand on Margaret's forehead and prayed. Prayed she would get well soon. Prayed she would feel my care.

***

Two days later while I spoon-fed Margaret some homemade soup, I heard the back door open. The last time I checked, Judson had been sitting on the porch. He wasn't his usual boisterous self, but I assumed he was concerned about his sister.

"Mama." I heard Judson's voice, small but clear. "Mama?"

When I went to check on him, my energetic son had sunk onto the floor. Another sick child? I reached down to help him onto the sofa. Fever wrapped his little body, and a rash covered his face. I lifted his shirt and saw tiny spots peppering his belly. The rash looked different than Margaret's. Not chicken pox. Measles?

Oh no. My babies!

Fremont sent for his mother, who knew how to cure most ailments. Mother Pope showed me how to make a baking soda paste to reduce the itching and how to make lemon water to stimulate their appetite. The good lady's presence could calm a stampeding buffalo herd headed toward a cliff, and her bedside demeanor brought peace where I lost control.

Love for my mother-in-law grew in bounds.

"I'll pray for their health, and I'll be praying for you too. Sometimes we all need a little reassurance to get through tough times." Mother Pope's words sent a tranquility dart straight to my soul. "Roses can't grow in the shade, dear. They need a bit of sunshine."

I prayed along with her, knowing only time and God could heal my sick children.

My mama came by with a pot of chicken and dumplings. "I can't stay, what with my job and your younger sisters at home. Children can be such a load."

She looked around at the unmade beds, clothes scattered on the floor, and dishes in the sink. "How do you get into these messes?" She shook her head in dismay and started toward the door. "Good thing you live close to family. You could never take care of these kids by yourself."

What had happened to make my mother so hard? Would she ever change? I hoped she'd become a sweet, understanding mom and see my family as precious as gold. We sure could use her support. But right then, I had more important work to do than wish for a better mother.

By the fourth day, they traded illnesses. Margaret came down with measles and Judson came down with chicken pox, only Judson was not halfway over the measles when the pox erupted on his belly. My bones already ached with weariness from getting up and down through the nights, cleaning, and worrying.

It had been only a few months since Keith's funeral. The baby who had taken my heart and left an empty spot as massive as the North Pole had died of unknown causes. I could not lose another child. I would not. My nerves grew taut as the tension rose each day the children remained sick, feeling as fragile and breakable as etched glass.

When I checked on Margaret around ten o'clock the next morning, she was sitting up in bed. "I'm hungry. Can I have cornbread and buttermilk?"

"Buttermilk?" I asked, relieved she looked better. "Are you sure?" We often ate leftover cornbread and sweet milk—but buttermilk? No one in the house touched the thickened sour drink.

Margaret insisted. "That's what Grandpa eats every evening before he goes to bed. He says it's good for you."

A smile came to my face. If the child wanted buttermilk, that was what she'd get, but I doubted if she'd like it.

Sure enough, she spit out the first bite. "Mommy, that's awful."

"You don't have to eat it, sweetie. Why don't you come into the kitchen and I'll make you some oatmeal?"

Wearing pajamas, she slipped into the warm kitchen and sat down at the breakfast table. Thankful she had made it through both illnesses, I put an extra spoonful of brown sugar on her oats and hugged her close. She recovered by the next day and lightened my burden considerably.

I checked Judson's temperature nearly every half hour and, by my thermometer, Judson's fever soared to a scary 102 degrees. We couldn't afford for a doctor to come to our house. Our cigar box was meant for the future, and I didn't want to delve into that again.

Then, Judson's temperature spiked to 104. Fremont's cousin Inez's newborn baby Marvin had caught the measles, and his fever had exploded.

He would never develop mentally past an infant's age, a tragedy that reverberated through the whole family.

I was frantic.

No. Not my child.

I panicked, my body going into full mom-speed. I'd do whatever it took to keep my boy alive. No matter what it might cost. Future or no future.

I picked up the rotary phone and held the mouthpiece to my ear. The switchboard operator asked, "What number, please?" I blurted out Dr. Fortson's four-digit number. Alarm edged through my voice as I explained the children's sicknesses.

The doctor came quickly and examined Judson. He gave the boy a shot and told me to keep him out of the sunlight. He said to put the child into a tub of ice water off and on throughout the day to bring his fever down.

I paid him from our cigar box, counting the money slowly into his hand. Then I followed his words religiously.

That evening, I paced, and my fear grew, threatening to overtake my mind. I stayed close to the young one, hovering over him like a mama bear for the next few days. Despite my efforts, Judson lay writhing on his bed, tossing in misery. I tended to him, stroking his forehead, wiping perspiration off his brow, feeding him broth, and laying wet towels on his hot body. I didn't leave his bedside except for necessary housework.

Two days later, Judson opened his eyes and asked for his toy truck. I gave a huge sigh of relief. That was my boy. Trucks were the biggest interest in his life.

The child would survive.

I kept Judson in bed for a few more days to make sure he had recovered because I didn't want a relapse. During the next week, I refused to let him wander outside until I finally relented to his begging and allowed him in the back yard during the warm afternoons.

Still stinging from my mother's heartless insult about my housekeeping, I swept, dusted, and sanitized the house the best I could. I washed dishes and clothes and ironed dresses. I boiled chicken for soup, tried not to worry, and allowed my son to heal, overworking myself and learning to cope no matter how hard life might get.

Fremont and I had agreed not go tell anyone about our plans, even though we whispered about it at night after the children slept. I had no idea what the next year held, or where we'd be living.

After God healed my son from his devastating illnesses, my trust expanded. Trust in the Lord I would need in the future—whatever the future held.

Chapter Seven

Fremont

A few weeks later, on a Saturday afternoon, we loaded the children into our old jalopy to visit Fairview Cemetery on Harrison and Independence Streets. A wide, roughly-hewn stone wall the length of the west section was built by the WPA in '37. It protected those buried in that cemetery the same way I tried to protect Sibyl and the kids.

I turned the vehicle toward the open, massive iron gate smack-dab in the middle of the rock wall, and then drove between thirteen-foot-tall rock pillars. Then I wound around a dirt road to the back of the cemetery and parked near Keith's grave.

The children sprang from the car while I took off my hat and stood in front of our baby's gravestone. I relished the sun on my shoulders and the crisp air blowing against my skin strong enough to ward off the worst of the Oklahoma heat. I breathed in heavily. A perfect day for an outing.

Sibyl ambled up beside me, her work dress flowing around her knees. We had purchased three plots because Sibyl and I planned to be buried beside our little son. I turned from the grave and kissed Sibyl's cheek.

Leaves and debris from a summer rain covered the area. "I'll get the rake and a sack," I yelled over my shoulder as I walked back to the Chevrolet and opened the trunk.

"I'll clean the stone." Sibyl grabbed towels, squatted before the marker, and began wiping soil off the sides.

I gathered leaves while Sibyl washed. When she finished, she began to trim weeds around the edge of the gravestone and dug a few holes to plant irises. When we visited next spring, large blooms of yellow and purple would greet us, reminding us of the joy and beauty Keith had brought to our lives. The thought made me smile.

Margaret helped us clean, her little hands getting as dirty as ours while Judson played nearby. Typical children, they didn't remain close for long and began running around, always within our sight.

I took a break from my raking and walked with the children down the cemetery roads, wandering in and out among the oak trees and graves. The two ran among the stones looking for letters that matched their names. Their shouts of discovery and wonderment floated on the warm air. We passed Dr. Brewster Higley's grave, the man who wrote *Home on the Range*. In the middle of the graveyard, we circled the mausoleum, a large white-washed, imposing building built in '29 that housed five hundred crypts surrounded by marble imported from Italy and solid brass gates, doors, and light fixtures. It held many well-known city family members such as the Cole and Rainey families. At least, that was what Sibyl had read to me from the newspaper.

When we returned, I spoke with the gentleman cleaning the marker next to Keith's. We had met Mr. Glenn before, an elderly widower who cleaned his wife's grave every Saturday. Mrs. America Glenn died last year in '38. The Layton gravestone sat on the other side of Keith's—Dosia and George Layton—he died in March a month before Keith. The McGlasson boy, Arthur, lay one gravesite over, having passed away recently at thirty-five years old.

I spread out an old quilt as Sibyl pulled out sandwiches. After a late afternoon picnic, I leaned back on my elbows, surveying our labor. We still had much left to do.

Toward sunset, and after more work, the grounds, once covered in dirt and leaves, looked clean and cheerful—not as drab or unkempt or unloved as before. I knew our Keith was no longer in that hole, his soul now in heaven, but it was a place I felt connected to him.

I stood in front of the grave, gazing at the flawless headstone.

Reading the script on the stone out loud, I could hardly get the words past the lump in my throat. *Fredrick Keith Pope, born July 3, 1937. Died*

April 22, 1939. Those few words were woefully inadequate to describe a child who'd been so full of life and had brought so much joy into the world.

Tears filled my eyes and trickled down my cheeks. My grief overflowed like it never did at home, and every time we came to the cemetery, I ended up responding the same way. I couldn't hold the moans back any longer and fell to my knees, draping my body over the stone, sobbing, my shoulders shaking. Why my boy?

How could we make plans to move away and abandon this baby in Shawnee? Would we always have an empty spot in our hearts?

Sibyl knelt beside me.

Finally, I spoke, my voice cracking. "We should have engraved 'Remarkable little guy. Loved by all.'"

She agreed and squeezed my hand.

We stayed for a long time at the cemetery to pull ourselves together before it was time to move on. We had two other children who needed our love and attention, so we finally turned away from the gravesite.

We packed our tools and picnic supplies into the Chevrolet, and I shook out the quilt and placed it over Margaret and Judson sitting in the backseat while Sibyl slid into the front. As we drove toward the cemetery entry, the sinking sun streaked across the vast sky in front of us. Brilliant reds and golds.

When we reached the iron gate, it was closed.

Locked.

***

I got out of the automobile and walked up to the gate.

I rattled it, checked the lock, and rattled it again. I shrugged. Yep. Locked up tight as a button.

We were stuck in the cemetery. I felt irresponsible and as careless as a foolish vagrant. Of all things, I had let my family get trapped in a ghostly cemetery at night.

The impressive rock wall protecting the front of the cemetery ran the whole length—four blocks—and the center iron gate set between huge posts was daunting. Even if I managed to climb over, what about Sibyl and the children? And the Chevy? I slipped back into the dark touring car and wrapped my hands around the steering wheel.

"Fremont, what are we going to do? We can't sleep in a graveyard!" Sibyl's voice quivered. "The children are tired and cold."

I looked in the back seat to where Margaret and Judson huddled together under the quilt. "Don't worry," I said. "There must be a way out."

I backed up the vehicle and drove around the cemetery, followed every lane, searched every edge of the acreage, but found no other exit. Sibyl was at the point of panic, which convinced me to stay calm. Only a few weeks ago, a young girl had been found murdered in the Ardmore Cemetery—a tragedy I kept to myself.

Sibyl trusted me. She believed I could solve this problem like I solved most problems in our lives, but I said a quick prayer in case I needed help. *"Lord, help us get out of this spooky place."* I never imagined I'd say a prayer like that. Would the Lord understand people getting locked in a graveyard? I would have chuckled if it hadn't been so serious. God probably shook his head at us.

Arriving back at the front gate, I turned the engine off and got out, the sunset fading into dreary.

Sibyl stepped beside me and glanced over her shoulder at the dark expanse of headstones. I turned around and, in the dim light, saw specs of light bouncing from the top of the stones. Eerie sounds slashed through the quiet and wind rustled the trees. Sibyl shivered and grabbed my arm so tight I'd have bruises.

Men weren't supposed to get spooked.

One light across the street shone like a beacon—the house beside the Shawnee Monument Works. Sibyl pointed to it and whispered as if the dead might hear. "Looks like people are awake over there."

"Maybe there's someone who can help."

"We can try."

"Margaret, come over here," I shouted. My brave girl ran to my side, ready to climb Mount Scott if I asked her to.

"I'll help you over the wall, and you can run across the street and knock on the door."

"No!" Sibyl said. "She can't do that. She has a dress on." I couldn't see my wife's face clearly, but her voice sounded loud enough. "A girl can't climb over a wall. I won't allow it."

"All right then. Judson, you're next in line, son. You get to climb over."

Judson, although usually scared of his own shadow, was excited to be chosen—maybe because he loved to climb. He ran to me, and I hoisted him onto the rock wall.

"Be careful now!" I said.

The boy plopped down on the other side with ease and grinned back at us before turning toward the road.

"Watch before you cross the street!" I hollered. Just last year a seven-year-old boy got struck by a car while running across Harrison Street near Fairview Cemetery—close to where we stood. Another tidbit I kept to myself. But Judson had already rushed across Harrison Street and jumped onto the porch. We watched him bang on the door.

A rumpled man appeared, shook his head, and disappeared inside the house.

Judson came running back to us—without looking up and down the street again. That child. He arrived out of breath, but it was too difficult to get him back over the wall, too steep on his side. The situation had gone from bad to worse. Now, it seemed impossible, and I felt as low as an old, lazy mutt, not competent to protect my own family. How could I ever take care of them in a town far away?

Then, the man across the road reappeared, moseying toward us.

"Can you help us?" I yelled, trying to hurry him.

He finally arrived, held out a key, and slowly unlocked the gate. "This happens every once in a while. That's why they gave me a key."

Times like this made our life dramatic—and made me thankful the Lord watched over us. I don't know what we would have done if the man hadn't been home. I breathed freely for the first time since we got locked in.

"Good thing I was here," the man said as he turned to go back home. "I changed my plans today and decided to wait 'til tomorrow to visit my mum in the city."

Sibyl patted my leg as we drove away. "I'm glad you never panic in emergencies."

I was glad she couldn't hear my racing heartbeat.

Chapter Eight

Sibyl

Two weeks later, while Fremont slept through the afternoon, Margaret, Judson, and I walked to visit Fremont's mother, a trek we often made before Keith died. Walking fast without the need of a baby buggy, we passed the Shawnee Milling Company, with its tall towers overshadowing the town. Judson, who had recovered quickly and now had more energy than a bucking horse, ran ahead to watch the delivery trucks pulling in with loads of grain, and I had to holler at him to slow down and wait for us.

Mother Pope's windows were propped open, and I smelled cinnamon from a block away, as if she'd expected us to drop by. She always knew what to say and how to help with my jumbled emotional state.

The cinnamon rolls smelled like wealth in the air, bringing back memories of my childhood when Papa purchased anything we wanted. Remembering the bag of peppermints and Lifesavers he used to bring home from Owl Drug Store could make my mouth water.

Those days seemed far away now.

Our savings fund had diminished because of the doctor visit and we'd begun to drop coins into it again. Money was so stretched that I wouldn't let the kids waste a bread crumb. They weren't allowed to eat part of an apple or orange and throw the rest away. Fremont and I had a thirty-dollar charge at the grocery store on Main Street close to Harrison, which we paid on a little each time he brought home a paycheck.

As we stepped up on the porch, I heard Mother Pope inside the house whistling, a talent I adored. She could make any tune sound like a musical bird singing from heaven. I opened the door.

"Hello, dears! Come on in. So glad to see you!" Mother's heartfelt greetings always encouraged me.

After the warm welcome, we followed Mother Pope into the kitchen, where she washed and dried a few plates. Though caring and compassionate, my mother-in-law, Mrs. Eva Katherine Pope, could not manage to keep her dishes clean. A stack of dirty dishes lay incessantly in her sink, and when she needed a clean plate, she'd go wash it up.

"Something smells like heaven." The children and I sat at the wooden dining table and watched her dish sugar-coated, mouth-watering cinnamon rolls onto three plates. I sniffed the concoction in the air and swooned, tasting the cinnamon before taking a bite.

When Mother set rolls in front of Margaret and Judson, they gobbled the food down as if they were starving urchins. Mine sat in front of me, untouched as I worried about how to share my thoughts. No one spoke.

A few minutes later, Mother got up and dished the children out another half cinnamon roll apiece, and I cringed. Not that she didn't make the best rolls in the world. She did. But the children would never eat their supper.

When they finished, Mother Pope gently washed their sticky faces and fingers.

"Margaret, take Judson outside to swing," I said, needing a few minutes to talk to Mother. Dad had hung an old tire from a tree limb beside the house where the children loved to play. We could hear them laughing from the dining room.

"Okay, honey, go ahead and unload your burdens." Mother pushed her glasses up and crossed her arms over her large chest as if she could wait forever. "I can tell you've got something on your mind that wants to jump out."

I warmed at her perception. Fremont got tired of delving into emotional heartaches, hashing out slivers of confusion even if it solved nothing. A conversation with him tended to be one-sided, but his mother always sensed my need to share and would listen.

I talked about how I hid from my friends and family. How I snapped at my children for no reason even while fearful for their health. How I felt responsible for my family and wanted to make sure they found God. How my life had slumped into a canyon, and I couldn't find a way to climb out.

However, some things I could not tell Mother Pope. I couldn't tell her I was disappointed in my mama. How Mama didn't understand and told me to "bury my feelings and keep going." I could use Mother's wisdom even there, but I wasn't sure how to ask for it without sounding disloyal toward Mama.

Even though my stomach ached, I thought I'd try a small bite of cinnamon roll. The sweetness coated my tongue, and I took a larger bite. Sweet honey. Mother made the best rolls I'd ever eaten.

"I don't know what to do with myself. Keith's death has taken the breath out of me." I explained how depressed I had been while sorting through Keith's clothing and keepsakes.

She ignored my complaints, served me a glass of sweet, iced tea, and chuckled. "That boy! Do you remember when he wandered into the back yard to pet the nanny-goat?"

I drowned my complaints deep inside, unhappy that she seemed to ignore my distress. She wasn't usually like that. Then I realized…this story was about Keith. The Popes had bought a goat to supply milk for our children. Keith loved goat milk and had it over his cereal in his little yellow bowl.

Mother chortled, recalling Keith and his antics. "The goat was tied to a stake to clean up the garden. Keith tried to pet him and, naturally, he got too close. Lands o' living. We watched from the kitchen window when that goat nudged Keith and made him plop to the ground on his back end."

Holding a napkin to my mouth, I snickered at the memory.

"Keith pulled himself up, and the goat nudged him again. Keith fell down but got back up four or five times. Every time that poor child tried to stand up, the goat knocked him down again."

"That's my boy." I laughed out loud. "He was always bringing a bright spot to my days."

"Girl, it was hilarious to watch his persistence. When he finally started to get frustrated, you rushed out to save him. My gracious, then he balked and didn't want to leave the goat's side."

We laughed together, companionable-like. In so many ways, Mother connected with me like it was a God-given link. She patted my hand. "Honey, I miss him too, like he was my own. That baby brought a light to everyone he met, and he sure found a place in this old woman's heart."

Mother's love for Keith shone through, as did her love for me and my family.

I placed my hand over my chest. "Will the pain ever go away?"

"No, but it'll lessen. Just dwell on the good he brought to all of us."

My boy's exuberant spirit had blessed my life, and as I ached for more memories of him, I determined not to forget the ones we had. Even if I couldn't hold my boy, I could hold his recollections close to my heart and move on. It was time.

Chapter Nine

August 1939

Fremont

My dad worked with the tenacity of a bulldog. Made from the same sturdy cloth, I labored alongside him to provide food for the coming winter. We spent the afternoon weeding the monster garden, hoeing row after row of green beans, and watering the fruit trees until they could hold no more. I disliked the grueling work, preferring to fiddle with some old Chevy engine or pull apart a mechanical gadget to see how it worked.

"Son, let's go get a swig of that cool water. No sense it dryin' up before we get our fair share."

I'd never heard such sweet words. After following him to the water well by the back porch, I grabbed the rope and lowered the bucket down into the well, then drew up the best tasting liquid known to mankind. Dad picked up the tin ladle and dipped it into the cool, clear water.

Swigging a mouthful, he let the water run down his chin and onto his overalls. "Sure tastes good after a hard day's work." He handed the ladle back to me.

After we drank our share, I poured the remaining water over my head, the coolness soothing my aching bones. Sitting down on a log nearby, we rested in the shade.

I told Dad about getting my family locked in the cemetery after dark and the antics it took to get us out. We laughed together, and I figured the story would stay in the family's lore for years, repeated over and over.

Then neither of us spoke for a good five minutes. I broke our silence when I blurted out the question I'd been mulling over for the past few weeks. "Dad, how do you get over the hurts in life?"

Dad leaned back and looked at me as if I were a chimpanzee, the question coming out of nowhere like it did. "I'd be hard-pressed to answer that without more to go on. What're you getting at?"

"Keith dying and all. The way life throws grenades, blasts your world, and expects you to live like it didn't happen." My heart had been so broken, I feared the pain would never leave, even though in front of Sibyl, my mother, and everyone else, I had to act strong and pretend I could manage. The stress was breaking me.

"The good Lord never said we'd have no pain in this life. Life is going to happen. Good and bad comes to all of us."

Usually, my dad and I joked around while we worked, but I was in a sober mood. Serious conversations with him were usually short and direct, and I dawdled to get my point across. "How do we get over it? The bad times?"

Dad was quiet for a long time. I didn't rush him. The answer was too important.

Before responding, Dad looked up at the clear, expansive blue sky for a few minutes. "Is something else bothering you? Something you ain't said yet?"

I rubbed my hands together to keep them from twitching. Nervous, I didn't want to admit the real reason I still grieved, but I plunged ahead, needing to say the words aloud. "What if it's my fault Keith died? What if God is punishing me?"

My normally jovial dad stood and looked around at the wood-frame house, the picket fence, the post oak trees, the well-tended garden.

I waited.

"Why do you think God is punishing you, boy?"

"Sibyl and I did wrong before we married, her getting pregnant and all. I sinned, and God knew it. Maybe Keith's death was the price, the punishment for my wrongs. Like King David, God took his son because he'd been immoral."

"Seems as I remember, David didn't repent 'til afterward. And as I recall, you asked for forgiveness right away."

Once making the first confession, I figured I may as well tell it all. "Another thing. I turned away and wasn't going to church like I should, going about my business day to day like he weren't important. Maybe this is God's way of getting my attention. What do you think he wants me to do?"

I expected Dad to jump in with a lecture about how God doesn't take a baby's life in retribution, how life is precious, or that God is full of love and compassion and would never punish but instead, woo me back to him. But Dad put his dirty hands into his overall pockets, dragging the straps down, and bit his lip.

"Got a story for you," he said. "Heard it at my pappy's farm long ago. This here young lad was a mite playful and didn't take life too seriously. He wandered around the fields like he was king, doing whatever he wanted. Racing horses. Climbing catalpa trees and swinging from limb to limb. Catching rattlers. Things like that. Thought nothing of it. He'd been taught better. Knew he shoulda minded his pap, but he was having a good time of it.

"One day, he rode his horse over the hill a mile down toward a creek where a pretty little gal lived. He wasn't supposed to be there, mind you, and he knew it. He stopped in the woods and saw this lil' gal bathing in the clear water. You know what that'll do to a man. The picture sent shivers down his body. Embarrassed, tempted, or whatever, he knew he'd done wrong and backed that horse out of the woods quicker'n a stampede of buffalo and headed home. Now, he didn't purposefully do wrong, but that picture in his head never left him."

My dad had entertained me with stories since I could remember, but I'd never heard this one.

Dad continued talking like I wasn't standing there covered with red dirt and sweat, chewing on a straw. "Like sin, a picture gets stuck in your brain. Won't leave you alone whether you intentionally done wrong or not. If you asked Jesus to forgive you like I heard you do, then he'll wipe that slate clean and you can start over."

I considered his words and nodded.

"You gotta ask the good Lord to make your wrong into something right." This middle-aged dad of mine removed his straw hat and wiped his brow with his bandana before he turned to me. "That's what God did for you. Took your wrong and made it blossom. Gave you a sweet little wife and a cute baby, didn't he?"

My heart still nagged, and the pain still lived, but the pressure released. God wasn't punishing me. He'd forgiven me and was pushing Sibyl and me further along on our journey.

Dad strode back toward the corn stalks.

"Wait. I have one more question," I yelled.

He stopped and turned around. "Yeah, son."

"That story. Is that true? I mean—is it another fairy tale from your days in Waco?"

"Can't say exactly. But your mother sure looks pretty when she gets her hair wet and it hangs down around her waist."

I couldn't help the grin on my face.

"And just to be clear, God don't expect you to always do right and, son, you might have to pay the consequences. But he didn't take your baby because of what you did. He loved Keith and he loves us all. Some things we may never understand. And as I recall, God blessed King David with a slew more chilluns."

My dad's longest speech ever.

Chapter Ten

The world was changing, and war rumors over the Crosley radio claimed Germany threatened to invade its neighbor country of Poland. Japan attacked China, and then China pushed back. Even though those countries were far away from our little town in Oklahoma, my interest was piqued.

I read every pertinent newspaper article from the *Shawnee Morning* and the *Shawnee Evening News* and watched fuzzy newsreels and listened to President Roosevelt static on our tube radio. Nonstop information from KGFF. It seemed everyone, including family, friends, and neighbors, prayed for the war across the ocean not to reach our home front.

Fremont didn't understand, but I didn't want to leave Shawnee until our siblings were in a better place in life, hopefully within a few months. I determined to influence them toward God and his love. Fremont's sisters, Irene and Ruth, and my sisters, Marjorie, Blanche, and Frances, were five of the most strong-willed, obstinate, contrary females I ever saw. It would take a miracle to get them grown and settled in a proper place. Settled was the hard part.

As the oldest of the sisters, I believed I could influence them better than anyone. Fremont thought girls were mysterious creatures and he hated to get involved in their squabbles. I became adamant about sharing our faith with them before we moved, even if he disagreed with me.

One evening, Fremont and I sat together on our front porch, swaying back and forth on the wooden swing, one of our favorite evening pastimes. We enjoyed times like this by ourselves while the kids stayed at his parents' house. Leaning close to him, I smelled the tantalizing aroma of Old Spice cologne.

I opened Blanche's new Caldron Yearbook in front of us. Blanche had left the book saying she would pick it up later. Our generous contribution to the yearbook had taken away from our savings fund and set back our moving date, but it was a simple way to support my sister.

The senior class members in the yearbook were listed in scholastic order instead of alphabetically. I excitedly pointed to the first page. "There's Blanche, third from the top." Who wouldn't be impressed? Out of two hundred and fifty-some students graduating in '39 from Shawnee High School, my sister was listed right after the valedictorian and salutatorian. A smart girl—who knew she was smart.

Fremont's voice held a positive tone. "Even through all the drama of your parents' divorce, the depression years, and Keith's death, that girl stayed focused on her studies. That's good news."

Each student had a quote under their name and Fremont read the words out loud under Blanche Trimble. "'Honor Society. Very quiet and not afraid. But she is very 'sat' in her ways.'"

I giggled like a schoolgirl. "The yearbook writers were closer to the truth than they knew. Blanche has always been set in her ways."

"That she is." His booming guffaw overshadowed my little twitter.

Searching for Fremont's sister's picture, I flipped through the pages, recognizing several students. Toward the back of the senior pages, I stopped turning. Irene was listed third place from the last in scholastic standing. A murkiness surrounded me as I leaned back and straightened my dress over my lap. "Laura Irene Pope." I cocked my head.

Neither of us spoke for a few minutes and I thought about his sister's lack of academic interest as he pumped the swing with his feet.

Irene's scholastic abilities did not seem to matter to Fremont. "I love my little sister whatever she does. She's had a hard time of it in school.

Clever enough, but her interests lie in people and family and living life to the fullest—not in book work."

I shrugged and spoke to myself. "What will she do now?"

Fremont raised his eyebrows. "All she wants is to get married. Weeks ago, she said getting good grades was a waste of time. Maybe her sharp sense of humor and good attitude will get her through life."

I agreed. "With her big blue eyes and all those curves, she's bound to attract a promising young man."

"Hopefully," Fremont said. "But she'll never make as good a match as you did."

I punched him in the arm. "Ah-huh. Just like the match you made." How I loved being married to this man.

"Two for two. Can't go wrong with that. You know you lighten my life quicker than sweetcakes."

My thoughts returned to our sisters' prospects. While Irene valued beauty and social standing, Blanche loved school and bookwork, not considering anyone as smart as herself. Blanche's tall, scrawny shape and long nose didn't bode well for catching a mate, even if she did have clear skin and wit as sharp as a tack. She seemed more interested in pursuing a career.

"Irene has a better chance at attracting an upright gentleman," Fremont said, our thoughts traveling the same line.

Our two high school graduates had chosen such different paths. As opposite as the Trimbles to the Popes, which was fine with me. I simply wanted them to follow God's plan and not their own. Which might be difficult to convey.

Fremont turned the yearbook page. Defending his sister the same way I defended my sisters, he said, "Irene will be happy with a simple life." I realized those words applied to Fremont too. He would be satisfied with a nice quiet home, a good wife, and healthy, obedient children.

Our marriage also had its opposites, its ups and downs. I was restless and yearned for a greater purpose in life. I wanted to help my family, but underneath I felt edgy, waiting for something more. Moving out of Shawnee would allow give me to discover what I wanted without the problems associated with my relatives. Just as soon as our sisters learned to make better choices.

"People are so different. Do you think the Lord will show us how to help others?" I thought of my parents. "Even the challenging ones?"

"Of course, he can help us. And as for Irene, I hope she meets a decent fellow."

"There're a lot of bad dudes out there. Too bad she'll never find someone to love her as much as you love me." I tried to hide my smile.

"That's my girl." Fremont kissed me soundly. "True. I love you to the brightest star and back. And if we had the dough, I'd shower you with gifts to prove it."

My husband had a heart of gold. Hopefully, our sisters would settle into a life of their own, and we could continue with plans to move, family issues or not.

Then doubts surrounded me. Should we wait a few more years before we moved? Fremont hadn't found a new job and we hadn't talked about it lately. I wanted to leave town but what about those who needed us?

Maybe we shouldn't leave Shawnee. Maybe I could talk Fremont into postponing our plans. After all, our families and friends lived here.

Chapter Eleven

Fremont

The third weekend in August my good buddy Isaac Taylor dropped by to see us. When I was a strapping young boy, my family lived in Pauls Valley, a flicker of a town an hour's drive south of Shawnee. We moved away from there but kept in touch with some of our Pauls Valley neighbors like the Taylors.

When Isaac arrived, we put together an impromptu get-together. Not like a big shindig or anything, that would have taken too much time, but we invited our sisters, Irene and Blanche, and a couple of friends over for hamburgers. Isaac brought his younger brother, Harvie.

Sibyl, anxious as always before an event, rushed around like a jackrabbit. Every friend would pitch in to bring food, so the financial burden didn't lay on one family. Stopping at the table, she took time to season the hamburger patties while Isaac and I set up a card table and chairs under a shade tree in the back.

Our friends, Effie and Doug Douglas, and their brood of three marched into the backyard soon after I started cooking on the outdoor grill. They stopped beside me.

"Sorry, we're late. We planned to come early to help, but you know how it is." Effie set her youngest child on the grass and held out a paper bag. "I brought tomatoes. Where do I put them?"

"Go ask my wife. She's cooking up a storm, and I'm sure she can find something for you to do."

Effie yelled before she got to Sibyl. "I can slice tomatoes or shred lettuce, but don't torture me with onions."

"You always get the good jobs." Sibyl turned and put her hands on her hips before she chortled and investigated the bag. "These tomatoes look delicious. Did you grow them?"

"You know better than that. I can't grow a dandelion. Mother has an abundant garden, and she shares with us."

"Nice in-laws."

Doug, watching me move the burgers around on the grill, grinned. "Can't let those two get together often. We'd never survive if they ganged up on us boys." Effie and Doug could lighten up a party quicker than a bowl of cherries. Merriment thrived at times like this.

Sibyl yelled toward the back-screen door. "Irene, can you bring out the pickles and mayonnaise and mustard?"

Irene walked outside and let the screen door slam behind her. "What did you say?" She was wearing a new knee-length dress for the occasion, but her hair, frizzed from the humidity, almost ruined the effect.

"Oh, never mind. I'll get them." Sibyl set down an onion, wiped her hands on her apron, and went into the kitchen. Carrying a tray of condiments, she returned and set the tray down and began arranging food on the card table. Normally, I wouldn't have noticed what she was doing, but she had been so nervous before the party, I wanted to make sure she didn't need anything.

A few minutes later, I tossed the charred hamburger patties onto a platter and scanned the yard. A dozen friends laughed together, children and Patches, our brown and white terrier, ran in and out among the adults, and the table was loaded with mouth-watering food. God's goodness overwhelmed me.

"Here, here." I used my commanding voice to quiet the chatter. "Let's bless this spread before the flies get it."

We bowed our heads, and I voiced a prayer. "Lord, thank you for the goodness of friends and family. Bless each one and this abundance of food. In Jesus' name. Amen." Happiness comes unexpectedly sometimes, and this was one of those times.

We grabbed plates and made our own hamburgers. Some guy put two hunks of meat on his bun and then loaded it down with a juicy tomato slice, green lettuce pulled from the garden, pickles dilled last fall, and a dab of mustard. I'm not saying who, but it could have been me.

Between a couple of camping stools, the dining room chairs, and a log, everyone found seats in the shade.

I sat beside Isaac's brother, and it took a few minutes to begin a serious conversation with him. Harvie Taylor was a relaxed sort of fellow, a happy, jovial guy who did more listening than talking. After a few pleasantries, I took a big swig of sweet-iced tea and asked, "What are your plans for the future?"

"Depends on this war business." Harvie pulled his shoulders back, a stalk of hair falling into his eyes. "I may join the army. I always dreamed of being a military man."

Conversation about the war was not always acceptable at social gatherings, even though the war was constantly on everyone's mind, but Harvie opened it up.

"What do you think's going on overseas?" Sibyl asked, always eager to discuss world events. Others turned and joined in the conversation.

"Japan invaded Mongolia," said Carl Alexander, whose wife Opal brought the delicious baked beans.

"I heard part of England was darkened for an air raid test."

"British bombers tried to prove their air power by flying to France and back, but, as we all know, the U.S. has the best air force in the world."

Agreement all around.

"President Roosevelt says war is imminent, but some senators say we have nothing to worry about."

"Do we? Do we have nothing to worry about?" asked Doug.

"I love military men." Irene interrupted before anyone could answer, effectively ending the political conversation. "Where do you work?" She sat at Harvie's left and batted her eyes at him.

We might never know if we had anything to worry about.

"I work on C-47s at the Douglas Aircraft Factory in Midwest City." His voice was staccato, curt.

"Oh! C-47s? You must tell me about it. A man in uniform makes me proud." She leaned forward, her cleavage showing more than was proper.

"I don't wear a uniform," said Harvie.

"I bet you will someday. You'll make it high up in the government." She continued babbling. Talkative Irene could carry on a conversation with a mannequin. "My friend married a military man, and they had the most beautiful wedding a girl could want."

We swiveled as a group and looked at Irene in surprise. That I remember, she had never voiced that she liked a man in a military uniform, nor had she recently attended a wedding. This flighty girl knew nothing about the airplanes they serviced in Midwest City and had never cared. What was my sister talking about?

Irene didn't notice the rest of us gaping at her because her gaze was fixated on Harvie's handsome boyish face. Her big blue eyes danced when she got excited and they were doing a jig right then. Those eyes could hypnotize any man who looked at her.

Within a few minutes, Irene took Harvie's hand and said, "I've met a couple of military men lately. Maybe you know them. Have you heard of …?" She dragged Harvie around to the front of the house to the porch swing. Seemed Harvie opened up to her because they talked and laughed for the next hour, cackling loudly enough for us to hear in the backyard.

Oh dear, this young man would be putty in Irene's hands even if he were five years older than her eighteen years. I hoped he would pass my parents' approval. Not keen on whether a man was responsible or not, Irene tended to look at a man's face, or maybe his earning potential, and I hoped that wasn't the case here.

By the time the party broke up, Irene and Harvie had disappeared into the night. Was it too much to hope that one of our sisters had met someone decent to take care of her?

Chapter Twelve

September 1939

Fremont

Sibyl and I discussed whether we should take a vacation. We'd agreed to save money and our Havana box was almost half full, but a weekend reprieve seemed more important than anything else at that moment. Unfortunately, it meant we'd have to put off planning a move for a little longer. Although her family chaos has smoothed out for the moment, Sibyl needed a break, and I had extended myself at work. My nighttime job as a guard drained me, and as a shade-tree mechanic, I had so many broken down cars lined up to repair, I'd never finish.

Neither of us had been to a beach and we could drive to Galveston, Texas, the nearest beachfront with sand and saltwater, paying only for gasoline. Effie and Doug said they'd loan us camping equipment, which included a tent, cots, and a portable kerosene stove. All we would need to take were linens, clothing, and food.

"I've been thinking, and I'm not sure we should go." Sibyl hesitated, I assumed feeling sad after Keith's death, tiredness peeking around the edges of her eyes. "I'd prefer to stay home and hibernate."

"You need this. It'll be good to get away." I took a deep breath, realizing I needed to get away as much as Sibyl did.

"Why don't you take the children and go without me?"

Was she bonkers? "I can't imagine taking care of the kids by myself. Besides, I don't want to leave you home alone." I really needed this vacation, but I could never take a trip on my own with the children. "And we promised to take Blanche and Irene to the beach as their high school graduation gift. Remember? They're looking forward to it."

In my black-and-white world, we should keep our word, and knowing my wife, she would be drawn to helping the girls. This would give her a chance to talk with them.

"You're right. Okay. Okay. We'll go."

Within an hour, Sibyl had pulled out a pen and paper and began to write lists of what we needed to take. Lists helped her focus. That woman made lists of foods and medical supplies and camping gear that would make an accountant cringe. And as we planned, we got more and more excited about the trip, determined to enjoy this vacation.

I changed the oil and aired up the tires of our worn '26 Chevy touring car, whistling as I shined and waxed the automobile's curves in the driveway. The gleam of the black sedan brought pride. The family vehicle, a benefit of working at the dealership, had cost $200, an amount we paid out over a year.

When the day came to pack the motorcar, Sibyl was overly prepared, as always. "Here's the blankets and pillows," she said, handing the bundle to me. "They can go inside the car. And I packed only one suitcase for all of us. Do you think that'll be enough?"

She barely waited for my response. "Did you tell Blanche and Irene to bring only one bag?"

"Yes."

"Were you able to get the tent and cots into the trunk?"

"Yes."

"Did you pack the swimming gear?"

"Yes."

"Will it be cold on the beach?"

"Honey, you worry too much. There'll be a store down there if we forget anything."

Sibyl packed a lunch and, if I knew anything about her, I could guess that the box would include everything edible in the kitchen—bread, ham, cheese, peanut butter and jelly, pickles, boiled eggs—with another picnic bag for the next day. I filled a jug with clean water and stuffed it in with a bag of potatoes, which we would bake.

After spending an hour loading the Chevrolet, we drove to pick up Blanche and Irene. They were waiting eagerly, practically on the curbs in front of their houses. I think they were as enthusiastic as we were. The car was full to overcrowded, what with two adults, two teenagers, and two children. The teens sat in the back seat with Margaret between them, while Judson rode in front with us.

At first, Sibyl led the children in songs, trying to keep them entertained. After an hour of singing, *She'll Be Coming Around the Mountain*, I exclaimed, "Don't you think we drug that goat to death?"

Sibyl laughed. "How about the Judy Garland song, *Over the Rainbow*?" Shouts of agreement echoed, and another round of choruses began. Finally, the vehicle quieted, and the children fell asleep.

I looked in my rearview mirror. Our sisters were as different as a wolf and a hyena, neither friendly with each other nor anyone else. Irene, who normally couldn't stop talking to beat the band, had remained quiet most of the trip, and that worried me. "How're you doing back there, sister?"

Growling meant Irene wanted to be left alone, but Sibyl didn't take the hint. "What are your favorite movies?" she asked but neither girl answered, so she turned her head around to see into the back seat and addressed Blanche. "What about you? I know you like movies."

"I like that old movie, *Things to Come*."

"The science-fiction based on the H. G. Wells novel?" Sibyl asked. "That's hard-boiled, isn't it?"

Blanche quoted in a spooky slow-drawn voice, "'The year is 1940...and it's Christmas in Everytown. Crowds gather in the streets to buy last-minute gifts and turkeys. Newsboys declare, 'World on the Brink of War!'"

Blanche's flair for drama amazed me. Maybe she *could* be an actress.

Irene snorted. "I'd never go see that movie. Mother would be horrified if I even mentioned it."

Blanche's voice filled the car. "It was engaging. Lived up to its potential."

"I heard it was dark and thought-provoking," Irene said, "Full of science, war, and a declining society."

"That too—with greed and power." Blanche dramatized the words. "Ah, the dream of utopian power. H. G. Wells dotes on brilliance like I do."

The film sounded too much like Hitler and the situation in Europe for my taste. And the utopian words of Mr. Trimble. Not a good thought.

Sibyl shook her head and spoke to Irene. "How about you? What movies do you like?"

Ignoring the question, Irene exclaimed with a gravelly voice, "I wish I hadn't come. This is going to be a drag without Harvie."

"Can't you forget about him for a few days?" Blanche rolled down her window, and wind whished through the Chevy.

"At least I have a boyfriend." Irene's snide remark revealed that this spunky girl's normal sense of humor had disappeared. She had started dating Harvie Taylor but got upset because Mother insisted that she take a boy to church before dating him. Irene hated the idea—but I liked it.

Harvie Taylor was a quiet man, especially around the talkative Irene, but when he did talk, he was witty and funny. I respected him and thought he'd be good for Irene. However, the way my sister carried on and flirted, I wasn't sure she was ready to settle down to marriage.

Silence filled the car again when Blanche rolled up her window. I could hear Margaret breathing as she slept, a sound as sweet as sugar cane blowing in the wind.

We made several fuel stops at little two-tank gas stations before we finally stopped at a rest area for a picnic lunch. I unloaded the box full of sandwich fixings, and we let the children run and play.

For the rest of the journey, I focused on my driving. I'd like to say the trip got easier, but it didn't. Irene began talking again, and, once she started, it became impossible for anyone else to say a word. At least her tales were entertaining. I had heard her chatterbox stories since she was old enough to quote Mother, but Sibyl and the children had not.

Anytime Sibyl addressed one sister, the other would cross her arms, either jealous or frustrated—I couldn't tell which from my view in the rearview mirror.

Why had they agreed to come? They clearly didn't like each other.

Sibyl looked at me and raised her eyebrows. She wanted to have some serious talk time with the girls, but I doubted this trip would give her the opportunity.

The almost ten-hour trip through the big state of Texas seemed as long as a trip to California and back.

***

When we arrived in Galveston, we chose a camping place close to the showers placed along the beach. I set up the tent and put the cots inside while Sibyl pulled out the bedding.

The cooling gulf water thrilled me, bringing a refreshing breeze during the summer heat. I plopped on my straw hat, sat on a cot stool, and wiggled my bare toes in the sand while Sibyl managed the children. She put hats on their heads, covered them with sunscreen, and warned them to stay in the shade as much as possible. How was shade possible for children at the beach?

After watching the little ones tiptoe toward the waves, I couldn't sit still any longer and began chasing them through the water. Before long, we were whooping and hollering, Judson running in circles around me.

Blanche and Irene waved as they passed us on the beach.

"Where're you going?" I shouted at them.

"We're walking to the shop booths," Irene yelled over her shoulder.

Blanche's bathing suit was more modest than Irene's which showed more of her back, but both girls strutted about like little peacocks in their wool swim shorts. Blanche turned back to look at me. "Irene doesn't want to tell you that we're actually looking for fellows."

"It was her idea." Irene pointed at Blanche. "She's the one who needs to find a beau."

"I don't need a man!" Even Blanche, though not as happy-go-lucky as Irene, couldn't stay despondent in this beautiful setting. "But we can still look!"

The girls' humor was infectious, the lightheartedness linking our little group together.

"Don't be long. Supper will be ready about dark," I said, as they sauntered out of sight.

When the kids and I made our way back toward camp, Sibyl was resting under an umbrella. I did a double take. My wife looked even better in a swimsuit than she did in a fancy Sunday dress. How did I ever get such a gorgeous lady?

"Look at the shells we found!" Margaret proudly pulled seashells and pebbles out of her bag, scattering white sand over the blanket as she lay the treasures beside her mother.

"You've been beachcombing." Sibyl picked up a few shells to examine.

Judson dragged over an assortment of driftwood he had collected.

"Hey, kids. Run down toward the beach and start a sandcastle. I'm going to sit with your mom for a few minutes."

Sibyl shouted after them as they sprinted toward the gulf. "Be careful and don't go in the water!" She looked at me, her eyes sparkling. "Yes. In case you ask, I'd love to come back to this Island City any time you want." Getting out of Shawnee and leaving our family's worries had helped clear our heads and gave us time to spend with our siblings.

I sat on the blanket beside Sibyl in the sand. As a cool breeze fanned the smell of seawater toward us, we sat in silence, holding hands, mine swallowing hers, and I felt the need to pull her close. She responded and lay her head on my shoulder, staring out over the ocean. Life was even loftier sitting on a sandy beach than swinging on a front porch swing.

"It's so quiet and peaceful here, gazing out into the sunset," said Sibyl.

"Hmm. Wouldn't it be wonderful to settle here? Shake the sand from our britches every evening and watch the waves roll in?" My daydreams could occasionally rival Sibyl's. "Which reminds me, we should discuss moving away from Shawnee."

"We do need to talk about it." Sibyl turned around to face me and looked like she had been waiting for this discussion for months—maybe she had. Moving had become our dream, our vision for the future.

"How much money do we have in the box?" I leaned toward her.

Sibyl, who counted the coins every week, frowned. "Not much. The Havana bank account is barely half full."

"That might be enough if I can find a good paying job in another town."

Sibyl's eyes clouded over as she spoke. "It may take a while. However, I've thought of several ways to earn money. I can crochet doilies and sell them. I'll need to buy extra thread, but you know how ladies are crazy about decorating with lace."

I hoped to earn a few bucks by repairing neighbors' old jalopies but felt like a cad if I charged people more than a few bucks. There could be a better way to help out. "That garage across town needs an extra hand. I heard it pays well."

Sibyl huffed and shook her head. "And stay gone from home more than you do now? I'd rather you didn't."

"All right. We'll skip that idea. But without more money and a new job, we won't be able to move this fall. Although, if we save a few more nickels, we could still move by December." I said, my hope rising. "Just think. We could be setting up a Christmas tree in a new home by then. What do you say?"

Sibyl paused, turned, and gazed out over the wide horizon. "We'd have to be careful with spending."

Her hesitation made me believe she was not ready to move away from her family. My heart sank a little at the thought. Would we ever leave town? No, of course, we'd move someday. I just wanted it to be sooner rather than later. "It's settled then. Barring any emergencies, early December will be a good time to uproot our family to a new home."

"Mama won't like it." Her voice sounded lower than the deep ocean. "She claims she still needs our help."

"Ah. Sibyl. We don't have to tell her yet. Even so, Blanche is grown and can help her."

"If she can find a job in this depressing economy."

Why was my wife so worried? Her mother earned more than I did. "Are you sure you want to move?"

"Of course, I do."

The way she answered didn't make me feel better, although I had faith she'd blossom into a starfish if we left this town and our families. We both needed a new start. I would not give up.

She leaned back against me, her soft hair caressing my face, and we watched the sun lower as the golden glow of evening began.

"Are you ready for me to start a fire?" I finally asked, noticing the time. "You get the hot dogs out, and I'll help Margaret and Judson gather sticks. The girls should be back soon."

"You're a good man," Sibyl said, pulling me back for a quick kiss. "I'm glad the Lord brought us together."

"And tonight, we're going to enjoy every moment." I patted her leg, jumped up, and yelled, "Come on, little fellows. Who wants to help build a fire for a wiener roast?" Screams all around.

The girls returned, and the six of us roasted hot dogs and ate around a lively fire before Sibyl brought out marshmallows. The night filled with jokes, giggles, and plenty of good old-fashioned laughter. I felt more relaxed than I had in months.

***

We left three days later, and the fun didn't last through the trip back home, I hate to say. It sounded like a cat and dog fight in the back seat.

Blanche and Irene had refused to use sunscreen, a concoction of half oil and half vinegar Sibyl mixed up. It worked for the rest of us, even if it smelled like rotten taters. Because of their stubbornness, the teens suffered severe sunburns, from their cherry-red faces to the blisters on their backs, all the way down to their pinkie toes. During the car ride, they screamed at Sibyl, at each other, and at themselves for going on the trip in the first place.

Misery rode in the back seat of our big old Chevy, and try as I might, it was impossible to ignore.

Sibyl wanted to travel through Shreveport on the way home because none of us had been there before, and, to my dismay, we did. I stopped at a Piggly Wiggly store, where Sibyl purchased baking soda to make a paste for the girls' sunburns. We checked into a hotel, and I could have kicked myself for not bringing enough money for two rooms. I set up cots and pallets for extra bedding.

In the middle of the night, I heard Blanche and Irene sneak out the door. Sibyl dressed and followed them while I turned over to go back to sleep. The next morning, I heard all about their rendezvous. The girls went to an all-night restaurant, where the three sat around drinking coffee, discussing life, and getting little sleep. Sibyl had her helpful girls' talk, saying neither one listened too well, and I didn't miss a thing.

Margaret and Judson took turns sitting in the back seat as we headed home through Texas. A squirming, rambunctious boy, squished between Irene and Blanche, didn't soothe their pain, especially when they tried to sleep. I focused on the road in front of me, but screams, groans, and complaints made it sound like the world was about to end.

Like bees swarmed.

Like rattlesnakes attacked.

Like I promised myself to never go on a vacation again. Sibyl could counsel all she wanted, but our sisters, like some people, were hard to be around. From now on, swimming at Shawnee's Garrett Lake would be enough excitement for me. And moving away from this harrowing family would be heaven.

Chapter Thirteen

Sibyl

Blanche sat at my dining room table with drawing paper and colored pencils, doodling and sketching. She heaved a sigh as if a thousand-pound stone sat on her shoulders. "I can't find a job. I have no experience, and no one will hire someone without experience. Those government nincompoops have no idea what it's like on the streets. I'm sure you don't either."

Her words rankled. Knowing how she easily flew into a tizzy, I rehearsed Mother Pope's words of wisdom in my mind, telling myself to ignore a slur, but it didn't stick. My response was hasty. "Surely an intelligent single woman can find decent work if she searches hard enough. Where have you looked?" I pushed aside the newspaper to wipe off the table in front of her. I hoped to get the kitchen spotless before the children came in from playing with Patches.

The look Blanche gave me could have withered a cactus. "I've looked *everywhere.* I went to Southwestern Bell and Coves Plant, and the Indian Sanatorium south of town. Even they didn't need office help."

"The tuberculosis hospital?"

She ignored my question but kept listing local businesses on her fingers. "Warren's Hardware, Marquis Furniture, Rosenfeld's Jewelry. I'll do almost any kind of work, but absolutely nothing is available."

"Why don't you enroll in college?" I asked. "You won a scholarship to OBU." When she didn't respond, I continued. "We could take a trolley there tomorrow afternoon and see the beautiful fountains at the oval. My mother-in-law helped raise funds for the WMU women's dorm, and it might be fun to tour it."

"Oklahoma Baptist would *not* be my first choice. Anyway, I would need a job to pay for books and expenses—which is not happening in this dad-blamed depression."

"My Sunday School class can loan you money. They loaned your friend Mary Jo Caron funds."

"Are you serious?" Blanche sounded disgusted as she stuck her sharp red pencil in the air, shaking it with each phrase. "They loaned money to another friend of mine and asked for it back because some spy saw her at a dance. I don't dance—not much anyway—but I'm not going to take the money and be told how to live my life." She resumed her sketching. "Art is the only thing I want to do."

I loved art as much as she did, but in the struggling economy, Blanche needed a paying job. She couldn't support herself by painting calm rivers and snow-covered mountains. I scrubbed the countertop, muttering under my breath, "Art classes were a waste of time. You can't earn a cent drawing pictures."

"What did you say?" Blanche stopped drawing.

I paused. I shouldn't have said words to inflame Blanche, but she needed a job. A paying job. I rolled my eyes in exasperation and turned away to start the meal. "You should've taken classes like typing or dressmaking. You didn't even take a home economics class."

After the last decade of near starvation, fear of not having enough money remained intact in me, a fear Blanche didn't seem to share. But then she didn't have small children and a husband to worry about.

I regretted my unkind thoughts. I couldn't criticize Blanche. Who was I to tell her to not want more out of life? I struggled with the same thing, trying to discern what God wanted me to do. At least she was pursuing what she wanted.

And, truthfully, I had to admit she was a talented artist. Her dress designs could compete with Coco Chanel's famous little black dresses. Because Blanche wanted to create fashions in Paris, she'd taken a high school French class, but all she'd learned were a few French words like *merci* and *excusez moi*.

Blanche looked up from her drawing pad. Dedicated, she spent hours at her art, trying different methods, paints, and mediums. "My art teacher said I was the most talented artist she ever taught. I loved Mrs. Tapp. She was the best teacher in the world."

I took off my apron and sat across from Blanche at the shaky kitchen table, the rickety one we couldn't afford to replace. I determined to try harder to communicate. "Why was she the best?" I remembered the teacher as absentminded, wearing clothes from the dump, and often seen in public wearing shoes that didn't match.

"She not only taught art, but she also taught manners and how to behave like a human being. She treated me more decently than most people do. Sure, she dressed a little odd and students made fun of her hats, but she was an individual, and her attire proved it."

Mrs. Tapp did have a good streak in her. One of her students had been born with an arm folded up and locked in place from birth, but her destitute parents couldn't afford to help her. Mrs. Tapp took the girl to Oklahoma University Hospital to have her arm operated on, and then the girl could straighten her arm and lift it to shoulder height.

Good stories like that should be in the newspaper.

***

Instead of good stories, the Shawnee paper printed such depressing news that when the U.S. declared neutrality in the war, we, as citizens, breathed sighs of relief. But peace was precarious and anxiety high.

I wanted peace. I wanted good news. I wanted to know how folks bought war bonds, planted victory gardens, donated to charity, and volunteered in a relief line. I wanted our young men to be safe and my friends and family to not be drafted, but the indications were not in our favor.

I also wanted Blanche to find a decent job. Then, she could better take care of my mother and herself if we left town. I meant, *when* we left town.

Governor Red Philips considered the New Deal to be federal interference in the state, but despite his objection, government jobs found their way to Oklahoma, and with those jobs, Blanche and I began to hope. The Works Progress Administration, or WPA, employed adults for projects like the Woodland Park Pool, sandstone retaining walls in town, and the City Hall Annex. A few summers ago, Fremont and his dad had labored with the government's CCC program at the Twin Lake's Dam.

Young people could get paid through the National Youth Administration or NYA for training, and Blanche was one of the lucky ones. She screamed for joy when they offered her a training job in a sewing room where women, ages sixteen to twenty-four, made clothes for the needy.

At the end of Blanche's first week at work, I agreed to meet her at Woodland Park for lunch. Margaret, Judson, and I meandered through downtown Shawnee, which had changed drastically in the past decade. No more Indians in shawls sitting under the awnings and few horses tied to posts. The long lines of unemployed bedraggled men and women were gone however, a few individuals remained, and old men still sat in the shade smoking cigarettes. I missed the clack of the trolley.

We arrived at Woodland Park and strolled down the beautiful shady walkways to a concrete picnic table and sat down. I could see the south side of the three-story brick Municipal Building where Blanche worked.

She finally pranced down the sidewalk, swinging her pocketbook, her calf-length dress swaying around her, her hair waved to perfection.

"How's your new job?" I asked as Margaret moved over to let her sit down.

"It's work. I train in a room with thirty-two girls, but I can look out my window and see children on the playground. I could see you."

"So, what I read is true? The NYA helps young women become self-supportive—like classes in gardening, canning, and nursing?"

"True as sunshine. I get paid eighteen dollars a month." Blanche tossed her head. "I like it. Keeps me busy and makes me feel worthwhile."

"That's a good salary. Better than most people make, but don't get too uppity, sis. You have a long way to go." I tossed Blanche an apple. "Remember, God provides."

"I'm not as ungrateful as you think. I've met a lot of girls, and even though I come from the upper-middle-class, I understand them. I'm like Daisy in *The Great Gatsby*." Blanche took a bite of the apple. "Mama understands my attitude even if you don't."

Those last words stung. Mama had never understood anything I did but seemed to have no trouble identifying with my sisters. I unwrapped two egg salad sandwiches and cut one in half for Margaret and Judson. "I made you a sandwich." I held one out to Blanche.

"I hate egg sandwiches." Blanche pulled a wrapped bologna sandwich from her pocketbook and set it on a napkin. "I brought my own lunch."

I thought of the way our family had flaunted our money in better times—the cut flowers mama had kept in the house, the latest fashions we'd worn. Blanche tended to think she was better than others. "Maybe you can make friends at work."

Blanche tossed her hair back and lifted her chin. "Most of the girls aren't just poor, they're uneducated, but we're learning together. When they make me the artist for the group, I'll get a raise! Twenty-two dollars a month. That's the least I deserve since I'm so smart."

Blanche. Blanche. No one said you were dumb. Arrogant maybe, but never dumb.

Chapter Fourteen

October 1939

Sibyl

The opportunity to have a sisterly talk with Marjorie—a serious sit-down, heart-to-heart chat, had been put off long enough. I wasn't sure if I could guide her toward sensibility, but that day my goal was to get my younger sister on the straight and narrow.

I waited on Main Street in front of Mammoths, admiring their window displays, saddened I couldn't purchase anything so stylish as padded shoulders and a tight-waisted, flared dress. New outfits were beyond our budget.

Marjorie joined me, dressed in a printed blue dress with a white collar, always trendy. We strolled through the aisles of Mammoths, whiffed the perfumes, tried on flashy beads, and wondered how anyone could afford the fine lacy slips folded on the top shelves in the back.

Later, we walked down the sidewalk and crossed the street to Owl's Drug Store. When we entered the glass doors, I noticed the scuffed, wooden floors, the sparkling glass countertops, and the youthful soda fountain jerk. Tall chairs scooted up against the bar, cozy as grandma's rockers.

"This is one of my favorite places, at least when I can afford to be frivolous," I said as we slid into the worn leather seats The almost empty diner meant we had our pick of tables, and we chose a booth near the back corner for privacy.

The charming young man behind the glass countertop came to get our order. He stared at Marjorie, her red lipstick and black eyeliner seeming to make him swoon like a love-sick farm boy. She winked at him, and I shook my head in dismay.

I ordered a slice of homemade lemon pie to share.

"I'm glad to be living back home, sis," Marjorie said. "You can't imagine what I went through in Phoenix with no family. I even started to miss the Green Frog Cafe, and you know what their food is like!"

She was interrupted by the waiter bringing the lemon pie, the young boy devouring my sister's fair face and flirtatious eyes. When he set the tray down, he leaned over her shoulder, a trifle too close in my opinion.

I ate a bite of my half of the pie, savoring the tart flavor. Not ready for seriousness, I slowly wiped meringue off my mouth. "There's nothing like Owl's for good dessert. Don't tell anyone I said that, especially my mother-in-law." The lemon pie was worth every penny I splurged.

Marjorie didn't waste time revealing the problems in her life. "I'm getting a divorce from Kelley."

I gasped, choking on a sip of water. "Must have been bad when you went back to Phoenix to get Larry." When she arrived in Oklahoma without her son, she told us her husband Kelley had kept him. She soon returned to Arizona to steal the boy back.

Marjorie leaned against the side of the booth and set her napkin down beside her plate. "When I got there, I went straight to the babysitter's house and snuck my kid out." She grinned like a cheetah. "Lovey, can't you see me doing that? Sneaking through the back door? Tiptoeing around? Since Larry and I had to hitchhike back to Oklahoma in such a hurry, I left my trunk full of clothes."

"You must have been quite a duo." I raised my eyebrows. "With your bleached blond, sassy looks and cute, little Larry sticking out his thumb to the drivers."

"I'll say. We had no problem getting rides." Her voice got quiet, and I sensed a sadness in her tone. "Thanks for coming to get us."

Marjorie and Larry had finagled rides back to Oklahoma, landing on Aunt Adah's doorstep in Marietta. Aunt Adah, Mama's older sister, a staunch Christian Scientist who was sorely disappointed in Marjorie, took her in for the night.

"Oh, yes. Aunt Adah called Mama, and I overheard their conversation." Mimicking Adah's voice, I quoted her. "'I *demand* you drive down this instant and carry this irresponsible girl back to Shawnee. I want no part of her tomfooleries. She's crazy as a Betsy bug.'"

Marjorie and I laughed. Mama begged Fremont and me to drive her from Shawnee to Marietta, a two-and-a-half-hour trek south, close to Red River.

"You looked like you'd been drowned in a desert with cactus poking you in the face." I didn't say Marjorie's thin, scratched face and old clothes at the time, so unlike her, revealed what she had gone through.

"Dearie, Kelley's out of my life for good."

The overhead lightbulb hanging in the drugstore flickered while Marjorie crossed her legs to show them off before smoothing down her starched dress. "I don't attract good men like you do. Fremont's a regular Joe. I always pick the duds, the rotten eggs. Like Mama does."

I gritted my teeth. "If that man lays a hand on my nephew, I'll drag him down Main Street myself."

My sister grinned. "I can see you doing that." Then she stopped, and seriousness passed over her face. "Oh, I'm sorry. Losing baby Keith makes you touchy."

Marjorie had never met my child, had not seen Keith through his birth, illness, or death. She was not there for the funeral. "You can't understand how bad it hurts to lose a child," I said. "That's why I beg you to appreciate Larry more."

The waiter interrupted our conversation and handed me a clean fork. I took another bite of the lemon pie, licking my lips. Special treats were scarce. "I know it's been tough for a ginchy girl like you, Marjorie. It's been tough around here too, but at least Fremont has a job. What are you going to do now?"

"Don't know, lovey. Got a meeting with an attorney tomorrow." Marjorie wiped her mouth with a napkin, smearing red lipstick as she did.

Tempted to reach over and wipe her cheek, I realized this was the time for that spiritual, big-sister lecture. "You don't have to live like this anymore. Larry needs stability, not to be dragged from place to place." Frustration laced my words, frustration, and concern. "You need to settle down and pay more attention to him."

"We're doing fine, sis."

"Why don't you go to church with us on Sunday? You might find some answers there—and some decent folks."

Marjorie cocked her head. "No thanks, sweetie. Church is not for me."

"You don't have to go out looking for someone to care about you. God loves you."

"Larry and I will make it."

A huge sigh came out of my mouth before I could stop it. I hoped to convince Marjorie to consider the Lord, at least for her son's sake, but she wanted nothing of my faith. I left the drugstore with a heaviness pulling at my heart, not glancing back when I heard Marjorie beckon the soda jerk over.

My wild sister. She sought love and comfort, mostly through enticing men—men with double-breasted jackets, wide lapels, and toe-capped shoes. Men cocky enough to sicken a bulldog. Marjorie would do anything to please them.

I was tired of domestic crises. Longing to tell my family about the Lord felt as heavy as a chain pulling me to the bottom of the ocean, but I determined to hold my breath and try harder. How could I help my sister without pushing her away?

I bit my lip. I would never be able to find peace until our family drama subsided, and at that moment I wanted run as far away from Shawnee as possible. The stress of walking a tightrope left my heart in shreds.

***

Six days a week, Fremont left for his security job around seven o'clock in the evening. Before he left, we had a few minutes to discuss the money in our Havana cigar box. Autumn had arrived. We had forty-two dollars and seventy-four cents, enough to get to another town, pay the first month's rent, and start over. He hoped to find another job soon.

After he left, I did last minute cleaning, put the children to bed, re-counted the money in the cigar box, and read. Mostly I read to pass the time and relieve the monotony. I was halfway through Earnest Hemingway's controversial book, *A Farewell to Arms,* when I heard a knock on the front door.

Marjorie burst in. "Hi, sis. Caught you with a book again, didn't I? What a boring way to spend a Friday night."

"What's going on?"

She smoothed her dress over her hips and slid onto a chair. "Do you remember years ago when I asked you to go dancing with me to cheer me up? What do you say, lovey? How about tonight? I need cheering up."

Even though the suggestion sounded outlandish, I thought hard for a minute. I craved excitement and missed the dances before marriage and children took over my life. What fun we'd had. When music entered my soul, I could swing all night, but go to a dance hall with her now? Had my sister lost her mind?

Having a rendezvous already planned, Marjorie persisted. "We can take Margaret and Judson to Mama's. Larry's there, and they'll have a good time." She patted her hair in place. "They'll be all right."

When my siblings and I were teens, we had many parties. We would stand around the kitchen and pull molasses taffy or so-called stretch candy, or I would play the piano while everyone danced the jitterbug and the hop, striping the shine right off Mama's hardwood floors.

Married life with Fremont was steady and comfortable, but I had to admit I sometimes missed the old days.

"We could boogie, sis," Marjorie said. "I know some cool guys who can swing you 'til you're so dizzy you can't stand up." She begged in her little girl voice, "We'd be back before midnight, and I'm sure the beer's still as good as always. You could blow your wig."

"What?"

Marjorie let out a chuckle, tossing back her long wavy hair. "Oh, love, that means get excited. You understand?"

I looked into Marjorie's dark-stained eyes that sparkled with naughtiness and understood better than I ever had. My sister's kind of excitement—the kind that could lead to heartache, danger, and disaster—would never be mine. Years ago, when we were kids in Clinton, Oklahoma, Marjorie and a neighbor boy stole matches from the kitchen and snuck outside. In their rashness, they caught a field on fire. The flames spread quickly, trapping us in the backyard, away from help. In her terror, Marjorie panicked and ran in circles like a wild animal trying to escape, unable to find her way out. I found my way down an alley to a neighbor's, banged on the back door, and pointed toward the blaze. Soon, a firetruck arrived and began to put out the flames.

Maybe my restless sister was still running, trying to escape fires of her own making, jogging in circles, refusing to listen to reason.

Marjorie and my differences had always existed. She fluttered around like a butterfly while I scurried about like a busy bee. Maybe if we'd been more open and accepting, we could've learned from each other. I could've taught Marjorie how to deny yourself for the sake of others, and she could've taught me the joy of embracing happiness. But that evening, neither of us would be learning any lessons.

"Sorry, sis," I said. "Not tonight."

Marjorie drew her mouth into a pout. "You don't like that I still dance and have all the boyfriends. Admit it, you're jealous of me. But then, how can you not be? I have all the fun."

I told myself I'd gotten past jealousy of my beautiful, self-absorbed sister years ago. But had I? Did I want to twirl around until I got dizzy and forget all the realities of life?

Margaret's whimper from the bedroom answered my questions. I could not rouse my sleeping children from their warm beds and drag them to their grandmother's.

At one point in our lives, Marjorie and I had danced to the same raucous songs. But God had tamed—refined—the music inside me. He had changed me, and his music lived at the center of my being. In the deepest part of me, my music held so much more meaning than one night's cacophonies of sound.

Marjorie danced for a different reason than I did. "Thanks for inviting me, but even if it weren't for the children, I couldn't go." I patted my abdomen. "I haven't told Fremont yet, but I think I'm pregnant again."

Marjorie's mouth fell open. "Yo, sis! Well, I guess that settles that." She walked to the door, and with a good-bye flick of the fingers, disappeared into the darkness.

Fremont

Early Monday morning, Sibyl rushed to the toilet, vomiting. Had she over-worked herself, or caught something? Probably overdid taking care of the kids. I should have watched her closer.

Coming back into the bedroom, Sibyl ignored my raised eyebrows. "I'm fine now. And..." She patted her belly. "Another little one is on the way."

We're having another baby? I hoorayed a dozen times and pulled my wife into a hug big enough to squeeze the rind off a lemon. The best news I'd had in months. "This baby'll be born in a new home where we're going to start over." I didn't say we'd leave behind the memories of Keith in this house, or that we'd be away from family squabbles, but that's what I meant.

"We can't move now."

What?

"I don't want to be away from family while giving birth. We can move after this baby is born. I promise. I'll be ready by then."

I argued with Sibyl, pushed her to change her mind, pleaded that we shouldn't put it off, but my arguments were useless, and disappointment felt as heavy as when I ate too many day-old biscuits, weighing a thousand tons. The timing *never* seemed to work out the way I'd planned.

That night, I asked the good Lord to take care of the baby Sibyl was carrying, and for patience. It wasn't the right time for a move, but when would it be? Hopefully, by spring, assuming nothing major happened between now and then. Life could be so downright frustrating.

1940
Chapter Fifteen
January 1940

Fremont

The 1940s arrived with promises of improved weather, an end to the drought, and threats of war. I didn't subscribe to any of it. Newsreels, radio, and the newspaper all jumped in trying to be the first to let us know what went on in our world, and from their point of view, humankind was on the brink of annihilation.

Christmas had been bittersweet. Different. No Keith running around, no toddler to chase. Maybe that was why we'd splurged on gifts for the kids, buying them presents like never before. Margaret got the first baby doll she ever had. How a child could love a plastic imitation of a baby so much, I'd never understand. Judson was thrilled with his peashooter and cork pop gun and bounced with more energy than a wild Billy goat let loose in a field of daisies. I managed that bit of peashooter ingeniousness.

January woes arrived before I could shout to two. Sibyl's mama couldn't afford the mortgage payment on her house on Beard Street, and the bank foreclosed—not without discussion and arguments, I imagine. The bungalow house Mr. Trimble built in '27 held many memories, but it had no place in Mrs. Trimble's tight-budgeted future.

Where could she go? Besides her, Blanche, Frances, and Grandpa Bennett, she had four boarders: a sociable elderly couple; Mr. Haney, a frumpy old gentleman; and Mrs. Peterson, a pleasant but lackadaisical widow. Mrs. Trimble couldn't turn out the boarders, now could she?

The old First Baptist Church parsonage on North Broadway stood empty. From what we heard, the preacher didn't like the run-down house that had sat vacant for years, so the church bought a new house for him.

The church agreed to rent the old parsonage to Mrs. Trimble.

"I'm grateful," she told us. "The church isn't using the building and leased it to me cheap. Unfortunately, we have tons of work to do because it's unlivable."

Unlivable was an understatement. Four blocks closer to downtown Shawnee, the house looked big enough for Mrs. Trimble's family and every tenant she ever had. Huge, beautiful birch trees lined the walkway, but the rest was disastrous. My dad's cow pasture would've been more accommodating.

The next weekend, the womenfolk scrubbed the house from the light fixtures to the baseboards. Sibyl cleaned the oven and threw out trash from closets while I did repairs and painted the bedrooms, groaning, stretching, and getting paint on my old khakis. It felt good to help my in-laws, even if their negative chatter made me wish I could close my ears.

We finished the cleaning and painting within three days and then pulled up the living room rugs. I declare, wood parquet floors lay underneath. That refinishing job looked bigger than Kansas, but the girls didn't seem to mind. I like to think I did most of the work—sanding the wood by hand, re-staining it, wiping a sealer on top—but it took all of us. Three full days of labor later, we gazed at the most gorgeous geometric floor design I'd ever seen.

***

"I can't believe the transformation!" said Sibyl. "Look at this house."

The family stood on the sidewalk wearing jackets to shield us from the south wind. We studied the remarkable-looking dwelling. Tired faces and aching muscles didn't deter our pleasure. We did it.

"I didn't want to leave our old house." Mrs. Trimble placed her hands on her hips and scanned the place. "But look at this. We now have a clean spacious building that will hold us all."

Moving day came, and chaos reigned like a scary Hitchcock movie.

We moved most of the items by hand, walking the several blocks instead of using our car. The elderly boarders moved the same day as Mrs. Trimble, enlisting relatives and friends to help. With all the people, we bumped into each other, stepped on toes, got items in the wrong room, and rearranged the already chaotic.

Grandpa was underfoot. When he offered to do a little carpentry repair, I led him to the back yard near a pile of used lumber. Exhaustion took over, but we kept moving, traipsing up and down the sidewalk until all that was left was the heavy furniture and an icebox.

"Here, Fremont, move this end table over there." Sibyl was hugging her stomach. When she caught my eye, she mouthed, "Almost finished." She looked exhausted.

"Why don't you sit and rest a bit?"

Sibyl slumped into a chair, and I stroked her hair. Her face was pale, her eyes droopy.

Mrs. Trimble appeared around the corner.

"What are you doing about the icebox?" I asked. "And the sofa?"

"Don't worry. I hired a moving truck for the larger items."

"Well, hallelujah for that." I started to grin but held it back when Mrs. Trimble eyed me.

Mrs. Trimble, Blanche, and Frances's living quarters were no better than what they'd had in the previous house. They kept only two bedrooms, one for Mama and Frances, and one for Blanche and Grandpa Bennett, twin cots in the same room.

"Now we have to clean the backyard," said Mrs. Trimble.

Mine wasn't the only groan in that room.

"Next weekend," she said.

We heaved a sigh of relief.

***

The following Saturday, with the weather clear but chilly, Sibyl and I pitched in to help Blanche in the backyard while Mrs. Trimble and Frances worked inside the house. Unlike the luscious yard and garden the Trimbles left behind, this plot was in major disrepair. Covered with trash, old newspapers, and tree limbs, with broken machinery parts scattered about, the place looked worse than a junkyard.

We stayed busy all weekend getting the yard presentable, dumping useless flowerpots, picking up tossed tin cans, and pulling weeds out of the flower beds. I trimmed bushes and pushed the lawnmower over the immense lawn, which included a terrace toward the back. Margaret seemed excited about helping, doing her share, but her main job was watching Judson and Larry, making sure the rascals didn't wander off or get tangled up in the broken fence trying to escape.

Sibyl tired more easily than usual, but I was smart enough not to tease her about shirking work, insisting she rest often. We spent hours picking up, raking, and carrying trash to the alley for pickup. We pulled a million weeds, and by the time we finished the yard looked almost in order. Almost. Everything in our life was *almost*.

***

The next day, wearing coats and hats, we met Mrs. Trimble and the girls at the northwest corner of Woodland Park before trekking over to their old Beard Street home. Sibyl's mama had enlisted us to dig a few of the flowers from their former yard. Mrs. Trimble rationalized that, with no one to water them, the flowers would die before spring.

"This house holds more memories than Mama's photo album," Blanche said as we rounded the corner.

"Papa built this house." Sibyl's voice was low and smooth. "We lived here while I went to high school and college." She pointed to the window on the north side. "That's where Marjorie and I snuck out to dance at the Blue Bird."

We stepped up to the front porch and I remarked, "And this is where you and I sat courting. Swinging. Holding hands—and kissing." I leaned over and gave Sibyl a sloppy kiss.

Sibyl responded, but before I could sneak another kiss, she was hiking toward the back yard.

I rushed to open the gate, and she walked through and leaned against the fence post, breathing heavily, and we hadn't even started working yet.

Dead branches lay against the wall, stark and bleak as the overturned picnic table on the side porch. A neglected yard now, like my in-law's marriage.

Mrs. Trimble appeared beside me. "Papa ruined everything. We would still be living here if it weren't for him. That man embodies the worst of humankind."

Even though I didn't care for Mr. Trimble, I cringed at her denunciations. Family should be more loyal to each other.

Mrs. Trimble glanced at Sibyl. "Is something wrong with you? You aren't pregnant again, are you?"

Sibyl hesitated. "I'm not sure."

Mrs. Trimble looked at her askance. Sibyl's mother could make my heart sink faster than quicksand. She wanted to shame my wife, while I was trying to pull her away and give her more dignity.

"Okay. I think so," Sibyl admitted.

"When were you going to tell me? When the cows come home? Were you so embarrassed you wanted to keep it a secret?" Mrs. Trimble's look could have slain an army. "What am I going to do with you? Surely, you know how to stop having children. What are you going to do if Fremont leaves you with all these kids like your papa left me?"

I cleared my throat, reminding her I was standing right there. Not that she could have missed me. I put my arm around Sibyl and pulled her toward me. Her pregnancy was wonderful news. "You don't have to worry. I'm never leaving Sibyl, and I'll take care of her like I promised."

"All men say that."

I let my arm drop. Although her words didn't surprise me, my heart fell. My mother-in-law should be joyful about a new grandbaby. She disapproved of our marriage, disapproved of Sibyl, and now she disapproved of our unborn child? "Wait a minute. We consider this child a gift from God."

Mrs. Trimble turned back to the flower bed. She humphed, speaking over her shoulder to Blanche. "Get a few more of those irises, Lord knows, your papa spent a fortune on them. Take several in case they don't stay alive." Mrs. Trimble handed a rhizome to Blanche but directed her gaze at

Sibyl. "And having another baby in this forsaken day and age is the epitome of stupidity."

I took a step forward, ready to defend our little family, wanting to say that her family was in shambles, and we weren't about to take advice from the likes of her. That I would never do what Mr. Trimble had done, but then I was not married to a shrew either. I wanted to say all those things so badly, my jaw ached from the pressure of keeping it shut. How my sweet, tenderhearted wife could have come from that shrill woman and her arrogant ex-husband, I would never understand.

Sibyl pulled me back toward her, and we followed them on the sidewalk toward their new house. Sibyl wiped away the tears in her eyes and tried to continue a decent conversation. "Your house will look better with flowers in the yard."

Her arms loaded with bulbs, Mrs. Trimble mumbled, "Stupid, I say. Just stupid. But at least you have plenty of room for another kid. That's more than we have, what with Gramps and the boarders."

How did my caring wife deal with such a mother? One who didn't offer approval but instead gave derisive words, words that stung like scorpions. Never much of a talker, I handled negative emotions by hiding like a possum at nighttime, coming out only when it felt safe. I settled my face into a passive look, knowing this was not the time to discuss leaving Shawnee, but a move to another town would get us away from the damaging influence of her family.

I wanted Sibyl to know I'd protect her from hurtful darts, be her guardian, and even if no one else jumped for joy, she and I would adore this new baby. A different child could never fill the empty spot of the one we'd lost, but God had blessed us. It would be a joy to have a little one in the house again, even if that meant we'd have to delay moving.

I couldn't help myself any longer and jumped on top of the rock retaining wall. I yelled to the rooftops, "We're having another baby!"

Laughing, Sibyl pulled me back down. "You're crazier than a loon." But her smile told me she didn't mind my brand of crazy. She looked at me like a hero from heaven while her family stomped away.

Chapter Sixteen

"Hurry or we'll be late for the performance!"

My prompt and efficient husband always seemed to be dressed and have his hair slicked back with Brylcreem before I took out my pin curls.

"I'm coming," I called to him, knowing I was telling a bald-faced lie. I still had to find Margaret's shoes, comb Judson's mop, wash the last dishes, not to mention, put on a little lipstick and face powder.

Frances's dance performance was scheduled for seven o'clock at the Bison Theater on Main Street. The group would be the entertainment for an electric company event, and the performers' families were invited.

Mama had taken in extra washing to pay for Frances's ballet dance lessons, and I admired her for working at several jobs to take care of my sisters' needs. My slim, pretty little sister had taken tap, toe, and ballet the past year at Wanda Stamp's downtown studio. When Mrs. Stamp recognized Frances's talent, she'd offered her a job teaching new students in exchange for lessons, which helped Mama a lot.

Mama and Blanche were waiting under the Bison theatre marquee when we arrived, and we hurried inside as a group.

"Mrs. Stamp thinks Frances is talented and should continue dancing lessons," Mama whispered to me as I scooted through a row of chairs and got Margaret and Judson situated. "But she's moving to Ardmore and wants Frances to travel there every week for lessons."

Mama straightened her broad-brimmed hat before taking a seat in the thousand-seat auditorium. Blanche sat on the other side of her, and the children and Fremont on the other side of me.

"Ardmore's almost a hundred miles away. That's a long trip for dance lessons." I looked around and lowered my voice. "She'd have to ride a train. Can't you find another teacher in Shawnee?"

"No teacher I can afford. Frances loves dancing, and I'd hate to take it away from her. Plus, she needs these lessons." Dr. Fortson had told Mama that dancing would help straighten Frances's left, turned-in foot. Frances wore special Re-Mix sandals with straps to correct her ankle. Pigeon-toed, Doc called it.

"And she loves this teacher. There's not another one like her in town. Do you remember that dance rail in our house?"

Nodding, I put my pocketbook on the floor and my hand on Judson's head to keep him quiet.

"Mrs. Stamp's husband installed it so Frances could practice at home. Wasn't that a generous thing to do?"

Someone tapped Mama on the back and asked her to remove her hat since the big feather blocked their view. A new year meant new hats, and most women in the room wore the stylish smaller ones.

"She must think Frances is good," I said.

"Oh, she *is* good. Mrs. Stamp claimed she could easily be a professional."

The dance troupe vaulted onto the stage. A dozen young girls in pink tutus and tights stood in a line. Frances especially looked cute in her outfit with a matching bow in her dark hair and I wished I had a picture of her.

Judson squirmed, tying and untying his shoes, and in his unusually deep voice, he asked how long the show would last, sounding like a little old man.

Mama leaned over and scowled. "Shh...can't you keep that boy quiet?"

I put my arm around him as if to protect him from the words, but what do you do with a boy who can't sit still? Some children were simply more boisterous than others, and Judson was one of those. If Mama expected a well-behaved child, she'd met her match in her grandson.

I pointed toward two redheaded girls standing beside Frances. "Are those the twins she always talks about?"

"Yes, Joyce and Joy. They've been in her dance class for a while now."

We watched as Frances and the other girls glided, twirled, and jumped in the air. The performance was outstanding, although I'm not sure Fremont and Judson enjoyed it as much as the ladies did.

After the performance, Frances ran to greet us and gave hugs all around, her face glowing with excitement. Thankfully, she lived in a bubble, trying to ignore the negativity. Helping Frances with dance lessons showed Mama's willingness to make sacrifices—if only Mama wasn't so bitter about Papa and disappointed in me.

"You did such a great job that I'll take you to the movies this weekend," I said, hugging Frances again. "How about that?"

Frances's favorite movie was *Mother Carey's Chickens*, based on the novel by Kate Douglas Wiggin. "I've seen it twice already," she said, "but I'd love to go again."

I hadn't seen the flick yet, but after reading the book, my interest had been piqued.

Talk of the war in Europe was all around us, but life had to go on—like Frances had gone on after Papa left, trying so hard to have a normal childhood. Her young heart had been affected as much as the rest of us.

How could I move away from her? How could I abandon my young, innocent sister to this sour and harsh family life? She needed me.

But how could I tell Fremont I didn't want to move. His heart was set on it.

Chapter Seventeen

February 1940

Fremont

Margaret and Judson spent many weekends at my folks' house. We often left the children with them from Saturday afternoon until after church on Sunday. It gave Sibyl and me much needed private time, a chance to drag Main Street, or an opportunity to visit friends.

My mother loved having her grandkids visit. She'd kiss them when they arrived and treat them with freshly baked cookies and milk. Dad, with his overalls and a red bandana hanging out his back pocket, also loved having the kids around, even if he did more frolicking than taking care of their needs. He would sing *Oh, Susanna*, and *De Camptown Races*, songs I remembered from when I was a tot.

Such a lively, happy household compared to Sibyl's kin. As Mother used to say, "The best sermons are lived, not preached." Her wisdom made me smile.

We met the children at church, and after the services, drove to my family's house on Tennessee Street for the midday meal. The skies were cloudy, and rain had beat down all morning. The fresh, clean scent smelled like heaven in the air. However, the deluge had created slippery, muddy ruts in the dirt roads making it difficult to navigate the south side of Shawnee. My clunker slid around like a drunkard on skates. We parked on top of the hill at the dead-end of West Farrell and waited for the last burst of rain to stop before walking down the hill to Tennessee.

Margaret and Judson ran ahead of us along the wet pathway toward the front door. As Judson disappeared down the hill, Margaret darted straight toward a mud puddle. I held my breath as she stepped right into it. Oh, that child.

Sibyl turned to look at me. "See what your daughter's doing? She walked through that mud like she didn't see it at all!"

"A puddle is hard to resist."

"Margaret!" Sibyl yelled. "Get out of that mud! And go wash your shoes off at the well."

The child tried to take a step, but the red clay tugged on her oxfords. She stepped out of both shoes and turned around through the mud in her stocking feet.

Sibyl gasped.

When Margaret reached down into the muck for her lost shoes, mud splashed over her church dress. I've never seen a child so soiled, and I started laughing before moving to help her.

Sibyl didn't see the humor. "Those are her good Sunday go-to-meeting shoes, and that dress! It may be a hand-me-down, but we can't afford to replace it."

I picked up Margaret, disentangling her from the mud, and set her on solid ground. Then watched as she wiped her dirty hands on her dress, smearing it more.

"Why didn't you step over that mud puddle?" Sibyl's anger flared at times I couldn't understand. Then again, I didn't scrub the clothes.

Margaret reached up with her dirty hands and pushed curls out of her face, leaving her adorable face streaked with red clay.

I couldn't help but be tickled at our child's shenanigans. I wiped the mud off her face and glanced at Sibyl, who shook her head, trying to suppress amusement, her temper fading as quickly as it rose.

Margaret turned and ran toward the water well by the house.

Watching her, Sibyl shook her head. "I don't know why I'm so harsh. Why do those words come out of my mouth? But, think of it, both the shoes and dress will be useless except for rainy days like this one."

I had no solution to that.

We reached my folks' yard, and, since there was no running water in the house, I drew a bucket of water from the outside well. Sibyl began to clean Margaret's dress while I wiped at her shoes.

Mother opened the back door and poked her head out. "What in the world happened to Margaret?"

Dad stood right behind her, and I saw him smile behind his pipe, clearly enjoying the scene. "Children will be children."

"Ollie, hush. You shouldn't be laughing at her," scolded my mother, but I saw her hide a grin.

"Every path has some puddles." My dad, a lackadaisical philosopher, drew calmly on his pipe.

Sibyl and I finally got the child cleaned up, and we all traipsed into the kitchen. Mother planned on chicken and dumplings, and I sniffed the air as we entered the house. My stomach rumbled, and Sibyl poked me in the side with her elbow.

My family home had four rooms—a living room, a kitchen, and two bedrooms off to one side. The house seemed to shrink on rainy days when the kids and menfolk couldn't go out, but even overcrowded, it was pleasant. The wood stove created enough warmth for the whole place to feel cozy. My younger sisters, Irene and Ruth, were busy setting the table, helping Mother finalize the meal.

We sat around Mother's table—me on my second helping of chicken and dumplings, my dad telling his crazy jokes. "Judson," Dad said, "pass the 'lasses."

Judson cocked his head like a curious puppy. "You mean molasses, Grandpa?"

"How can you have mo-lasses if you ain't had no 'lasses' yet?"

The children giggled with delight. They loved his humor even if they had heard the joke a thousand times.

"Remember that time we tricked Mama?" Irene recounted the story. "Dad and I purchased some meat—six juicy slices of steak—and brought it home. Meat rarely found its way to our table, and Mother was thrilled."

Mother Pope rolled her eyes.

"The meal was delicious as always. Everyone ate a slice." Irene nodded toward her younger sister. "Even you, Ruth."

Ruth, a gorgeous seventeen-year-old with an angular face, perfect figure, and sweet personality could have been on a Broadway show. Although right then, her face didn't show pleasure but disgust. "That was not a good joke. Especially when Dad encouraged Mother and me to share that last serving."

Dad had a round, happy face, and his booming laughter rang throughout the room. He could hardly speak. "As I remember, you and your mother argued about who would get the last slice. You gave up dessert for that last piece of meat."

Irene couldn't help gloating. "I can't believe you fought over goat meat and you didn't even know it was goat meat. I'll never forget Ruth running out the door when she found out what it was. We could hear her vomiting from in here."

Mother frowned at Dad's smile. "You old codger. How could you pass goat meat off as beefsteak?"

"Irene and I bought it on sale. I knew you'd enjoy it if I didn't tell you what it was."

Mother looked askance at her wayward husband, and I knew what was coming. "You knew I didn't want to eat goat. You can play jokes on these children, but you've met your match with me." She shook her head. After living with Dad for forty years, she had learned to dish out pranks as well as anyone.

"But we got you back, Dad," Ruth said. "You refused to eat raw eggs, so after lunch, Mother made homemade ice cream and put raw eggs in it. And you ate two bowlfuls!"

Merriment reigned at the table for the next thirty minutes as we experienced the joy of an exuberantly happy family.

Sibyl and I had kept our secret for weeks, waiting for the right time to tell my folks. When the conversation lagged, I said, "Mother, we have an announcement."

"Don't just sit there," she said. "Do tell."

"Sibyl's going to have a baby."

Mother's face lit up, and she turned to Sibyl. "I guessed it when you looked so tired and nauseated. I'm happy for you, girl."

Sibyl beamed at my mother's approval, but then her face fell. "Mama didn't take the news well and certainly didn't approve." She hurried on without waiting for a comment. "And another thing. I've been doing a lot of physical labor, helping Mama move, so I hope I haven't hurt my baby."

I loved that Sibyl could share her worries with my mother.

Calm as always, Mother stood to take the dirty dishes from the table. "You'll be fine, dear. Just fine. Work will only make the baby stronger. And remember—this baby is a gift from the Lord."

My sweet, caring mother. I wanted to grab her and kiss her. Whereas Sibyl's mother always found fault, mine could lift our spirits like a cool breeze on a summer day.

Dad stepped into the living room and sat on the floor with the children, promising a game of rock, paper, scissors. A few minutes later, I peeked in and watched him entertain the kids. Margaret sat next to him, wearing one of Ruth's shirts, which swallowed her, while her clothes were drying. Through large blue eyes, she peered at her Grandpa and giggled. Judson, on the other hand, climbed onto his shoulders and rode him like a horse.

Watching the ruckus, my heart filled with happiness and apprehension. When the Lord called us away from here to a new place, to a new town, would we be able to leave such loving folks? How could I ever tell them our plans? So many reasons to stay in Shawnee. So many reasons to leave.

Sibyl wanted to share the good news of Christ wherever the Lord led, but not until her family was happier. Would she ever be free from her mama's bitterness, Marjorie's waywardness, and Blanche's hateful attitude toward the world? That was just the beginning of their issues. I wanted a family like mine—happy and taking problems in stride rather than succumbing to them and I was determined to have it.

My wife wanted to lift her family up, but more often than not, she got dragged down into their disputes. That would never lead to a content life or security for our kids.

As we rounded up the children to go home, Mother handed me a package wrapped in cheesecloth. "I churned fresh butter. Daisy has been extra generous with her milk lately." Then she handed me a basket. "And here's a dozen eggs."

I swallowed hard. My parents' generosity brought me to the brink of tears. Living in the same town had helped us in so many ways.

"Son, I'm delighted to hear about the new baby." Mother patted my shoulder. "You've got a lovely family, and I pray every day for God to take care of you all."

Gratitude flooded me—gratitude for my parent's acceptance and physical and emotional support while I scrambled to make ends meet and deal with an uncertain future. They understood I yearned to move at the same time bamboozled with another child. Complications came in droves.

I stood in my parents' doorway and held home-churned butter, fresh eggs, and Margaret's clean dress and shoes. Life could be good. Problems or no problems.

Chapter Eighteen

March 1940

Fremont

Sibyl and I loved nature and spending time with our best friends, Effie and Doug, so we decided to go camping together for the weekend. Platt National Park in the Oklahoma Arbuckle Mountains, about sixty miles south of Shawnee, held swimming holes, winding walking trails, and natural mineral springs. I hankered to travel to the foothills, where the forest would be in bloom.

Talk of moving away from Shawnee had faded between Sibyl and me, especially as she focused on taking care of family and children. I terribly wanted to relocate, and contemplated plans even if I didn't discuss it with her. My visions of the future were set, but I wasn't sure about hers. Maybe this trip to the mountains would remind her that we had plans to make. That we didn't want to live in Shawnee permanently.

Early Saturday morning, we followed the Douglas' Ford down Highway 177, through Stratford and Asher, arriving at the park by midmorning, and then drove around to where the CCC fellows had built covered pavilions and rock walls. With only one tent, for a second sleeping area, we strung a tarp between two trees. Effie and Sibyl set up mats and cots underneath the tarp.

The Douglas' had three kids nearly the same ages as ours, which meant we had six children between us, all under seven years old. Now that was a mess of little ones running around.

Good friends. Army cots. A watermelon. A cookstove. Hot dogs stuck on long sticks and cooked over the fire. Euphoria claimed me.

An unusually warm day, the children begged to wade in the cold creek water, and we headed toward the running stream. Sibyl and I sat on a rock by the creek's edge while Doug took off somewhere upstream fiddling with his fishing gear, maybe to Little Niagara Falls.

The children's laughter rang out like joyful music. Well, until they screamed about the icy water, and within minutes, jumped out. Margaret and Joyce wandered back to us, while Judson and Effie's boys, Robert and Dewayne, gathered sticks to use as swords.

Effie, a Pied Piper with children, yelled, "Come on kiddos! Let's go for a walk." She grabbed Sibyl's hand and pulled her along. "Come along with us."

The children's voices dimmed as they followed the ladies down a trail. My eyes closed, basking in the cool spring breeze. I must have fallen asleep, because next thing I knew, Judson was scrambling on top of me scattering sticks and leaves through the air.

"Daddy! Daddy! Look what I found!" he yelled. "A turtle shell." I sat up, and sure enough, that boy held the biggest shell I'd ever seen.

Several other children emptied their pockets to display prized pebbles, acorns, and bird feathers. I oohed and aahed over their treasures until Effie came to my rescue. "Let's see who can catch a butterfly!"

We should have kept that lady around more often.

After lunch, Doug pulled out his fishing pole and motioned me to get mine. We walked upstream to a waterfall, where Doug promised we could catch trout for supper. I hated to admit it, but I had never caught a fish. None. Ever. I could sit all day, follow all the fishing rules and advice, and still come up empty-handed, however, I did enjoy getting away from stress to sit with a fishing pole in my hand.

"Did you catch anything?" Effie asked Doug when we wandered back into camp.

"You betcha. Enough for supper and breakfast, too!" Doug, the best fishermen of the folks we ran with, held up a stringer of ten nice-sized trout, a crappie, and a huge white bass. He had an uncanny sense for finding a fish's hiding place.

No one had to ask how many fish I caught. None.

I stoked up the fire for supper thinking there was nothing like trout grilled over oak branches. I was right. While the adults feasted on fish and potato salad, the kids wolfed down hot dogs and chips. Watermelon for everyone.

Darkness fell, and we tucked the youngsters into their arranged sleeping places.

"I love this place, don't you, Fremont?" Wearing a jacket, Doug sat on a boulder, his brown hair falling across his forehead. "We should go back to that same fishing hole tomorrow."

I rubbed my chin. My whiskers grew as fast as dandelions. "That wasn't such a lucky spot for me. Maybe we can find a different place."

Doug threw his head back and hooted louder than a night owl. "Maybe it wasn't lucky for you, but I caught more than my share."

"Boys, boys." Effie turned toward the campfire and pulled a quilt around her shoulders. "Don't boast, Doug. You've been fishing all your life. Maybe you could give Fremont a lesson or two."

To end the fishing talk, I announced, "Hey, Sibyl and I have news to share. Anybody want to hear it?"

"Sure."

"Tell it!"

"We're going to have another baby!"

Sibyl's smile was bigger than the state of Texas. This would be our fourth child, and although missing Keith, the prospect of a new baby made me as happy as a white-tailed deer prancing through the Wichita Mountains.

"Fremont, you old buck, you. You didn't even say a word during all those hours fishing."

"Wanted to tell you both at the same time." I got up and threw another log on the dying fire. "I predict this one will be a girl."

Effie looked sheepish. "Guess I need to admit that I'm pregnant, too."

Her announcement was met with more cries of joy. The ladies had helped each other through previous pregnancies and were sure to help each other now. I remember baby Robert's birth.

Back in December '35, the Mammoth Department store was giving away several rooms of furniture to the family of the first baby born on or after January 1st. The Douglases, like the rest of us, lived in a tiny house and had next to nothing. Effie was absolutely set on getting that furniture. She went into labor at home on the morning of December 31st, but she wouldn't push when it was time, determined to make it to midnight. She didn't make it. Robert Douglas was born in the last two hours of the last day of the year, and he nearly lost his life because he was born blue and not breathing. Effie's sister called a doctor who arrived and gave instructions to wrap the baby in a blanket and lay him nearby. Instead, she performed mouth to mouth on the infant, and miraculously he began breathing on his own.

"What did your mama say about a new baby?" Effie asked Sibyl.

"Oh, you know my mama. She thinks Marjorie's the smart one with only one child." Sibyl raised her hands in a questioning gesture. "What can I say?"

"I declare, why would anyone not want another sweet baby around?" Effie made it seem as if anyone would be daft to disagree. "My youngest is walking around like a big girl now, and I'm ready for a new one."

I looked across the campfire to where Doug sat with his arm around Effie. In my heart, I wished they could always live nearby, right down the street from us. How could we move away from such good friends? They supported our lifestyle and had chosen the same path of having a big family.

I stared into the fire, the flames and uneasy thoughts heating my face. I wasn't sure how a new baby would affect our plans to move, but Mother said children were a blessing from God, and I say, a man can't have too many blessings.

Chapter Nineteen

Sibyl

Marjorie found a job in the ladies' department of Sears, Roebuck & Company. Their massive, two-story building was located downtown on Main Street. One unwritten benefit of her job was that she could rescue discarded or damaged items tossed to the alleyway, which meant she brought goods home for the family to mend or repair. One of her rescues was a fashionable straw hat with a modest brim for Mama. Thrilled with the fashion windfall, Mama paraded through town, shopping the sales, and showing off her new headpiece.

Marjorie and a girlfriend moved into a two-bedroom apartment above a storefront on East Main Street near the railroad tracks. Just as Marj got settled into her job and apartment and bought a few necessities, her boss fired her. Said he couldn't afford her anymore.

She couldn't find another job.

On a breezy February afternoon, I walked to Marjorie's apartment to check on her. Her greeting was all lightness and air as if she were riding a swing, suspended from a cloud. But I knew that couldn't be true.

"I saw your divorce notice in the paper," I said. "Hope you managed to get some child support from him."

"Nope. Don't want anything from that two-timing cat. Larry will be much better off without him. We both will."

I couldn't imagine a life without Fremont, a steady man who loved me. But Fremont wasn't Kelley, and unless Kelley changed, he would only be bad news for Marjorie and Larry. He had never supported them much anyway.

I knew she had to be low on cash and food. "Why don't you come to our house for supper. Brown beans and hot cornbread will fill your belly."

"Don't worry, sis. Life will turn around. Just wait and see."

By that, I assumed she meant a man would come along and offer her roses and sunshine.

"I ran into a gent last night at that shindig in Seminole. He's a regular hot potato on the dance floor and thinks I'm the dandiest dame he's ever seen."

The kind of men she attracted—men dressed in fancy duds who didn't stick around—would only use her and discard her like an empty cigarette pack. I feared she would attract another dolled up, ne'er-do-well, scratching the bottom of the barrel again. "What are you going to do now?"

"Don't be concerned about me, dearie. I'll make it, and if I must, I'll move back in with Mama again."

"How will you take care of Larry?" A handsome child with pink cheeks and long eyelashes that were the envy of every female, he seemed able to adapt to any situation, even though I often saw confusion in the eyes veiled behind those lashes.

"He's staying with Mama," Marjorie said. "She'll watch him. At least, he'll have a roof over his head and won't go hungry."

That would have been a blessing, except Mama's daylight hours were spent traipsing around town. She played bridge with friends, saying she needed a diversion, and many nights she attended women's club meetings. Singing at Eastern Star was also thrown into the mix. I didn't come right out and say Mama neglected her children, only stated the obvious. "Mama is gone an awful lot which means Blanche will be taking care of him."

Marjorie shrugged as if she didn't see a problem. "Larry makes friends easily, even with unpleasant people, so I'm sure he can win Blanche over."

I shook my head and stood to go. Maybe Marjorie was right to leave Kelley, a two-timing abuser, but divorce was destructive to a family. I was seeing the effect my parent's divorce had on my sister and her child. There was no joy in this household and I wondered if there ever would be again.

I longed for joyfulness but we would never find it until we distanced ourselves from our troubles. Or were we merely trying to run away from them?

Marjorie didn't hear anything I said, and it hurt to see her darting through life like a wild turkey, not able to see a fox lurking around the corner. I wanted to shoo the craziness from her skull because clearly, she wasn't thinking about the future. My sister's short-sightedness wasn't just unhealthy for her. I feared it would be harmful for little Larry.

Chapter Twenty

That next morning, after the children left for school, I grabbed my pocketbook to go shopping. Rumors were flying that the biggest store in the area would be going out of business. Mammoths, Shawnee's largest department store, had been around for forty-five years, almost since Shawnee became a viable town. Now, if rumors could be believed, Montgomery Ward would be purchasing it. Hopefully, there would be a big sale—a madhouse of barterers, more like it.

Mammoth's, the big red brick building on the southwest corner of Main and Bell, had the best window displays in town. Mannequins wore narrow-waisted dresses, shortened for the promising new decade, small hats cocked to one side, and handbags that matched leather pumps. I would have loved to buy such a pulled-together outfit.

A little later, I left, having found nothing I could afford, thinking I should wait until after my baby was born to purchase anything.

I stopped briefly at the Pottawatomie County Bookstore and purchased *The Grapes of Wrath*. Reading offered an escape from a chaotic life. Fremont accused me of spending too much money on books, and he didn't even know half of what I bought from my savings.

Finding myself only a few blocks from Mama's new home, I decided to drop in and ask her to take a walk with me. The springlike weather was fetching, and flowers would soon arrive like a belle preparing for an exciting ball. Stopping at the small Sunshine Grocery Store on the northeast corner of Beard and Dewey, I picked up soda crackers and Sugar Daddy candies, and then raised the lid of the red metal Coca Cola icebox and pulled out two ice-cold pops.

Mama agreed to stroll with me through Redbud Park, my favorite park. Located in a quiet neighborhood on North Beard Street near West Dill, I seldom came to this small park because it had no playground for the children. I usually took them to Woodland or Boy Scout Park.

We walked through the splendid arched gateway where lovely jonquils bloomed along a path, and redbud trees lined the walkway.

Almost immediately, Mama launched into to her favorite topic—Papa. "I have news about your papa in case you're interested. You seem to take up for him."

My good mood deflated. "What news?"

"Your Papa can't seem to stay out of trouble. His legal problems are not over because that Barnett case is still going on."

"I wish the scandal would blow over. It's a never-ending thorn," I said. "We don't need any more publicity."

Papa, as a state banking auditor, had examined—and closed—banks during the thirties. He had been so intertwined in the statewide banking corruption that he might never recover. Disappointment in his behavior dogged me daily. Accusations of misconduct. Negative newspaper coverage. A corrupt auditor amidst hundreds of bank closings.

"Gossip will be what it will be." Mama's voice rose. Anger is a difficult emotion to ignore, and her temper could explode as quickly as a firecracker. "I get so mad every time I think about what your papa did to our family. How could he? He's a sleaze bag."

I pulled my scarf tighter around my chin as we walked across the narrow bridge.

"I don't want to ever see that man's face again, and my children better not speak to him." Mama continued to spit the words out for the next ten minutes.

I kept my head down and kept walking. My parents' friction continued long after the court adjourned, and Mama, unforgiving, would never find peace until she set it aside.

A rare flash of bravery pushed me to speak. "Instead of focusing on Papa so much, look at all you have. You have Blanche and Frances and Marjorie. And me and your grandkids."

"Fine for you to say. You have a good man who loves you."

She was right, but I was still shocked by her words. Mama had never called Fremont a good man before. Was she softening? Maybe this would be a good time to tell her about God and how much he loved her. "Mama, I know you don't like talking about church and the Lord, but he understands your problems."

Mama stopped and stared at the ducks in the creek. "How can God know what it's like to be abandoned? If my husband left me, who's to say God won't leave me. I don't buy it. Now don't get me wrong, I still believe he's out there somewhere, just not interested in me."

My mouth fell open. Mama thought God might leave her? How would I feel if Fremont left me like Papa left Mama? Fremont would never do that, would he? Could any man be trusted, or had Mama been right in saying men didn't care about women and their feelings?

I took a deep breath and reigned in those ridiculous and dangerous thoughts. Fremont was *not* Papa, and I resented the way Mama could raise such doubts in me. And God did care. He had pulled me through the fire and back more than once, always there for me. Instead of continuing to mull over life, I slowed down, breathed deeply, and enjoyed the remainder of the walk.

We arrived back at the park entrance and I kissed Mama good-bye on the cheek.

She pulled back. "Now do what's right about Papa and avoid him. You haven't always been an obedient daughter. You won't listen when I tell you not to spend so much time down at that church. Don't want you to become fanatical." Bitterness flowed through her words.

I hadn't been involved in church since Keith died. Why was Mama telling me what to do? *Control* seemed a strong word, but *influence*, perhaps? Our lives intertwined like the branches above us.

A knot wound tight around my chest, a confused mixture of fear and pain. Tears came quickly. How would I be the bold, outspoken, and confident person I wanted to be if rejected all the time?

My relationship with Mama rolled from good to bad and back in no consistent time frame, and there were times when she could be quite frustrating.

Familial ties were harder to manage than I expected, and I certainly couldn't tell Mama that Fremont hoped we would move away from Shawnee soon.

I rushed home where my husband would listen to my hurts.

Chapter Twenty-One

April 1940

Sibyl

Mid-morning two days later, Papa waltzed into our small house. He had a habit of suddenly appearing at the most inopportune times.

"Your flowers look good, Sibyl. I've always loved irises." Years before, Papa had collected an amazing assortment of irises from around the states and created the most beautiful back yard in Pott County. That was before he abandoned the house and everyone in it.

"Thanks, Papa." I reveled in his compliment, not mentioning the rhizomes were ones he had purchased from California.

"Can't stay long. Got a few minutes before a meeting downtown." He frowned, drawing his thin upper lip into a straight line. "Business meetings are the bane of society, invented to irk decent folk."

He looked around our living room with its scattered toys and crochet pieces stacked on a chair. To make our home warm and cozy, I had spent hours since the last time he came wallpapering and sewing new curtains, but he didn't comment on the improvements.

I wore a loose, printed cotton frock around the house, sleeveless because the weather was warm. It hung below my knees but was unsuitable clothing for a visitor, especially for Papa. I motioned for him to take a seat on the couch. He declined. Dressed in an immaculate suit with a matching vest and tie, he acted like his fancy duds might get soiled. He glanced disapprovingly at Judson, who looked like a street urchin, dirty from his tousled hair down to his bare feet.

Papa had a new position at the Reconstruction Finance Corporation, or RFC, an independent agency started by Hoover in '32 to stimulate bank loans. The job called for him to make loans to banks, railroads, mortgage corporations, and loan associations.

"Who're you meeting with?" I pulled Judson onto my lap to keep him still, holding him tight around the waist while he squirmed against my growing belly.

"The Home Building and Loan Association."

"Isn't that where the Barnett made an illegal transaction?"

Back in 1935, State Commissioner W. J. Barnett bought stock in Shawnee's Home Building and Loan Association for three fourths its face value. Barnett, accused of corruption, made a profit on the transaction. Papa was the primary witness against him.

"I read you went to court again. Is that true?" I had read an article in the April 7, 1940 newspaper. "And they called forty-two witnesses and it lasted six days?"

Judson wrangled in my arms. I let him go, and he dashed out the back door, Margaret following. The sound of Patches' barking carried through the open windows.

"A stupid waste of time," Papa said. "This debacle has dragged on for years now. I insist the thirteen thousand missing funds went to the Ardmore Bank, although the records have been stolen or hidden. It's plain as day. I saw the carbon tape from the entry machine myself."

"Will there be more trials?"

Papa paced. "No doubt. It's a fiasco. Numerous banks filed accusations, and the commissioner is way in over his head. He'll be sitting in jail until he's a hundred and twenty years old."

"How much were you involved?" I could have bitten my tongue, but the words spewed out and kept coming. "I mean, many people think Barnett was set up. Is that possible?"

Papa took off his hat and fanned himself before speaking in his authoritative voice. "Of course, I was involved. I audited the bank, for mercy's sake. Barnett claims I destroyed bank records in my possession as a state banking officer. Records that might have shown the man's innocence. Humbug. His claims are poppycock meant to prolong this disgusting affair."

His voice carried the harshness I remembered as a little girl when I left my shoes on the stairs or accidentally broke one of Mama's good dishes. "It's difficult to understand the situation, child," he continued. "Don't reach any conclusions. You don't know the background."

"Papa, I am *not* a child. I understand more than you think." I took in a slow, steady breath. My father never realized how much he irritated me. When I needed more information than what I got from the newspapers and gossipers, I eavesdropped, like when I played Sherlock Holmes and snuck through alleys years before. I had learned a lot about Papa and Commissioner Barnett. They were great buddies—before this legal battle. Now, they claimed the other was at fault.

"Best forget about the case," said Papa. " Nothing to worry about. Ask those bankers if I was fair or not. Come to think of it, don't ask them. Auditors like me are their sworn enemies."

Could I trust Papa? Was he telling the truth about the case? I might never know. My dander rose as I stood, but before hostile words could come out of my mouth, Judson flew in the back door with our terrier, Patches, on his heels. Chaos came in the form of me chasing the dog and the dog chasing Judson while Margaret stood in the middle of the room trying to catch the dog as he ran by. That dog and a boy could create a ton of mischief.

Finally, Margaret opened the back door and yelled, "Come on, Judson."

Judson and Patches sprung after Margaret through the back door, and it was quiet again.

"Is it always like this?" Papa had stepped toward the front door during the turmoil.

I wanted him to mention my coming baby, but he hadn't said any words of encouragement, so I replied, "Sometimes."

My anger gone, I reflected on the words Papa had not said. He seemed deceptive about the lawsuit, but maybe that was his nature. He'd certainly hidden girlfriends from Mama through the years.

Although disappointed in Papa, I wanted to confront him with his falsehoods and deceitfulness and rescue him from a blinded lifestyle that hurt everyone around him. He might be a scoundrel, but he was still my papa, and God would surely answer my prayers for him to change his life. Soon, I hoped.

***

As Papa turned to go, the front door flew open, and Blanche appeared in a tizzy. Her hair was disheveled, and she breathed heavily. Obviously, she'd come from her house on the north side of town.

Blanche saw Papa and turned to face him. "What are you doing here? You can't come visit your two youngest daughters, but you come see Sibyl?" Blanche's voice held bitterness which barely concealed a mountain-sized volume of pain.

My body tensed. Would Blanche tell Mama about seeing Papa at my house? I would never hear the last of it if she did, not with Mama's sour state of mind.

"I'll come by your house next week." He was lying. He never visited when he said he would.

Blanche reared her head back. "It doesn't matter." Her voice was too loud in the small space. "I don't want to see you anyway."

An awkward silence jumped through the room.

"I have to go now. Can't be late." Always avoiding his family, Papa rushed out the door, his emotions locked as tight as a turtle in his shell.

Blanche walked into the kitchen and began to make herself a sandwich as if nothing had occurred, laying out two slices of bread and putting a piece of bologna on top. "Do you have any pickles? A sandwich isn't good without pickles."

"No, we don't have pickles, and you don't need to tell Mama that Papa was here."

My sister shrugged. "I don't know what I'll do." She walked out the front door with her sandwich. She would probably hold Papa's presence over my head or let the news out at the most inopportune time.

My conscience told me I should keep the communication lines open with Papa, no matter what others thought, no matter that my mama disapproved.

I knew Papa wasn't the man I'd once thought, the man I'd idolized as a kid, but he had sunk farther than I realized.

***

I was preparing peanut butter and jelly sandwiches for the children when I stopped the knife midway in the air and squeezed my eyes shut, thinking about Papa's duplicity and all the scandals surrounding him. My faith in him had already fallen but now it plummeted like the '29 stock market crash. He could not always be trusted.

Continuing to prepare the lunches, I recalled an incident when I was young. Papa and I forded a creek in his motorcar to visit kinfolk near Ketchum. When Papa traveled, he wore a poor-boy cap with a bill instead of his high-class fedora or homburg. On a dirt road about halfway there, a grungy unkempt man stepped in front of our flivver. Papa slammed on the brakes.

Papa looked nervous, which made me nervous, and when the fellow motioned Papa to roll down his window, he quietly slid his wallet to me. "Hide it," he hissed.

Was this man a burglar?

Another man stepped from behind a grove of trees and walked over to Papa's car window. A decent looking fellow, he sported a starched white shirt with the sleeves rolled up.

Papa stepped out of the car and slapped the clean-looking man on the back. "Glad to see you, Elmer. Just knew I was a goner."

"Sorry about that. Thought you were a robber, what with the ball cap and all. I'm out here trying to catch a few."

The men shook hands and walked a few steps from the car, but even at that young age, my eavesdropping skills were keen.

"Haven't seen you at a Klan meeting lately."

"Been meeting with a group down south. Still dedicated to the cause," said Papa, the only voice I could distinguish.

"Did you hear about that traitor over in Maud?"

Then the men whispered, and I couldn't hear any more.

Finally, Papa practically ran back to the car and gunned the engine to leave.

"Who was that?" I asked. "What meeting did he mean?" The only Klan I knew was the Ku Klux Klan.

"I don't have a clue."

Papa was not always what he seemed to be. He pretended when convenient. For example, when I asked him about the KKK hood Frances found in our shed after he left Mama, he denied any knowledge of it. But who else could've put it there?

Papa tended to wear a smile, especially in public, and act as if his life was rosy. Maybe his upbringing made him distrustful, but whatever the reason, Papa never relaxed. He avoided issues. Always defended himself, and always pretended. And even though I couldn't trust his words and hated the way he treated family—I didn't want his soul on my conscience. Lord willing, someday Papa would understand that he walked down the wrong path.

In the meantime, I certainly didn't want his influence in my life or in my children's lives.

Chapter Twenty-Two

Fremont

I couldn't understand Mrs. Trimble's and Marjorie's nutty relationship. It went up and down at the speed of a bouncing ball.

Sibyl's mama had been so angry at Marjorie for testifying against her in the divorce three years ago that they didn't speak for months. Mrs. Trimble didn't consider that Marjorie needed her papa's financial help after her surgery. The girl had looked sick as a dog during the divorce and had so many medical bills she could never have pulled herself out of the pit without his help. She *had* to testify against her mama, or her papa would have let her drown. My heart ached over the pain caused to Sibyl's family.

Later, when Marjorie came traipsing back from Phoenix with Larry, Mrs. Trimble acted as if nothing had happened and all was normal between them again.

My mother-in-law loved to cook mouth-watering meals for family gatherings, and one Saturday in late April, Sibyl, the children, and I drove to her house, carrying a pan of hot rolls.

When we walked into the kitchen, Marjorie and Mrs. Trimble were busy, steam rising around them like fog. Mrs. Trimble turned on the burner to heat the grease for fried chicken, while Marjorie put potatoes in a pan to boil. Calvis, Sibyl's brother, and his wife, Evie, lived in Oklahoma City, thirty miles due west, and would be arriving around one o'clock, just in time to eat.

Sibyl pitched in to help, making iced tea while Marjorie set the table. The two younger sisters disappeared somewhere in the house, probably entertaining the ragamuffins, Larry, Margaret, and Judson, while I went to sit on the front porch to chat with Grandpa Bennett.

Mrs. Trimble was the best cook I'd ever known, excluding my mother, meaning she could've made a feast out of rotten 'taters and day-old bread. Gramps and I returned to the kitchen when Sibyl yelled that the chicken and potatoes were dished up and ready to be served.

"Hi, Mama!" Calvis shouted as he walked through the front door.

Mrs. Trimble and the rest of us hurried from the dining room to the living room to welcome him.

He took off his hat and pecked his mama on the cheek. "Jeepers, something smells heavenly."

His wife, Evie, trailed in behind him, followed by a good-looking fellow with blond, windblown hair. The blond guy propped himself against the doorpost.

Marjorie set down a stack of plates, rushed over to this stranger, and embraced him in a cozy hug. "Hi, sweetie." She gave him a long passionate kiss right there in front of the whole stinking family.

We stared. We had never met this fellow before. How did Marjorie know him?

I couldn't believe Sibyl's sister could be so openly affectionate, but then I shouldn't have been surprised. She'd been a flirt since I'd known her. Sibyl told me about the dances they went to years before and how Marj would dance with any guy with two legs, batting her tinted eyelashes at every male in the room, many of whom stared at her half-exposed bosom.

Marjorie turned around. "Meet Sammy. Isn't he a dear? I met him at a night club up in the City where he plays in the orchestra. You know how I love to dance."

"This is your new boyfriend?" Mrs. Trimble asked.

"Of course. Ain't he a darling? I wanted you to meet my dream man."

I exchanged glances with Sibyl before pulling out a chair for her. Marjorie and Sammy sat across from us. Despite the awkward beginning,

114

good food and talk flowed easily around the dinner table and continued as the siblings reminisced about the fun times, times when they were youngsters.

Marjorie was the one who brought up her father. "Remember when Papa came home from a business trip and scared Frances to pieces?"

"He usually brought gifts, but this time, he walked in empty-handed," Blanche added for the newcomer's sake.

"Papa claimed he brought home an alligator," Frances said as she took a second helping of potatoes. "An alligator!"

"She screamed like a banshee and refused to go out to the car."

We all laughed at the hoax, even Grandpa Bennett. I glanced at Sibyl beside me. I tended to be nervous at these family gatherings, not sure what tempers might flare or what nasty words might come out, but I enjoyed myself, laughing along with the rest.

"How about when Mama got bit by a poisonous spider?" Marjorie said with her mouth full. "When we lived on Beard Street? She was deathly ill for over two weeks, and we all worried about her."

"Yeah, I remember Papa had to cook for us. He baked a huge fish that was scrumptious," said Blanche.

"Delectable."

The new fellow Sammy set his fork down and spoke for the first time. "That doesn't sound like the man I know. I've never seen him cook anything for anybody."

Everyone stopped talking. All eyes stared at him.

"You know Malcolm?" I asked.

Sammy nodded. "He's married to my mother."

"You're Gladys's son?" Frances mumbled.

"Papa's stepson!"

Sammy shrugged as if he didn't know what he had done wrong.

Shock filled the room. Calvis had brought Papa's wife's son to Mama's house? Gladys, the woman who'd broken up their marriage? I hadn't known she had a son, much less one the same age as Marjorie, and now to think she was dating him, the child of the family's enemy.

This was going too far. Way too far.

Mrs. Trimble scooted her chair back only seconds before everyone else did. She stood with her hands on her hips. "Calvis Junior. Did you know about this?"

Sibyl's brother looked guilty, as did Marjorie. They knew. None of it made sense. Surely, they didn't expect Mrs. Trimble to accept this fellow, knowing she'd never recovered from the divorce where Gladys was the "other woman." Never forgotten the public betrayal, shame, and outright rejection. Perhaps Marjorie didn't mean to announce the big news yet— that she was dating Papa's stepson.

"You're awful." Mrs. Trimble's voice rose to treble level, and she practically jumped over the table at Marjorie, knocking over the gravy bowl. "You bring that tramp's son into this house? What were you thinking? Get out! All of you! Get out of this house right now!"

Calvis, Evie, Marjorie, and Sammy backed away from the table, their food halfway eaten. We heard Mrs. Trimble yelling all the way to the front door. She probably wouldn't speak to Marjorie for months, and then they would become all lovey-dovey again. The push-and-pull thing.

I looked at Sibyl. Her eyes were wide, her jaw dropped. I knew how she felt.

Mrs. Trimble stomped back through to the kitchen, her face red and her eyes flashing darts at anyone in her way. The divorce and Mr. Trimble's remarriage remained as fresh on our minds as this morning news, mostly because Mrs. Trimble wouldn't let us forget it. This was the most dysfunctional family in the world and I so much wanted a calm life.

God would have to work extra hard to tame this bunch.

Sibyl

After the impertinent guests had been banished, I helped Mama clean up. Her temper was on the edge of erupting again, and she clomped around like an enraged grizzly bear.

"How could Marjorie do that? She knows what I think about her papa." Spittle flew from her mouth. "He's the worst man on this planet, and that's saying something. Why—"

"Calm down, Mama." I was relieved her anger wasn't targeted at me.

She continued to rant. "Nobody cares what I've gone through all these years, least of all Marjorie. Even when she knows that worthless excuse of a husband and father left me for another woman and won't support his rightful wife and children, she brings that tramp's son into my house! To my house! For dinner! Can you believe that?"

"Hold on—"

"It's all that man's fault. Your papa is downright shameless, marrying that hussy of a woman. How could he?" Pots and pans clanged as Mama slung them around.

Marjorie had to have known how Mama would react. Even if Sammy had been a dream guy, she had no business exposing the family to such pain.

"Maybe…" I began again but stopped. Patronizing words wouldn't help.

"Maybe what? Have you ever had a man discount you?" Mama's eyes burned with pain and anger. "I can hardly afford the rent since your papa pays only twenty-five dollars a month in child support. When he pays."

Blanche, sitting at the counter watching us work, jumped to her feet. "Mama, I understand you, even if Sibyl doesn't. She's on Papa's side and doesn't care about us."

"How can you say I don't care!" My voice rose, but I couldn't help it. Once an argument began in the Trimble household, it didn't stop until malicious words and tears erupted. My begging for peace would only make it worse.

Now was the opportunity Blanche had been waiting for. She delivered her crushing blow. "Did you know Papa visits her?"

Mama turned on me in a flash, her eyes saying what her mouth did not.

Blanche began spewing hateful insults toward me, and Mama screamed for her to be quiet.

At Blanche's betrayal, I felt steam rising in me, but before I released it in a torrent of self-defense or hot invectives or a downpour of tears, I lowered my head and took a deep breath. At that moment, I prayed for self-control, for understanding and wisdom. And at that moment, I saw how badly my mother had been hurt. She'd used the word *discounted* to describe the way Papa had treated her, and she'd been exactly right. He'd left her, disregarded her, rejected her. Had marked her at less than valuable. She had a right to be angry.

Mama got her speech back and spoke with venom. "You've been talking to your papa, have you?"

I didn't want to lie but I certainly didn't want to tell her that Papa occasionally stopped by my house. That would only hurt her worse. My silence spoke louder than my words would have.

Mama's voice lowered. "You don't care about us. Pretending to understand my heartache. Ha. I see the real you—you don't give a flip about my feelings. You're as bad as Marjorie."

My voice caught, and I stuttered, "I love you, Mama. I wouldn't do anything to hurt you."

"You're hurting us by speaking to Papa," Mama blurted. "You don't care who you hurt, do you? Not even your own family."

Lord, was this a test of my faith? The familiar flow of tears began—tears that came often when I was with my family. I looked at Mama. Even if she didn't think I cared, I would bite back the mean words. God's kind of love didn't hurt others, no matter what they'd done.

My mother's pain flashed all over her. What came off as anger and judgment, I believed, was only masking her deep hurt. She'd been rejected, and everything she did now was a reaction to that. Maybe she didn't hate me. Maybe she feared me. Feared that I would reject her like Papa had rejected her. Like a scared dog backed into a corner, Mama always came out fighting.

Things might never be perfect between Mama and me, but at least I could understand better.

Mama faced me in the middle of the kitchen, and her accusations began again. It didn't seem like she knew the intense hurt she caused me. She just thought I was being emotional. The understanding and patience I extended didn't mean I had to like being belittled. By the time Fremont came into the kitchen with the children, I was crying again. Sobbing like a hurt puppy.

Fremont had grown used to my tearful outbursts in front of my family. "Sibyl, it's time to leave." He pulled me toward the door, hurrying the children in front of us.

On the drive home, despair flooded my heart, and the tears flowed freely. Would Mama and I ever be able to work through the anger and frustration? I couldn't take much more of this discord.

I wanted out. Maybe Fremont was right. We needed to break the apron ties, step away, and disconnect from these broken relationships.

My thoughts about leaving Shawnee went back and forth as capricious as a teeter totter.

Chapter Twenty-Three

May 1940

Sibyl

I picked up the phone, but before I got the *hello* out of my mouth, Marjorie started talking, rambling on like a chipmunk. "It's Sammy. We broke up after that awful dinner at Mama's house, but he kept calling me and calling me, wanting to talk, asking me to go out with him...and...and..." Her voice cracked, her words coming too fast. "I kept refusing to see him on account of not hurting Mama, but we stayed friends—so to speak."

My tough, happy-go-lucky sister was distraught.

"I spent hours listening...listening to him whine about his lousy life. About feeling no good, useless..." Her voice pitched even higher. "I told him to do something like go back to school or get a job, to do anything to find his way in life. I didn't know—"

"Whoa, slow down. What happened?"

"It's Sammy."

"And..."

"Sammy committed suicide...last night."

I felt sick and knew she must feel worse than I did. "I'm so sorry, Marj."

"Sis, I tried to encourage him. Oh, lovey, I'm devastated. It's all my fault."

"No. It can't be your fault."

"That's noble for you to say, sis, but I got busy and didn't have time to talk to him, and I ignored him. Not intentionally, of course." Marjorie's voice broke again. "But I met a new fellow, and…you know how it is."

I knew my sister and how she collected boyfriends, but she shouldn't take the blame for this. "Sammy was a troubled young man. Didn't you tell me he was depressed, and he racked up some gambling debt? That would have been worrying, to say the least."

She didn't answer right away, and I could hear her crying. I didn't press her. "Thanks, sis," she finally said.

"Have you talked to Mama?" I asked.

"I don't dare tell Mama. But I had to tell someone, sweetie, that's all. I'll be okay." Marjorie clearly was not okay.

"Will you go with me to the funeral?" Her words were so low they were barely audible as if she feared my answer. "I don't know who else to ask."

After we talked more, I hung up the phone and stared out the window at the desolate, dry road, and remembered Mother Pope's words. "Don't be too quick to judge." I didn't know everything about Sammy or Marjorie or what she was going through. My heart went out to her. To Gladys, too. Much as I disliked the woman, nobody deserved that kind of heartache.

Lord, help my sister. Please. She needs you.

My whole family needs you.

I wanted to bring hope to my parents and siblings, to my husband and sweet children. If the Lord wanted Fremont and me to move elsewhere by summer, his plans needed to be clear-cut and well-defined. Loud enough to be heard through the chaos because my heart was pulled two ways. My family, difficult though they were, desperately needed me, and here I was, planning to move away and find a more secure place to live. How could I do that to the ones I loved? How can a person find themselves or stay sane in the midst of a family like this?

I pulled my shoulders back. I would not give in to the despair inside me.

***

Marjorie and I slipped into the back of the small group of people gathered for the graveside service. We could see Papa holding Gladys up near Sammy's casket. Gladys, stoic, wearing an ankle-length black dress with matching hat and gloves, dabbed at her eyes underneath the dark netting.

Having lost my child, I could almost imagine what she was going through. No mother should have to experience her child's death.

The simple service was over quickly, and people began to leave. When most attendees were gone, I turned to go, but Marjorie started walking toward the front, and I latched onto her arm. "What are you doing?"

"I need to speak to her—to apologize. I should have done something." Marjorie shook my arm loose and walked toward the flower-covered casket, and I followed.

Glady's face changed from grief to irritation when she saw us.

Marjorie, a vibrant girl out of place wearing black, spoke as soon as she reached our stepmother. "I'm so sorry about Sammy."

Gladys's chest expanded like a balloon about to burst. "I can't believe you showed your face here. Sammy told me how you led him on and crushed his heart. Wouldn't talk to him because of your mother."

"It wasn't like that," Marjorie said. "I cared about him."

"You should be mortified by this, I say."

Marjorie took a step back and almost bumped into me. "We were good friends. I'm sorry."

Papa, standing behind Gladys, gave us a nasty look. "I think you both should go—and don't come around for a while." He took Glady's elbow and led her away.

As Marjorie and I ambled back to the car, her hurting words continued. "It's all my fault. All my fault. I'm so ashamed. I had no clue he hurt that much. Sis, I should have talked to him more."

"From what you told me, he was already depressed, and there was nothing you could have done."

As I watched Gladys and Papa drive away, I could do nothing more but hold my sister and be glad I was there for her. Glad I still lived nearby.

122

Chapter Twenty-Four

June 1940

I loved having Mother Pope to myself, especially to watch her bake. She usually made cobblers—cherry was my favorite—but today she was twisting lemons on a metal hand juicer for a lemon pie. Finished with the lemons, she put a cornstarch and water mixture over a burner and stirred.

We chatted about the day, the weather, the children, and the goings-on at church. Nothing deep at first, but as we talked, my anxiety rose. I had so much I wanted to discuss with her. Marjorie had another boyfriend and frustration with her was near the top of the list. My sister's foolishness could make me blush. My mother was my next concern. I couldn't seem to influence my family at all. Relationships, especially close ones, could be as perplexing as baking pies in a potbellied stove.

Mother poured the lemon juice, sugar, and a beaten egg into the cornstarch mix and stirred it over the heat to let it thicken. Soon, a perfect yellow concoction appeared that she poured into a flaky, homemade piecrust. Oh my, would edible wonders never cease.

I grabbed a pencil and paper and began to furiously write down the ingredients for Mother's lemon pie. Recipes kept me focused on something other than my exasperation.

I stood and turned on the flame to heat water for washing dishes. Mother always poured boiling water over her cleaned, rinsed dishes.

She handed me an empty basket. "Sibyl, I need a few more eggs for the meringue. Would you gather some while we wait for the pie to bake? I'll watch the water."

Mother kept Rock Island Red hens in a henhouse and gathered their eggs every day. She kept them under her bed in a box to stay cool before selling them to neighbors or the mom-and-pop grocer over on Forrest Street.

I set down a dirty dish. "Sure. Margaret, come along with me."

The child followed me out the back door, and we passed the water well and entered the wired chicken coop, which held twenty to thirty chickens. Margaret and I moved fluffy hens off their nests or reached underneath them to retrieve the eggs, patting their feathers as we did so.

The cowshed was farther down the hill, and even though the Popes lived on the southwest edge of Shawnee, their fifteen acres carried a country-farm feeling. Their gentle Jersey cow with a brown face and huge, sad-looking eyes supplied nearly five gallons of rich milk a day, plenty for the Popes and family and neighbors.

We rushed back toward the welcoming kitchen. Carrying the basket, I opened the door and stomped dirt off my shoes while handing the eggs to Mother Pope. I ushered her and Judson into the back room to play.

Mother cracked two eggs and separated the yolks from the whites. She spun the whites with a hand beater to make meringue for the top of the lemon pie. The constant clickety-clack sound made talking difficult. I licked my lips. The pie would be as yummy as sand plum jelly on freshly baked bread.

Mother turned to me after she finished, the beater still in her hand. "You can go ahead and talk now. I know there's thoughts in that busy head of yours, and I'm prepared to listen."

Words were ready to jump from my mouth. Now would be the time to talk to her about my mother's bitterness and Marjorie's problems. "When Mama gets angry and blows up and disapproves of everything and screams at me, I feel less than dirt. Like a stupid, useless dishrag." I could hear my dejected tone and tried to change it. "Afterward, I sob like a baby, like the world is going to end, even though I know her temper always passes. But how can a mother be so trying? Does God want me to simply sit and take it?"

"Your mama's words may be hurtful, but she's had a tough time of it." Mother put down the beater and wiped her hands on her apron. "Some people don't see the pain they cause."

"True." A pause between us never felt uncomfortable. "Are you saying I should listen to her even though I feel like throttling her?"

"God loves her as much as he loves you." Mother Pope and I shared a look, the kind that meant you understood each other.

"Marjorie upsets me even more than Mama. She knew better than to bring Gladys's son to visit. That was thoughtless and downright inconsiderate. And even after what happened with Sammy, she's out dating some other hoodlum."

While I checked on the kids, Mother took the dessert out of the oven and put it on the shelf to cool. When I walked back into the kitchen, the aroma of lemon pastry surrounded me. I longed to scoop up that golden-brown dessert and carry it home with me. I also longed for life to be as sweet and lovely as that lemon meringue pie.

"The Good Lord says tribulation works patience." Mother spoke gently, not like she was delivering a sermon. "I know it isn't always easy to hold your feelings in check. Marjorie has been a trial for you, and your anger on your mama's behalf might be justified, but you're not likely to change your family's behavior with disapproval or lectures or anger. So, for now, I'd bear it if I were you. It's a burden, I know, but set boundaries and keep praying for 'em." She untied her apron and hung it on a wall peg. "You and Fremont come by tomorrow for some pie. Lemon was always his favorite."

I loved Mother Pope for her wisdom, for her willingness to share it, and for her calming demeanor. And I have to admit, I also loved her for her lemon pie.

***

On Tuesday night, the children and I sat home alone. I disliked that Fremont worked nights, but I couldn't complain. I mean, he had a job, after all. Being eight months pregnant in the summer heat made me irritable, my emotions jumping up and down faster than a grasshopper in a cornfield. I moped around, feeling sorry for myself, lonely as a wallflower at a prom dance, sad as a lonesome dove. Now there's a pitiful description.

Calvary Church was holding a two-week revival, and I considered attending, but the weight of family life fell on my shoulders, sapping my energy.

About six o'clock, Effie Douglas knocked on the door and marched in, her passel of children following her. She appeared more pregnant than I did. "Sibyl, how are you doing?" She looked me up and down. "You need to get out. You've been stuck in this house for too long."

Years ago, when Fremont had invited Doug over to our house, he couldn't have known how Doug's wife would become my best friend. We attended circles together. Laughed together. Cooked together. Sobbed on each other's shoulders. If anyone understood me, it was Effie.

"You go on and get dressed," she insisted. "I'll tend to the kids."

Thirty minutes before, a rattlesnake couldn't have budged me from my house, but at Effie's insistence, I pushed myself from the chair and walked into the bedroom to get ready.

***

After rushing down Farrell Street to Market, we arrived late for the revival service. A deacon opened the heavy door, and we entered Calvary Baptist Church, two women heavy with child and Margaret and Judson and Effie's three children trailing behind us.

"Let's sit in the back." I didn't want anyone to approach me. Faking smiles would be tiring.

We slid onto an oak pew bolted to the floor, and I scooted in between my children, unsure if they could sit still through the next hour.

The singing had already started—gospel hymns, the kind I loved to sing. I tapped my foot—reminded of happy times playing the piano while my family sang around me. Music, especially church music, ran deep as a river in me and joy flooded my heart.

Women in front of us cooled themselves with fans provided by Gaskill Funeral Home. I picked up one and glanced at the words printed on it: "This Do in Remembrance of Me." Did that mean we must remember Christ when fanning away the stifling heat?

Cavalry's old-time revival drew a crowd. On the second week it ran, attendance averaged over two hundred people, the highest on record since the church started in 1920. I heard the revival meeting brought visitors from smaller towns surrounding Shawnee: Earlsboro, Bethel, Maud, Tecumseh. Guests from as far away as Dale and Meeker. I looked around and noticed people I'd never seen before.

Other details caught my attention—the white-washed ceiling above the pastor's head where the fan rotated precariously at full speed; the baptistry behind the pulpit with a picture of the Jordan River hanging over it; the choir chair where I used to sit; the side of the auditorium where curtains created overflow classrooms.

After the music, Pastor Sewell introduced a student preacher from Oklahoma Baptist University, the college on the north side of Shawnee founded thirty years ago. The gospel preaching touched me deeply, and tears streamed down my face as the evangelist spoke about Jesus loving all people. Why was I so emotional?

Did God realize my struggle with family? That I was being crushed by the stress? Did he have important work for Fremont and me? Work someplace beyond Shawnee?

God's presence washed over me like warm water on a cool day. Peace settled deep in my soul with a reassurance that God did have a plan for my life. He had specific tasks, specific dreams just for me. I prayed for strength to do whatever he wanted, hoping a precise plan of action would alleviate my anxiety.

"Are you okay, dear?" Effie looked over Margaret's head, worry lines creasing her forehead.

I nodded.

At the end of the service, several people professed their faith or rededicated their lives to the Lord. Conviction, reconciliation, and excitement filled the building with spiritual sparks. People loitered for an hour after the last stanza of *Just as I Am*.

By the time we stood to leave, Judson had fallen asleep. I woke him, and he leaned against me as we turned to go with Effie and her sleepy kids.

Anna, a friend of mine since high school, came up to us and glanced at my overlarge stomach. "So good to see you. You must be busy with your family." She touched my shoulder. "I'd love to have Margaret spend the day with me. After the revival is over, of course." Married and with no children of her own, Anna adored my little girl.

I looked at my daughter, who gazed up at me in anticipation. Had I been so preoccupied with my issues that I neglected her? A mature child, she appeared so self-sufficient and didn't seem to need coddling or scolding as Judson did.

"Please, Mommy."

Margaret would have a wonderful time as the center of Anna's attention for a whole day. A good friend is even more special when they love your children.

***

That night after arriving home and putting the children to bed, I got on my knees and prayed. *Lord, help me follow you.*

I heard nothing, not a single small nudging from God. I fought off disappointment, yearning for Fremont's kind of godliness, believing his deeply religious family heard from God all the time.

Please, heal my heart. I've been struggling with my family for a long time, trying to manage, and I can't go on like this.

I scolded myself. Many people around the world didn't have the blessings I did. My heart ached as I thought of lost souls who needed Jesus—who felt emptier than me. I'd never wanted my daily life to be focused on housewife chores—cleaning house, cooking beans, scrubbing cast iron skillets. Surely this wasn't all I'd been called to do.

Frustration surged through me. I was weary of dealing with my family's bitterness. When younger, I'd longed to improve society through political activities, but now I yearned to follow in the footsteps of Apostle Paul and encourage others with the gospel. Oh, to experience the outside world, to get away from the pressure of caring for my senseless family, and realize my full potential. My heart pounded, and the Lord's wisdom touched me. I'd read that morning, Romans 4:20. *He staggered not at the promise of God through unbelief; but was strong in the faith, giving glory to God.*

"I want to be strong in the faith, Lord," I prayed. "Help me know if we should stay or go, and I'll follow."

Even as I made that commitment, I wondered: Was I being honest? My anxious heart wanted to leave Shawnee and have the freedom to start fresh. I hoped, sincerely hoped, God would allow us to move to a different town. I never wanted to get so caught up in my family's ranting that I couldn't hear his voice, but did I have the strength to do what God wanted? I wavered, uncertain.

I rose from my kneeling position with one last prayer: *God, what do you want us to do?*

Nothing. I would have to wait for my answer.

In the meantime, there was work to do.

Chapter Twenty-Five

July 1940

Fremont

Sibyl and I decided not to have more children after our third one, but Keith's tragic death changed our minds. Miserable from the heat, in the summer of '40, I watched her stomach pooch out more than with any of her other pregnancies. I was certain the baby would be a girl. I never knew the basis, but my predictions had been right so far.

It was July 22, 1940, two weeks after Sibyl's thirtieth birthday. The birth looked to be proceeding as normal, but though the midwife told me everything was going as well as expected, all the same, I jiggled the change in my pocket and paced the front porch until I wore a path in the gray paint.

I went to the kitchen and counted out cigar box money to pay the midwife and doctor. I left the amount in a neat pile on the old, wobbly table, leaving little in the box. I pushed away thoughts of funds needed in the near future, funds we were saving to move.

Dr. Fortson arrived late in the afternoon and an hour later, the baby was born.

Joy flooded over me. The good Lord blessed us with a new daughter, and Sibyl didn't know it yet, but I was going to spoil this little tyke rotten.

All of our babies were born on their due date—exactly on their due date. It was uncanny how my sweet wife could predict the time so closely. I, on the other hand, could predict the baby's sex. Our new child was indeed a girl—Carol Jeanne Pope. Doug's wife Effie had delivered a baby a month earlier, but that infant came a week late, and Doug's prediction of its sex had been wrong. Take that, my friend!

Carol had dark blue eyes and a soft covering of black hair, like all our babies. I assumed, also like all our babies, she would quickly lose her hair and become as bald as her Grandpa Pope for a short time.

I had taken Margaret and Judson to spend the night with my parents, and the day after Carol was born, they scrambled into the house, eager to get a glimpse of their new sibling.

Margaret squealed when she saw the tiny bundle in my arms and yelled, "Keith!"

My heart dropped. This infant was born in the same house as Keith, exactly fifteen months to the day after we'd lost him. Broken by my daughter's enthusiasm, I said, "No. This isn't Keith. This is a new baby." I knelt down so Margaret could take a peek at her new little sister. Margaret *oohed* softly and patted Carol's cheek.

Our Sunday School class brought casseroles and cakes as if they thought we were on the verge of starvation. Or maybe they'd heard about my appetite. Regardless, their intentions were noble, and their offerings appreciated.

My mother came and cleaned the house from top to bottom and brought my favorite soup, chicken noodle. Several afternoons later, Sibyl's mama brought supper. Even though she'd complained about our big family, she surprised me by being there when we needed her. She told silly stories and played with the kids, making them giggle as she made funny faces and crossed her eyes. I was glad to see the children and their grandmother laughing together.

During that visit, Margaret came to me wiggling her front tooth. "Look, Daddy! My toof is loose."

"Ah, it looks like it's time to pull it out."

Margaret had a dozen questions. "Will it hurt? Will it grow back? Will I talk funny?"

"Slow down, child. Let's see what we can do." After much coaxing, cajoling, and sweet-talking, I tied a string around the loose tooth and pulled it out. The ordeal was over quickly, and Margaret cried for only a few seconds. Our firstborn lost her first tooth a few days after Sibyl gave birth to our fourth child. Margaret was growing up quickly. It seemed just yesterday she was a newborn herself.

"You've been a brave girl," I told her. "Let's go wash that tooth for the tooth fairy."

Margaret, not only a physically strong little kid but naturally calm and level-headed like me, her daddy, patiently learned how to hold the baby gently. She also learned how to fold diapers, which I appreciated because I'd been enlisted as official diaper-folder.

Judson was another story. That boy romped through the backyard with his energetic dog. He was even more rambunctious in public—pulling loose from my hand, darting between people, shouting at the top of his lungs. I dreaded taking him out. He had the energy of three boys and the courage of a racecar driver. Watching him at play one afternoon, I recalled a news story from a few weeks before about a guy who fell from a Rock Island freight car and the train had run over him. I shuddered as I thought of my daredevil days, riding the rails as a hobo before I came to my senses. If my rowdy boy was anything like me—and by all indications he was— I'd have to keep a close eye on him.

And pray he'd outgrow the rowdiness like I did.

That evening after Sibyl's mama left, I cradled our new baby Carol. I had one more precious soul to protect and watch over. I looked at the newborn cuddled in my arms, and she gazed back at me with wide, trusting eyes.

Love for my little family rushed through me, and I prayed one of the most fervent and sincere prayers of my life: *Lord, protect my children from harm and help me lead them the right way.*

Chapter Twenty-Six

August 1940

Fremont

For the first time in weeks, a dust storm passed by leaving mounds of dirt around the windowsills, under the doors, and through cracks in the walls. The air felt like powdered chalk and tasted like it too. I was relieved when it blew over quickly. While the powder settled, Sibyl dusted and swept, and I opened the doors and windows to bring in fresh air.

The hope of autumn filled my mind even if I couldn't smell it yet. Autumn meant a time for change. For action.

Margaret turned seven years old on August the nineteenth. Oklahoma was sweltering hot, so I hoped for a breeze as we set up card tables under the shady oak trees in our back yard for the birthday celebration. Breeze or not, it was cooler outside than in our house, which felt hotter than the Sahara.

Afterward, Margaret begged to spend the night with Grandpa Pope so she could wake up early and help him milk the cows.

Every morning before dawn, Dad climbed out of bed, pulled on his overalls, and grabbed a pail to go out and milk his old Jersey cow. I remembered his words, "Trouble with a milk cow is she won't stay milked." I agreed because I'd been roused in the early morning dawn most of my growing up years.

After Dad brought in the bucket of warm milk, Mother would strain it with cheesecloth, pour it into glass bottles, and seal the bottle with caps. She'd set a jug of milk on the front porch and pick up the clean quart bottle someone had placed there. Later the full milk jug would be gone, and a dime left. Just like magic, she received ten cents for a quart of milk.

The next day, near on midmorning, and appreciating the clear air, Sibyl and I walked instead of driving to my parents' house to pick up Margaret and collect milk for our own use.

We walked toward Tennessee Street, pushing our fancy new baby carriage with wheels as shiny as new car spokes. The carriage, out of our price range, had been a gift from Papa. Baby Carol lay inside, while Judson ran around us in circles. After the strangling thickness of yesterday's dust, this outing with the sun shining over a big, wide sky felt like liberty.

Apparently, Sibyl didn't share my enthusiasm. "This feels like a hundred-mile trek," she said. "Let's stop and get a drink."

I knew she must be tired and for good reason. The weather was sweltering, and she'd just had a baby the month before. We bought a cola from one of the many mom-and-pop stores set up in houses along the way.

Before we reached the end of Farrell Street, we saw Mother squatting beside her house, wearing a straw hat and work gloves, and carrying a bucket. I guessed it to be blackberry picking time and hoped the smell wafting through the air meant a blackberry pie was baking in the oven.

Judson ran to greet her. "Grandma! Grandma! Can I help?" He danced around like a wiry monkey. She handed him a bucket and explained how to determine which berries were ripe enough to pick.

I pushed the carriage to the shade while Sibyl plopped down on the porch swing. Margaret rushed around the corner and saw us. "Daddy! Grandpa got me out of bed this morning before the sun woke up. The cow wasn't even awake."

I laughed at my child. "Well, pretty little milkmaid, do you want to come back and help again tomorrow morning?"

"Don't be silly, Daddy. I don't *ever* want to do that again."

Smart girl.

"How's the baby doing?" Mother came over and peeked at Carol's sweet little, pink face. "I see you've decided to get outdoors. I wouldn't want to be cooped up after the dust storm, either. But do you think this heat is safe for the baby? And is it too much for you, Sibyl?"

Sibyl didn't appear to hear the questions, so I wiped sweat from my forehead and answered for her. "Carol's fine. She seems to love the outdoors, and Sibyl's a little tired, but she insisted on walking."

Mother raised her eyebrows as if she questioned our sanity and sat in the swing beside Sibyl. As I took a seat on the concrete porch steps, Mother asked Sibyl, "Did you hear Irene and Harvie got engaged? What do you think about that?"

Like me, Irene was born in the backwoods of Waco, Oklahoma, a poor farmer's kid, but for years she insisted that she'd marry a "society" man someday. Harvie Taylor, the youngest son of a doctor, qualified.

"I'm happy for her," I said.

"We've known his family for years—ever since we lived in Pauls Valley when Fremont was a boy. Irene's beside herself, acting like she's the only one who ever fell in love, mooning over that boy as she does." Mother's deep-chested laughter made me smile.

"Have they set a date?" Sibyl turned to Mother.

"Not yet. I hope they can wait long enough for a church wedding. We don't need any hanky-panky going on."

"Harvie's an honest fellow if you ask me, but I'm not sure Irene's ready to settle down yet." I voiced my concern. Irene had gone through a dozen boyfriends last year. Would she accept responsibility when she still loved to giggle and dance and flirt?

"Oh, don't worry," Mother said. "He's lucky to have her. She can't help that she can charm a grizzly bear. She's beautiful, don't you think so?"

Mother was biased, as any mother would be, I guess, but what she said was true. Irene had an attractive round face with the biggest, bluest eyes I'd ever seen.

"I've been praying for that girl since she was born, praying for her to find a decent fellow. I think this is the one." Mother stepped over and gently lifted Carol from the carriage. She returned to the swing and whistled a lullaby as she rocked the baby back and forth."

"Did you hear about Ruth bringing one of the Castleman guys to meet Blanche?" Sibyl asked. "What do you know about him?"

"That was Don Castleman." Mother laughed to herself. "We have a slew of relatives on my side of the family back in Missouri. I'm the youngest of the Osborne David Castleman clan."

Seventeen siblings, indeed. I had met dozens of relatives through the years and couldn't remember the names of most of them.

"Don's a distant nephew, but matchmaking can be a dangerous business." Mother shook her head, even though she'd done her share of matchmaking in the past. "It's like sticking a lighted match to a bale of hay."

I changed the subject to something safer. "Is that blackberry pie done yet?"

***

At supper that night, Sibyl said, "I wish my family were more loving, like yours," She took a few bites of potatoes and shook her head. "I know it's unrealistic and every family's different, but couldn't my relatives be kinder and more caring? Maybe it's time to leave our troubles behind."

My eyes opened wide. Maybe Sibyl *did* want to move. I'd been unsure she could leave her mother but maybe now she was willing. Most of our problems would dissolve if I could provide a better living. Blazes, it ate at my sense of manhood that I couldn't give Sibyl everything she desired.

Irene married Harvie Taylor on August 29, 1940, in a small church wedding because my folks couldn't afford a big one. Sibyl and I attended the informal reception of cake and punch and merriment, watching Irene giggle throughout the evening.

The newlyweds moved to an apartment in Oklahoma City across the street from a Methodist Church and near Harvie's work at Midwest Air Base.

I never saw a couple so happy, laughing through life without holding back. I hoped it would last.

Chapter Twenty-Seven

Sibyl

My youngest sister Frances contracted scarlet fever and was quarantined for ten days. A teenager, she would hate missing school and seeing her friends. I called Mama, remembering how distraught I'd been over Keith and my children's illnesses. "Is there anything I can do?"

Mama's voice revealed her weariness, which I suspected was both physical and mental. "Blanche and Larry will have to move out of the house," she whined. "I don't want them to catch it, and you don't have enough room with all those kids."

She was right. We had no room for more people in our tiny house.

Mama's long sigh came through the phone. "I'll send them to Marjorie's. Her roommate moved out so she has an extra bed."

Blanche and Larry packed small bags and moved to Marjorie's apartment. As expected, it didn't take long for Blanche and Marjorie to find something to argue about. Those two couldn't see eye to eye on how to run a comb through their hair. The neighbors probably got an ear full, and Blanche quickly moved back home.

Frances recovered within the week, and later Frances shared her ordeal with me on our back porch. "Blanche was supposed to take care of me, but she wouldn't even get me a glass of water. Told me to get it myself."

"I'm sorry, dear. I'm sure Blanche's bedside manners leave a lot to be desired."

"One afternoon when Mama was gone, I woke up crying from a bad dream."

I put my arm around her. Comforting didn't come easily for me, either, but I had to let her know someone cared. "What was the dream?"

"I dreamed Mama died," said Frances, sobbing on my shoulder. "I was at her funeral and I thought she would never come back home. I got so scared I started shaking, and when I told Blanche about it, she said I was silly and to shut up."

I hugged Frances tight as anger rose in me. Part of it was directed at Blanche, but the bulk of my wrath was reserved for Mama. After all, Frances wasn't Blanche's child; she was Mama's. And that woman had all the mothering instincts of a turtle that lays her eggs and swims away.

***

Aunt Adah suggested Marjorie move to Lawton, where jobs were plentiful, and Aunt Adah usually knew what she was talking about. Fort Sill, an army base established in 1869, had a thriving town around it. Lawton was a two-and-a-half-hour drive from Shawnee down Highways 9 and 62—a longer trip by bus.

Marjorie moved and found a job right away at a photography shop, carefully hand-tinting black-and-white photos. She, like Blanche, was talented in art, and the photographs she displayed were charming. She applied her skill to several of our family pictures.

Larry stayed with Mama in Shawnee, where he'd been staying on and off for the past year. Marjorie wanted to save money and get settled before taking her son down to Lawton.

Despite his precarious childhood, Larry, a sullen boy when he first returned from New Mexico, was back to being an amiable kid, although a bit unruly. He liked to play gin rummy with Mama's boarders—until he lost. He would then go next door to play cards with their neighbor, an elderly lady who would let him win and give him stale sugar cookies. Even with no stability in his life, Larry's buoyancy could not be contained—until he caught the measles, and Mama scared him half to death by telling him he might go blind if light got into his eyes. He had to stay in his room with the shades pulled and wear colored glasses.

When I visited him, I found him with a quilt pulled over his head, afraid to peek out. I tried to reassure him. "You'll be okay in a few days. Just take it easy."

His body was as resilient as his spirit, and he recovered quickly.

Larry enjoyed living with his grandma and two aunts. After all, he could do whatever he wanted and go wherever he wished as long as he returned home before sunset. The same age as my Margaret—whom I wouldn't let go more than a half a block away—Larry would wander the streets all day long. Quite the man about town, he talked to acquaintances and strangers alike, played ball with friends, visited the library, and sometimes— a lot of times—forgot about the time.

A few days after Larry recovered from the measles, Mama called me late at night. Fremont had left for his night job, the sun had long since set, and I had crawled into bed.

"Larry hasn't come home! I tell you, that boy will be the death of me yet."

"I'll be right there. Now call the police." I threw on clothes, called a neighbor to sit with the children, and scurried over to her house.

In a panic, Mama paced the floor, pausing frequently to peer out the window. As she and I waited, I prayed silently. Where was he? Had he been snatched up? Was he lying hurt somewhere?

Mama was beside herself. She ranted about Marjorie leaving the boy, about Larry not being responsible, about a town unsafe after dark.

Just after midnight, a knock exploded on the door.

Mama rushed to open it and a burly policeman stood in the doorway.

"Did you find him? Is he all right? Where is he?"

Seeing only the policeman, I felt my heart lodge in my throat. We couldn't lose that boy. Then Larry poked his head out from behind the big man.

I breathed a huge sigh of relief and pressed him to my chest in a big hug. "What happened to you, child? We were worried to high heavens."

Larry pulled away from my grasp. The impish boy didn't look contrite even if he did look bedraggled and anxious. Poor child looked like an abandoned waif. Dirt stained his face and clothes, and his brown hair, badly in need of a cut, stuck out in all directions because of multiple cowlicks. He stuck out his chest. "I was talking to a bum at Woodland Park. I know I wasn't supposed to, but…." He lowered his head.

"What? Why did you do such a foolish thing?" Mama scowled at him, her hands on her hips. "I told you to stay away from those people."

He melted and when he spoke again, he sounded close to tears. "The fella looked like he needed a bite to eat, so I gave him the crackers in my pocket."

I smiled, understanding his need to help others, and admiring his brave deed.

Mama's eyes narrowed in disapproval. "And that's why you were out so late?"

"It got dark, and I was scared I'd get in trouble. I was afraid to come home, so I hid in the park."

"Gadding about! You were out gadding about and scaring me out of my wits!" Mama's voice rose. "You go straight to bed, young man. There'll be no supper for you."

Larry broke into sobs and ran up the stairs.

The shouting brought Blanche into the living room. "You're a terrible mom," she hurled. "That's no way to treat a child. I'm taking him some food, and you can't stop me." She disappeared into the kitchen and quickly reappeared with a sandwich and stomped up the stairs. "I'm better at mothering than you are."

Mama's eyes grew cold. "Her behavior is all your papa's fault. He's the one who ran off and left her. I'd be acting up, too, if I were Blanche."

I had no response to that comment. Truth was, I could see both sides. Mama *was* a rotten mother at times. She tended to shirk her responsibilities—neglecting Frances, letting Larry run wild, and allowing Blanche to act as if she were in charge. But as a mother myself, I could understand Mama's fear and anger and worry. Her family was important, and a missing child can be a horrible nightmare. "Maybe we should say a prayer, thanking God that Larry is home safe now."

"Always bringing God up, aren't you? Maybe He should have brought the boy home hours ago."

My family's obstinance left me drained. I tended to be sensitive and cry when their words hurt me, but I yearned for my loved ones to see God at work in their lives. Mother was near my heart and I loved her no end, but her stubbornness left a boulder of hurt.

My flailing attempts at helping were not enough. I prayed for my family constantly.

My faith was growing daily, but it still had a long way to go. Sometimes I doubted prayer was enough to heal my broken family. Or direct the path Fremont and I should take.

Chapter Twenty-Eight

October 1940

We didn't move that fall as Fremont had hoped, mostly because we didn't have enough money saved, but also because my husband hadn't found another job. He had even travelled to an Oklahoma City car dealership, To no avail. I don't know if I was glad or sad. He was so sure about leaving Shawnee and I flopped back and forth, going from guilt to excitement about the future. A few more months in Shawnee were fine with me.

Two weeks later, I walked down Main Street where many drug stores, cafes, and soda fountains lined the sidewalk. Owl's Drug Store made the best homemade pimento cheese in the country, while Lantz Drug made the best cherry limeades and the Aldridge Hotel had the fanciest décor.

I arrived at the Aldridge Building—a beautiful ornamental structure ten stories tall with two hundred rooms above us. As I looked around at the interior of the hotel, one of Shawnee's finest, I hoped no one saw me enter. The last thing I needed was for Mama to hear of me meeting with her worst enemy. I made my way to a table in the small coffee shop where Papa sat in the booth, drinking black coffee.

As I ordered, he began our conversation by complaining about the installation of parking meters on Main Street.

I sipped my Coca-Cola and studied his face. I hadn't seen him since Sammy's funeral, but his small, deep-set eyes hadn't changed much and, except for more stress lines around his thin lips, he looked the same. He might not be famous, but he was well-known in Oklahoma, and not for his goodness.

Papa had wanted to meet in private, without the children present to disturb us. "My life has taken a downturn," he said after we discussed the family.

"I thought you were doing well at the RFC."

The RFC was an independent agency of the federal government, chartered to alleviate financial panic, though I'd never put much faith in it.

Papa grimaced. "They've gone broke."

"Broke?" Scandals abounded, but how could a government organization go broke? Then the personal consequence of his news dawned on me. "So that means…"

"Yes, I lost my job…been laid off. A complete disaster." Papa frowned, and deep wrinkles creased his forehead. "Top people were accused of wrongdoing. Personally, I blame their pride and disorganization. Greedy men at the top. Bah!"

The waitress refilled our drinks, interrupting our conversation.

Papa resumed after she left. "I'm still waiting to get reimbursed for my last expense report. It may take litigation. In fact, all the executives may get sued over this."

Papa was smart enough to finagle money from any organization he was associated with. He kept a journal of his expenses and could add multiple numbers in his head faster than a calculator. He had given each of his children a ledger book and taught us to keep track of our money. I have to admit, his training helped me manage the finances for our household. I hoped against hope he was not involved in another scandal.

For years, I'd yearned for a father I could trust and respect, one who hugged and laughed and cried with me, but I'd had to accept that my papa was not that kind of man. A doting father he was not.

Wanting to know my papa's viewpoint on the current political state, I changed the subject. "What do you think about the war in Europe?" I kept my voice low as I formed circles with my finger on the tablecloth.

"With reason and justice, we should try to save mankind, but we've done a poor job overcoming evil. As it is, we're destroying ourselves. Don't need the Germans for that."

Once Papa started talking about his beliefs, he could talk for hours. "Living together in peace means sharing the wealth, of course. We both know that social improvement from generation to generation will bring about evils's final destruction. The eventual salvation of the human race. That's how it's meant to work."

"What do you mean?" I scrunched my eyes to understand.

"Evil has continued to grow and thrive. Everywhere. Even in our own country. We should think about teaching people how to live so we can save mankind from self-destruction."

"Self-destruction?"

"Our first task is to restrain workers of iniquity so they can't expand their activities. We must unite the people of goodwill from around the world and eliminate the evil ones."

I coughed into my napkin, wondering if I fell on the evil or the good side. Although I'd heard his theories before, they seemed cold-blooded. Eliminate all evil people? Didn't he see that evil existed in all of us and no one was perfect? Even him.

I could never agree with my papa's theories. Someone had to be in charge of deciding what was evil and what was good. But before I could respond, he asked, "How do you and Fremont plan to pull yourself up out of the your destructive lifestyle? Improve your situation?"

That question I could respond to. "We're planning to move away from Shawnee."

He hmphed. "You have it backward. You should improve your position first and later go wherever you want." Papa shook his head in disapproval. "Now is definitely not the time to be moving."

What could I say to that? He didn't ask why we wanted to move, or when, or where. Although I didn't know the details because I ignored Fremont the last time he tried to talk about moving, it would have been nice if Papa had asked instead of quickly dismissing our vision.

I watched as he slid out of the booth and went to pay for the drinks. He cut an imposing figure—a handsome, well-dressed, arrogant man. A man I couldn't trust.

Fremont

The court case involving Papa found its way into the newspapers, and Sibyl, like the studious daughter she was, scrutinized every article to find out what was happening in his world. While she gobbled up every tidbit of information and eavesdropped on conversations, I didn't give a hoot about Papa's role. I'd lost faith in that man long ago.

On Saturday night, I listened obediently for the umpteenth time while Sibyl read another Shawnee News article and summarized the facts for me. My Bible lay on the end table, ready for me to study Sunday's lesson.

Sibyl mumbled out loud. "According to this, Papa obtained a written statement from Fisher—an employee of the Shawnee Home Building and Loan Association. It's about the stock transfers that indicted Barnett. And from what I gather, Fisher's statement is crucial to Papa's testament."

With the children playing on the floor and the baby taking a nap, I sat on the sofa trying to concentrate. Evidently, the hatred between Trimble and his old boss, State Commissioner Barnett, flourished. The banking scandal had not been settled, and it impacted several other Oklahoma banks. More bad news. I picked up my Bible to read.

A few minutes later, Sibyl interrupted me again. "Listen to this, Fremont."

I sighed and set down my Bible.

"During the trial, when the document was presented to Fisher on the witness stand, he said the statement gave the wrong impression. It was inaccurate and Fisher did *not* want to sign it." Sibyl looked at me, a frown on her face. "Can you believe that? Fisher never wanted to sign the statement about the alleged stock transfer in the first place."

I wanted to advise her to not get worked up, that anxiety solved nothing, but how could Sibyl not be upset? Her papa was her papa, and news of him floated through the newspapers like loose feathers.

She went on. "According to this article, Fisher called the inaccuracies to Papa's attention, but Papa threatened to place the company in bankruptcy if he didn't sign."

"You mean your father threatened Fisher?"

Her eyes widened when she looked at me but quickly resumed reading. "Fisher refused to sign until he discussed it with Wells, a Shawnee attorney. Naturally, neither Fisher nor Wells wanted the company to go bankrupt, and so he signed the statement although it was false."

This embezzlement situation was nasty…and complicated. I was tired of the whole fiasco and couldn't understand why Sibyl wanted anything to do with her father.

That relationship was as unhealthy as the one with her mother.

Sibyl

I folded the newspaper and laid it on my lap.

How could my papa, the person I'd idolized while growing up, be so dishonest? Had he really threatened men to sign an inaccurate document?

When we were small, Marjorie and I rode with Papa to Bowie, Texas. We traveled in the first car our family owned, a '16 Ford Model T with Eisen glass windows and heavy cloth snapped on as a permanent roof. A beauty in our eyes. The ride to Bowie had been fun, and Marjorie and I giggled together in the back seat.

Papa's father, Grandpa William Slaughter Trimble, had lost his farm and lived above his dry goods store, W. S. Trimble Groceries, where glass jars rested on shelves, Chase & Sanborn coffee cans and tall wooden barrels stood on dirt floors. Grandpa would scoop the contents from the barrels of corn and beans and slide them into canvas bags. In the front of the store, he sold supplies to old men and wheat farmers while bootlegged whiskey flowed out the back door.

I liked Grandpa Trimble. He'd revel us with stories about how he'd been a shoe salesman, a clerk, and once upon a time a horseback postal rider. Then he'd give us Mary Jane candies, a treat we cherished.

On that day Papa argued with his father, over what I didn't know. But the trip home was much different from the one there. Neither Marjorie nor I uttered a word, wary of Papa. He ranted about how he hated the poor Bowie farm where he grew up and was glad to be done with it. "My father lives in poverty, and I can't stand to see him content with a ramshackle existence."

Although we didn't fully understand Papa's words, we knew not to answer. "I'll never return to my roots," he said. "Never look at the past, I say. Look forward."

As I recalled that story, I wondered if Papa knew his father the way I knew mine. Like how I knew my papa liked collecting rhizomes and my mama swooned over new hats.

From what I could tell, Papa did not have a nurturing childhood. He was forced to wear a dress until he was six years old and, although many little boys wore dresses at that time, he never got over the shame. His family's poverty humiliated him, and he ran away from home at twelve. Maybe poverty had taught him to trust no one but himself. Maybe he tried to prove he was better than other people.

Even before that trip to Texas, Papa seemed distant from his original family. They never had reunions or kept in touch like Mama's family did. Papa seldom talked about his father, and we never went back to visit.

To me, Grandpa Trimble was a good man—a little eccentric, but a hard worker and always kind to his grandchildren. He was buried in Bowie, Texas, alongside his wife. Papa went by himself to the funeral and didn't talk about it when he got back.

Fremont, who was so close to his dad, would never understand why Papa didn't respect his father. Oh, Fremont would never say unkind words but would shake his head and sigh in disbelief whenever Grandpa Trimble and Papa's estranged relationship was mentioned.

I thought of when I was young and admired my father. My hero had fallen, then again, maybe he had never been a hero to begin with. I worried about Papa's salvation. I had to keep praying that God would one day open his eyes. I also prayed that the impetus to relocate would not overshadow prayers for him.

Chapter Twenty-Nine

November 1940

Fremont

Another November and we still had no definite strategies to leave Shawnee. Problems seemed to dog us and we seemed destined to remain in poverty. Although Sibyl claimed she wanted to move forward, she balked when I told her about my plans to take the family to California. She shut me down quickly, saying, in no uncertain terms, that it wasn't the right time. When was the right time? I felt stuck. Frustrated and stuck.

On the streets, heated arguments leading up to the presidential election could have meant another Civil War was on the horizon. Oklahomans were as divided as our families. Normally uninterested in politics, I knew more about this election than any other election in my lifetime. Sibyl put me to sleep reading newspaper articles out loud and tuning in to every political program she could find on the Crosley radio. Most of it I barely endured, although I did enjoy listening to Roosevelt's fireside chats.

I hoped Roosevelt would win. The leader who helped us through the Depression had my strong support. I personally believed he was a shoo-in for re-election, mostly because he promised to keep the U.S. out of the war—but not everyone agreed with me.

Sibyl didn't see the world as black-and-white as I did. I had heard about a job in Stillwater and wanted to check into it, but Sibyl said we should wait until after the elections. Something about how the decisions concerning war might affect the economy.

Hullabaloo.

One of our main disagreements concerned the New Deal. Sibyl argued that Roosevelt spent too much government money rescuing us, and I said he didn't spend enough. But then, she'd never been a hobo riding a rail to California, penniless and yearning for my mother's hoecakes.

No one had a clear picture.

On our way to the church to vote for the president, Sibyl and I discussed the issues, although I could hardly keep up with her deliberations.

Looking straight ahead, I broke into her chatter and asked, "Does your papa still think socialism's the best way?"

"It's been strong in Oklahoma for the last two decades. He claims our folks are primarily farmers and wage earners, and that they, plus the unemployed, don't trust the government. Says it's in bed with big business."

I looked at her and raised one eyebrow. "He's got that right. Many folks would rather kick a mule than trust Roosevelt. But what about you? Do you agree with him?"

"Papa has his own opinions. He's been a stout socialist for years and believes Norman Thomas is the best man for president." Sibyl raised her hand in a questioning manner. "But after being defeated three times, don't you think the man should give up by now?"

"You didn't answer my question. Do you agree with your papa?"

"I used to think the government should meet the people's every need, but not anymore. Who's going to pay for all the free stuff they promise? What motivation would people have to work? No. I don't agree with Papa. Haven't agreed with him in years."

I'd suspected that but wanted to hear her confirm it. I took her elbow and helped her over a hole in the sidewalk.

Sibyl scooted near me in line as we stopped at the voting area, and her voice got softer. "When I was young, I went with him to a political rally for Jack Walton, you know, the one who served the shortest term as our governor. The KKK grew during Walton's tenure, and, due to his disregard for the Constitution, he was removed from office. Papa didn't make a good choice when he supported Walton. He is not making a good choice now."

After we voted, we sauntered down Main Street on the way back home. I must say, my chest stuck out a bit, proud of the brilliant, well-informed wife hanging on my arm. Not only a classy lady, but she was also smarter than a white-tailed fox, using her thinking powers to reach logical conclusions.

The next day, Sibyl read me the voting results.

"Mrs. Mark McAllister won alternate delegate to the Republican National Convention from Oklahoma." Sibyl looked up, a wide smile on her face. "A woman! That's great news."

Republican businessman Wendell Wilkie had been defeated. I guess people didn't trust a successful businessman after all, perhaps because they thought wealthy people started the Great Depression.

Roosevelt won his third presidential run. First time a man was elected to a third term.

The world was looking up.

Sibyl

We watched newsreel after newsreel about the war and listened to the box radio until Fremont begged me to turn it off. Jews in Europe were in the crosshairs of the fighting. They were forbidden to buy, sell, or pawn valuables such as gold or silver and were ordered to report their money and valuables to the bank, where the loot would be confiscated. The Nazis prohibited Jews from owning radios, using vacation resorts, or placing notices in newspapers, among other restrictions. The Jewish people became the most destitute group in society.

Fremont and I had finally reached a place where we no longer felt as poor as Southern cotton pickers or the Jews in Germany. Those poor souls. We would never have deep pockets, but at least we didn't have to wonder if we had enough food to feed our family. Our cigar box was almost full. Thankfully, Fremont had a job, and even though I nagged him about needing school clothes for the children or vanilla flavoring for a cake, we were grateful for what we had.

And what we had was ours. No Nazis could come and demand our radio, or steal from our savings box, or keep us from going on vacation. We lived in a free republic.

Freedom to move if that's what we wanted.

Fremont insisted we needed to leave right away, but I put him off. Even though I wanted to get away from my unstable family and the distress they caused me—an argument still had my nerves on edge—life was smooth at the moment. I went back and forth so often about moving, I wasn't sure what I wanted. However, I didn't believe we should leave town with the war question pending.

In fact, the big question loomed like a storm cloud overhead. Would our country continue to only observe the war, watching the conflict from a distance, pretending it didn't relate to our personal lives? Or would we get involved? I followed the developments in Europe with rising interest, seeing the devastation and destruction, not only to nations but to societies, families, and individuals.

Like the world's tension strung out on a tightrope, tension escalated between me and my family. I thought of our many shortcomings and the havoc wreaked. Then I thought of our desire to move away from domestic turmoil. Were we simply hiding our heads in the sand like the U. S. seemed to do? Waiting for a crisis before we made a move?

Lord, where's the peace we need?

Chapter Thirty

Just before Thanksgiving, I baked Mama a new casserole dish and dropped by one evening to give it to her. I wanted to make peace before the holidays. No one was home—not Mama, Larry, or any of my sisters.

The boarders must have gone to bed early because no one showed up when I let myself in. I waited, expecting my family to walk through at any time. Margaret, Judson, and Carol were home with Fremont, so I took advantage of the quiet and sat down and propped my tired feet on a footstool.

Mama arrived just before sunset. "Where're the girls?" She yelled at me as if it were my fault nobody was home. "Where's Larry? That boy can disappear quicker than bubbles in bathwater."

"They were gone when I got here." I set my feet on the floor and stood, smoothing down my dress and shaking my head to loosen the cobwebs.

"They're missing!" Mama glanced through the window into the back yard, acting as if we'd never argued, never disagreed. "Since you're here, come help me find them."

She stepped onto the back porch and yelled in her powerful, operatic singing voice, "Blanche Harriett! Frances Marie!" The whole neighborhood—everyone from the alley mutt to the deaf man down the street—now knew Mama was home and looking for her daughters.

Frances and Blanche came running from Mrs. Goodpasture's house next door. "She invited us to supper."

Blanche wheezed, out of breath. "She makes the best chicken pot pie I've ever tasted."

"Why did you go and do that? I don't want the neighbors to think we're lowlifes without food. We'll make do."

Frances clutched Mama's arm. "Don't be mad, Mama. I only ate a little."

Mama shoved her away, and the girl's face fell a thousand feet. When Mama was upset, she wasn't one to tangle with.

I flinched. Busy doing other people's laundry by day and out gallivanting most evenings, Mama ignored her youngest daughter. Fourteen-year-old Frances needed attention as much as an orphaned calf needed to be hand-fed. My downcast little sister trudged into the house and plopped onto the sofa.

We followed her inside, Mama still scolding. "You just want to marry Mrs. Goodpasture's son, Blanche. That's why you went over there." She removed her hat and gloves.

Although the stress lines around Mama's eyes had increased, she was still a beautiful woman and worked hard to keep up appearances. Her clothes were homemade but—thanks to Blanche—expertly tailored after the latest styles seen in *Life* magazine. Fashion-conscious, she loved the new rage of a military-style including shoulder pads and straight skirts.

"I wouldn't have Thomas on any condition," Blanche said. "He's been a nasty kid ever since he was a boy and played with Calvis."

"He seems like a good kid to me," I said, "and not too bad looking either. Maybe you should get to know him better. Go out on a date."

"With that pyromaniac? Remember the fire that left a gaping hole in the storage shed? Thomas's fault. And the fire that burned the back pasture? All his doing. Does that tell you something about him?"

The mention of fires made my heart thump. No one, absolutely no one, liked uncontrollable fires, especially me. Ever since our backyard burned, fires had invaded my nightmares.

"A date is a date," Mama said dismissively. "Which reminds me, I have a date tomorrow night, so I won't be home until late. Don't wait up for me. I'll leave a pot of beans for supper."

The idea of my mother on a date shocked me into silence. Although Papa had remarried six months after their divorce, Mama had never hinted about dating. It felt awkward and I felt a sour taste in my mouth—my mother seeing another man.

Mama and Blanche stood several feet apart and glared at each other. Although tension rose between them at times, I'd never seen Blanche this angry and I sensed another family storm brewing. Not wanting to get caught in the controversy, I shuffled toward the door ready to flee.

Blanche, with the madness of an old wet hen flashing in her eyes, squawked at Mama. "Are you seeing that married man again? No decent woman would do such a thing."

"It's none of your business who I see."

I hoped I didn't hear right. My mother seeing a married man? Playing Gladys?

My sister threw her hands up. "Do you realize what you're doing? It makes me so angry I could..."

"I don't care if you're angry. Let's get this straight. You're the daughter, and I'm the mother. You can't boss me around." Mama called Blanche a few choice names, her voice as acerbic as a green plum. "You can't tell me what to do!"

"And all you care about is yourself!" Blanche's face was crimson as she stepped toward Mama.

My mouth fell open in shock.

Blanche's gaze could have seared a hole in the wall. "You're disgracing the whole family. You're a two-timing cheater, just like Papa."

Mama slapped Blanche so hard I not only heard the smack, but I felt the sting.

Blanche stood stunned for a moment as if she couldn't understand what happened. Then she slapped Mama back.

Without thinking, I stepped between my mother and sister, holding out my arms, a palm facing each one like a referee in a boxing match. They glared at each other, breathing hard, their hands clenched in fists.

No one spoke.

In the lull, I realized this was their fight, not mine. I had enough of my own issues to last a lifetime. "Why don't you both move back and take a deep breath." I dropped my arms and stepped back.

Mama and Blanche turned away from each other, and all I saw was Mama's cold shoulder. She probably wouldn't speak to me for weeks.

Then she turned to me, fire in her eyes. "Why should I ever listen to you? You and your papa don't care."

"I do care." I felt an overwhelming sorrow, the kind that travels from your head to your toes. Then tears came, flowing from a great hole that would open up around my family, bringing an outpouring of pain I couldn't control.

Blanche's mocking voice came next, "You can just stop the crying. You're always so emotional and you're not even hurt."

Could family problems get worse than slapping each other in anger? My heart felt heavier every time I experienced their tantrums or witnessed one of their fights. I would never forget their coming to blows. They seemed to thrive on the arguments and negativity.

For some reason, my hysterical crying could turn their anger toward me in a flash. I had to get out of there. One minute Mama loved me and the next she discounted me. I couldn't let her pull me into her bitterness.

I rushed back to Fremont, who could restore my calm. *Lord, bring peace to our family*, I begged on my way home.

The more I dwelt on my family's discord, the more I wondered if our problems would ever be resolved. Would Mama's bitterness destroy me? Would it destroy our family? I had forgotten that was one of the reasons we needed to get away.

Was God big enough to handle this?

Fremont

"Hello!" I yelled as I opened the door of my childhood home.

"Come on in, son," Mother said. "Just thinking about you—praying for you, that is. That's what I do while I'm sitting here churning butter. Praying for my young un's." Mother sat on a stool moving a broomstick-

155

like handle up and down in a large crockpot in front of her. She made the sweetest butter I ever tasted, churning how many pounds over the years?

"Where's Dad? I came to borrow a shovel."

"He's taken the truck out toward Waco. A fellow has a calf for sale, and your dad wants to raise another one to butcher. You can probably find the shovel in the garage."

"I'm in no hurry." I pulled up a chair beside her and sat down. Mother had always been easy to talk to, and it wasn't often I had a chance to speak to her alone because Sibyl and the kids were usually with me. When I did come alone, I helped Dad with the garden, mowed the grass, or cleared the underbrush in the back field.

"How're things over at your place?" Mother asked.

"Not bad. Just wish life wouldn't be so out-of-control."

"You mean with the children? A woman can get moody, you know. You should have figured that out by now."

"No, it's more than that. She tries hard to be kind to her family, but they keep tearing her apart, sour as all get out." I shook my head.

"What do you mean?"

"They get into squabbles. Always something or another. Usually not important stuff, but it escalates, and Sibyl ends up bawling all evening."

"That doesn't sound healthy." Mother took her hands off the handle, wiped them on her apron, and leaned back. I could tell she was tired, probably had churned for the better part of an hour.

"While I'm complaining, I tell you, she's a nervous wreck around her family. Sibyl's high-strung, I know, but the stress her family causes beats all I ever saw. I don't know what to say, and sure as I say something, it'll be the wrong thing." I scooted my chair around and moved the pottery churn in front of me. Shoving the handle up and down, I pounded the cream. "She's got a good heart and wants to help her relatives but getting upset around them doesn't bode well. She mulls it over at home, tense as a stray cat. I don't know what to do. It can't get any worse, can it?" I began to pound that milk like I was chopping wood.

"Whoa, son. No need to churn so fast." Mother's voice was lighthearted, and I knew she wasn't scolding.

I slowed down a bit, still agitated about unloading all my worries on my mother. "Don't get me wrong. She's a good Christian woman and all, and I'm quite proud of her for wanting to show her family godly love, but it's pulling her down." My speed must have quickened because the butter was getting harder to churn.

"Son, you can't fix it for her. That's something she has to work out for herself, meanwhile, you got some protecting to do. Sibyl's growing spiritually and wants to help her family, but she might need to step back from it."

My thoughts exactly. I didn't want Sibyl's family to come between us, but I'd never dealt with this kind of situation and was as frustrated as a foxhound chasing his tail.

"She needs you to support her—to be strong and pray. And don't run away because of her family. Follow God in this." Mother opened the lid of the churn and checked the butter. "I know these are trying times, but the good Lord can help you through."

Then my dear, sweet mother quoted a verse I'd heard her quote many times through the years. Isaiah 41:10. *Fear thou not; for I am with thee: be not dismayed; for I am thy God: I will strengthen thee; yea, I will help thee; yea, I will uphold thee with the right hand of my righteousness.*

I had almost forgotten about the strength of God. I needed to trust him more, even if it was difficult during the day-to-day turmoil. I leaned over and gave my mother a peck on the cheek. When I left, she was using a cheesecloth to strain the sweet butter from the sour buttermilk.

Chapter Thirty-One

December 1940

Fremont

While Sibyl and I rode the trolley around town or drank root beer at Richard's Drug Store or bought day-old bread at the Briscoe Home Bakery on Main Street, we heard lots of talk about the conflicts overseas. Even the fancy Christmas decorations lining Main Street that the children loved, couldn't get people's minds off the war. Thankfully, so far, President Roosevelt had kept us out of it.

Sibyl was more interested in politics than I was, but even I could feel the tension, the flashes of sparks in the air. Some people ignored the news, dismissing it as propaganda, but Sibyl didn't buy that. She informed me daily and listened to the tube radio every evening. Italy invaded Albania, and the blitz in England continued as four bombs exploded in London's theater district, injuring twenty people. Would England surrender?

Fear mounted throughout the country—fear of a rift that could shake our entire world. A cold winter draft of unrest.

The December temperature rose above freezing. Ice and I didn't get along too well, not since the recent storm where my car slid into a ditch and I nearly froze my toes off getting it out.

Sibyl, the kids, and I arrived early on Christmas morning to help Mrs. Trimble prepare the noon meal. Grandpa Bennett wandered aimlessly around the house, and I directed him to a chair in the living room.

Sibyl was setting the table with the good china, and, as I walked by her, she whispered, "This is the last time we'll use these nice dishes. Mama needs the money and is selling them." Papa had stopped the child support payments again.

I nodded, the tragedy of losing fancy dishes being lost on me, and I began to round up extra chairs for the table.

Marjorie arrived alone, having ridden a bus from Lawton, and just as the food landed on the table, Calvis burst through the front door, also alone. He removed his hat and hung it by the door. "I'm starving. Is dinner ready?"

"Where's Evie?" Mrs. Trimble asked.

"You don't want to know."

I couldn't speak for Mrs. Trimble, but I, for one, honestly didn't want to know about their marital problems. It was general knowledge that Calvis and Evie didn't see eye to eye on much of anything.

"Come on. Tell us," Blanche said.

Calvis scowled. "It's her fault. She wanted a new dress for Christmas, and I refused, so we had a row. That woman has no idea about finances."

There Calvis stood in his fancy new suspenders and shiny pointed-toe shoes. How could a sweet lady like Evie marry a man like Sibyl's head-strong brother?

"Evie, as I recall, never wears anything new. No wonder she was upset," said Sibyl.

"Humph." Calvis pulled out a chair and sat down.

The rest of us found seats at the table, and I voiced the prayer, thanking God for our family and this delicious meal. We men filled our plates, and then the ladies filled the children's plates, dishing up pickles and sweet potatoes and turkey and sage dressing and everything I loved about a good meal—the works.

Taking a swig of sweet, iced tea, I listened to the clatter of dishes and smelled the cinnamon and spices, reminded of God's goodness. We had made it through another year, trials, worries and all.

After everyone had eaten more than enough, I laid down my fork, leaned back in my chair, and patted my stomach. "Good food, Mrs.

Trimble. Mighty good. That is definitely the best grub I've eaten in a coon's age." Words I heard my dad speak many times.

Mrs. Trimble acknowledged my compliment with a smile.

Later, Calvis brought out gifts from Papa and Gladys. We'd agreed not to overdo buying Christmas gifts, our savings more important, but Calvis handed Frances, Blanche, Marjorie, and Sibyl packages, which they tore into.

Sibyl held up a wad of rabbit fur. What in blazes would she do with rabbit fur?

"Look, a detachable fur collar."

"Oh, now I see."

"You remember the fur department at Montgomery Ward?" Calvis asked. "That's where Gladys works. She collected fur scraps and made these by hand."

"Fur isn't sensible in this economy," said Mama. "She should've kept her gifts to herself."

With that comment weighing in the air and gift-giving time over, Calvis and I bundled up and ventured into the cold to inspect his recently purchased '38 Ford. He revved the engine to show it off. I heard a clanging sound and tried to fix it and might've gotten it done if the weather hadn't been so nasty.

Twenty minutes later, we rushed back inside, the cold air blowing in with us, our faces numb from the chill. We stomped our feet to get the snow off and hung our coats by the door. Mrs. Trimble brought us cups of hot coffee.

Margaret tugged at my hand. "Daddy, come look." She led me to the Christmas tree and pointed to a bird tucked into a back branch. "Shh...be quiet," she said, worried I'd startle it. To her, the fake bird was a miracle.

Margaret's sweetness and innocence contrasted starkly with the war talk Calvis initiated. "Rumor has it that we might fight beside the Red Army—against Hitler."

"Nonsense. Stalin supporters are sworn enemies of the West." I couldn't help but explain the obvious. "Where would we be if Stalin won? The Soviet Union hasn't been our friend for decades."

"Americans should keep their distance from the war." Blanche jumped into the conversation. "This fighting is serious business."

"I disagree." Sibyl raised her voice. "We *should* engage with Hitler. Our future, like everyone else's, is at stake. That being said, I don't want any of our family to be drafted."

"You're right. It's time for the President to step in and make a decision, one way or the other," Fremont said.

"Can't we have a family gathering without talk of war? Forget that for once." Mama clamped down on the discussion, but war was hard to ignore.

Anxiety grew. Tension stretched nerves to the point of snapping and opinions were skewed as to be meaningless. No one recognized the enormous hole the world was falling into.

***

I gathered the children, my beautiful wife, and leftover apple pie, and headed toward the car, not wanting to overstay our welcome at the Trimbles or get into any more arguments.

More than that, my folks were expecting us at their house for the evening meal. Mother would have gifts for the kids and offer homemade chocolate fudge and decorated cookies, and then we'd sit around and sing Christmas carols. Compared to Christmas lunch at the Trimbles, our evening would be a scene right out of a Norman Rockwell painting, and I looked forward to a relaxing time as the sun set.

On the short drive to Mother and Dad's, Margaret leaned over the back seat to be near us. That girl had grown like a dandelion, and I was reminded of last Christmas when she'd been an angel in the church play, looking so small in a white gown that swallowed her and hid her feet. I chuckled recalling the rest of that pageant. How five or six kids sang in front of a wooden frame made of two-by-fours with curtains attached and when the kids leaned on the frame, it tumbled backward. The entire church laughed before gasping at the kid's feet flying in the air.

That was last Christmas when fighting on the other side of the world was far removed. This year, anger over the world situation was like a storm forecast, spreading dread and fear of coming destruction. Reports of the fighting trickled in on newsreels every week, and none of the announcements were good. Men's anxieties, mothers' worries, and young peoples' uneasiness permeated every conversation.

If we went to war, would I be drafted? What would that mean for my family? Should we move now before a war started? What if I had to leave Sibyl? She might need to be close to her family. The military didn't draft married men with children, but that could change if the war became lengthy.

I pulled the motorcar into my parents' driveway. Through a frosty window, I saw the glow of candles on a cedar tree my daddy must've chopped down and lugged into the house a few days before.

Ah. Fremont, old buddy, listen to what your daddy told you. Worry about today and let the good Lord take care of tomorrow.

Peace—at least for the moment—settled over me. Peace that I hoped would last throughout the new year.

1941

Chapter Thirty-Two

January 1941

Fremont

A few Sundays after the holidays, Sibyl and the children and I went to my folks for lunch. My mother's cooking on a bad day could rival an Italian chef's. She fed us as if food would take all our troubles away. It didn't, but it helped. Plain old country cooking. Fried pork chops and buttered potatoes along with homemade bread and butter pickles and fresh canned corn—all just for us. Umm. Nothing smelled better than a home-cooked meal.

We ate our fill, and Mother brought out peach cobbler. Like an urchin who'd just been given a gold piece, my eyes widened with delight.

"Who wants some?" Mother held up a spoon to dish out the dessert right there at the table.

The first to speak up was Dad. "Give me a big ol' heaping bowl of those vittles. I don't reckon anyone else wants any."

"You already had your dessert today. You must've forgotten." Mother ignored Dad's plea and handed me a bowl filled to the rim. I tried to hide my smile from Dad.

Dad protested, his eyes drooping fake sadness. "No ma'am, you're mistaken about that. When did I have dessert?"

"That toast you had for breakfast," Mother said. "You loaded it down with so much butter and brown sugar I thought it was candy. If that isn't dessert, then my mama will turn over in her grave."

163

Dad's jolly laughter rang out. He most certainly liked his sweets, especially sugar cream pie with meringue, which he called calf slobbers. Peach cobbler, like Mother was dishing up, was his second favorite.

"Honey, if I covered the toast with sorghum molasses you might have a point, but otherwise, dish me up some of that there grub."

Mother smiled and gave him a large bowlful of cobbler covered with sweet cream.

After the meal, Dad snuck out the front door and sat on the porch swing. Mother Pope took a blanket and draped it over his lap, while Margaret and Judson snuggled around him. He began to tell stories. Some were true, but others obviously were embellished, tall as Uncle Louie's windmill.

He had outlandish sayings that entertained the kids. "When you see a frog up a tree, pull his tail and think of me." Or songs like "Mama's little baby loves shortnin', shortnin'. Mama's little baby loves shortnin' bread." Any silly song or story created a giggle from the grandkids, and it wasn't long before he had them rolling on the porch, roaring with laughter. We could hear the sound all through the house.

Mother, Sibyl, and Ruth were cleaning the dishes when I heard a horn honk.

I looked out the window and saw a shiny black, Ford sedan drive up. My cousins, Clyde and Inez, stepped out. Clyde opened the back door and lifted out their boy, Marvin, who had grown too big for Inez to carry. Clyde carried his lanky son indoor and set him gently on the floor.

When he was just days old, Marvin contracted measles and ran a high fever. It was clear at six years old that he'd never eat, walk, or use the toilet by himself. He had never talked, and probably never would.

Clyde and Inez sold their homestead near Bethel last month, and moved to Shawnee, buying a house next door to her parents, my Aunt Woodlie and Uncle Raleigh. They helped Inez, their only child, with Marvin, their only grandchild.

Both Clyde and I loved to work on automobiles, and though neither of us did much heavy labor on Sunday, we could take a gander under the hood of a car. We strode outside to check out my jalopy.

Clyde stepped in front of the Chevy engine. "What're you working on?" He spent hours in filling stations around town and knew more about auto mechanics than the Duryea Brothers, but I'd never let on I believed it.

"Putting in a new engine," I said. "Needs to be done by tomorrow."

"Blazes! You haven't started yet. No one can work that fast. What're you thinking?" A grin crossed his face when he heard me chortle.

We were close to the same height, and I looked him over. Like most mechanics, he had grease under his fingernails and tended to look rumpled. "You need broad shoulders like me for this kind of work." I pushed out my chest to look huskier.

Clyde slapped me on the back. "You don't say. Now if this car was a Ford, I might be all for helping you."

"No chance of that, but since you're here, stand in front of those headlights so I can see if they're working."

Between the two of us and with a pair of pliers, a screwdriver, and enough baling wire to do a job, we could fix anything on wheels. If a motorcar needed repairs, friends and family knew to take the broken-down machine to either of us.

One headlight was out. As I picked up the replacement bulb, I dropped my screwdriver.

"You always that clumsy around cars, boy?"

"Hey. I was driving my dad's car when I was only ten. 'Borrowed it,' you might say."

Clyde chuckled. "Did you get caught?"

"I maneuvered around some barrels beside the road over by Earlsboro once. Knocked those barrels down, and I was so proud of myself, but heavens to Betsy, I didn't know the barrels were filled with cement. I tried to get home before Dad because that fender was crumpled up like a squashed pumpkin."

Clyde doubled over with laughter.

Sibyl

After Fremont and Clyde went outside, Mother turned to Inez and asked, "Would you like some peach cobbler? It's the best I've ever made. I picked the peaches myself."

Inez, one of my favorite people, shook her head. "Although that does sound scrumptious, I can't eat a thing. We just finished dinner."

Mother slipped back into the kitchen, while Inez and I sat on the sofa. The youngest children, Carol and Marvin, played on the floor in front of us. I gave Carol a plastic bell, which she rang.

Inez and I had become good friends. Her sweet voice had a lilt that made everyone feel comforted, and I especially basked in the sound of it. "How are you doing?" I asked. "We missed you at church this morning."

"Clyde and I stayed home and let my parents go to the service." Inez paused and took a deep breath. "We've decided to alternate taking care of Marvin at home, and I think it's working out. At least that way, we can get out of the house occasionally and Marvin will be looked after all the time."

Marvin was a few months older than my Keith would have been. Was it better to lose a child like I did or have an incapacitated son like Marvin? I buried the thought in the back of my mind. Some questions couldn't be answered.

"Marvin likes to ride in the motorcar, so on Sunday afternoons, we go for a drive. We don't know many people in town yet, so we wound up here. This is the only place I feel comfortable getting Marvin out of the car."

Inez stood and scooted Marvin to a pallet in front of the screen door. The boy switched between playing with a large-toothed comb, which for some reason fascinated him, and staring out the door at the trees. Inez was trying to teach him to walk even though doctors said he would never be able to.

"Clyde said we should have more children—lead a more normal life," Inez blurted out as she returned to the sofa.

"What do you think?"

"He wants to put Marvin in a home." Tears pooled in Inez's eyes. "He thinks it'll be better for him...and for us."

I had no advice to give her. With three healthy children, I found myself bumbling my way through motherhood most of the time. I couldn't imagine the challenges of raising a handicapped child. "What do *you* want to do?" I asked.

"Marvin's my responsibility. I have no right to pass him off to someone else." Inez leaned toward me and whispered. "I can't imagine anyone taking care of him but me." Her voice took on a determination that surprised me. "I'll never have another baby, and I refuse to send this child away. I told Clyde that Marvin is the only child I'll ever have."

Inez, the meekest, most precious lady I'd ever met, was adamant. No, she would never put Marvin in a home. She would take care of him all his life, thank you very much.

In contrast, Clyde was a robust, outgoing male. He wanted a normal life with a normal wife and a house full of lively, 'normal' children.

How could they reconcile something this huge? How did any family reconcile their differences?

Chapter Thirty-Three

February 1941

Sibyl

Hitler and his army were becoming more and more aggressive.

However, I could not focus on the war because more urgent issues occupied my thoughts. I heard a neighbor boy died, and the doctor pronounced it pneumonia. Any child's illness flooded me with worry.

Two days after my neighbor lost her son, our baby Carol became seriously ill. Old fears came rushing back with the same agony I felt when Keith lay in the hospital. I panicked, remembering how his death had shaken our family.

My poor little Carol. When I couldn't get her fever down, I removed her clothing, gave her a wet towel bath, and fanned her. Nothing helped. I remembered little Marvin, who had been handicapped for life by a childhood fever.

In a panic, I called Doctor Fortson.

"I'm on the way," he said.

I breathed heavily to keep from fainting. Asthma from childhood had taught me to breathe deeply and calm myself, but at times like this, those strategies proved useless. I paced from Carol's room to the front window and back, taking deep breaths, waiting for the doctor to arrive.

Margaret and Judson were in school at Horace Mann Elementary on Draper Street near our house. A ten-year-old red brick building, the school had enclosed metal slides, used as fire escapes, angling down from the second story. The children arrived home only minutes before the doctor arrived, and I sent them into the back yard to play.

The doctor arrived and, before he would look at Carol, Margaret the acrobat walked into the house complaining of a hurt shoulder. Dad Pope had made her a bar, and she'd been hanging upside down by her knees and tumbled down the day before. At the time she seemed fine, but now tears streaked her pale face. As I put my hand on her back to lead her to the sofa, she screamed in pain. Through sobs, she told me about falling on her shoulder a second time.

Doctor Fortson, a tall, bespectacled gentleman, turned to Margaret. "What's wrong, child?"

"She isn't the patient," I said. "But she fell and seems to have hurt her arm."

Her wails got his immediate attention, and he sat on the couch to examine her. She had a broken collar bone. Dear child. I was so preoccupied with the baby's illness that I hadn't noticed the extent of her injuries. The doctor bound Margaret's arm in a sling and gave her something to alleviate the pain and help her sleep.

The doc examined Carol next and ran some tests. None of the children had been vaccinated, and I prayed she had not contracted some horrible disease.

If I hadn't been so exhausted from caring for the children, I would have gone to bed and cried myself to sleep. But I couldn't.

Raising kids was not for the meek and mild.

***

Doctor Fortson came back the next day with Carol's test results. Diphtheria.

On hearing the dreaded word, the blood drained from my face. I held my breath while my heart twisted into a painful knot.

No!

Carol could not be that sick. Not my baby girl. I could not lose another child.

169

The doctor gave Carol a toxin. "Where have you taken her?" he asked me. "No one in the area has tested positive for diphtheria."

"We went to a family reunion at Sulphur two weeks ago. Do you think that's where she contracted it?" I considered the irony. Had the family outing that lifted my spirits caused this threat to my baby's life?

Another thought occurred to me. Fremont and I had renovated our rent house in exchange for three months' free rent. While painting the inside, we'd removed the window screens—allowing flies to stream in. Margaret, Judson, and I shooed flies all day by flagging tea towels and herding the swarm toward an open door, but they came right back.

"Do flies spread diphtheria?" I asked.

"Anything is possible," said Doc Fortson. "There're several ways she could have gotten it, but our concern now is to get her well and keep it from spreading. Keep her away from others. Hopefully, we've caught it early, and she won't have a serious case."

The doctor hung a sign on the front door which read: *DIPTHERIA. These premises under quarantine. No person must leave this house or remove any article except by permission of an authorized person. Signed, The Board of Health.*

That night, after making sure the children were calm and sleeping, I limped to bed, exhausted. Fremont sat on the edge of the mattress beside me. "We'll have to make some changes because I have to go to work tomorrow. I can't stay inside."

"Oh no. I haven't thought of that. What if you get sick?"

"Now, honey." Fremont stroked my hair in the way that always calmed me. "That's something it won't do to worry about. What matters is Carol and getting her well."

Fremont

Diphtheria, extremely contagious, required our family to be quarantined for four whole weeks. Every time we had a cigar box full of dough, an emergency arose.

Mother brought food and set it on the front porch. We could hear her praying over our house like a mama duck praying for her ducklings. Meanwhile, Sibyl's mama called and lectured on how to take proper care of children so they wouldn't be exposed to diseases like this. As if we could have prevented it.

I couldn't take a break from my work as Norton's night watchman because my salary supported the family, therefore, I couldn't mingle with Sibyl or the children, which meant I was no help to them. An awful situation, but there was no getting around it.

We arranged for me to sleep in our bedroom while Sibyl slept with the children in their room. She brought me clean clothes and pushed them through a narrow opening in the door without touching me. I longed to grab her hand and feel the softness of her skin, but I didn't. I couldn't take any chances. My family needed me to stay healthy.

Carol's fever broke during the second night, and a weight lifted off me. My heartbeat returned to normal, and I could breathe freely again. Our baby would survive, and I thanked God over and over.

Sibyl knocked on the door of our bedroom. "Here's your supper, honey—meatloaf and gravy and fried potatoes."

I opened the door enough for her to slip the plate to me. "I feel so bad about this. Wish I could do something to help."

Sibyl merely shook her head, but I could see the worry in her eyes. "We're managing."

Margaret stood behind her, peeking around her skirt. "Hi, Daddy. Can you hug me good night?"

"Sorry, pumpkin, I can't. Have to wait a while."

"Can you tell me a story?"

"Now, that I can do." I sat by the closed door and spoke to Margaret and Judson as they sat on the other side of the door. I launched into a tall tale about my childhood and read *Hansel and Gretel* to keep them entertained, and then I asked Margaret, "How's your shoulder now?"

As a result of her broken collar bone, Margaret's arm was taped across her chest. She slid a note under the door with her unrestrained hand. "I'm better. Mama said to show this to you."

I unfolded the paper from her teacher and read, "Please instruct Margaret to do her schoolwork." I read the note again. "Margaret, why aren't doing your work?"

"I told the teacher I can't write because of my hurt arm."

"And what did your teacher say to that?"

Margaret's voice rose through the door. "The teacher didn't understand. She told me I can still write."

"Dear, you are right-handed. It's your left shoulder that's hurt."

"So, I can still write?"

I muffled my laugh and attempted a stern voice. "Yes, girl. You can still write. Now get your paper and start working."

When Sibyl took the tape off Margaret's arm three weeks later, the child couldn't straighten it. Sibyl worked the limb often, bending and straightening it to stretch the muscle. I wanted to help her learn how to use her arm again, but I was stuck in a room, feeling useless, lonelier than a bear hibernating through the winter.

I dwelt on how to keep my kin safe and make sure we had enough money for necessities—and emergencies. What if our savings had been depleted? How would we have paid the doctor?

I just had to work harder. I could do better if given half a chance.

When the quarantine days were over, the first thing I did was gather my wife and young 'uns in my arms for a tight hug.

I would do anything for my family. Anything.

Chapter Thirty-Four

March 1941

Sibyl

Saturday morning, Mama smoothed down the taffeta-ruffled apron over her loose high-waisted house dress. Her hair, pulled back into a kerchief, fluffed down to her shoulders.

I sat in a dining room chair watching her make a chocolate cake. No one interfered while Mama baked. A family rule. My rule, since I expected criticism to fly off her lips at any moment, was to do nothing to make Mama upset. Being around Mama was good until it wasn't.

"I don't think I'll ever cook as well as you do." My words were not meant to flatter, her recipes were probably gleaned from Irma's popular book, *The Joy of Cooking*. I simply hoped to get into her good graces.

I stood and glanced out the window at Margaret and Judson playing on the front porch. I heard a noise and turned.

Grandpa Bennett wandered into the kitchen in a daze, looking around the room like a lost two-year-old.

"What do you need, Dad?" Mama asked. "Do you want a biscuit or a cup of coffee?"

Grandpa's eyes were blank as if he couldn't remember what he wanted. He shook his head to clear it. "I'm looking for someone to play canasta."

"Canasta?"

"He enjoys playing cards with the spinster upstairs," explained Mama.

"Where's my wife? She beats me every time." Grandpa turned his head slowly as he looked around the room for his wife. My Grandma Bennett had been able to mend chest colds, nurse broken bones, and deliver babies, in addition to playing a mean game of canasta. She knew about medicinal herbs, read the Bible a lot, and had my big strapping Grandpa eating out of her hand. But she had died six years before, right after Fremont and I married.

"Grandma's not here," I said.

When Grandma and Grandpa Bennett were first married, he would hitch up his horse and buggy and take his petite wife to treat people in their homes. A godly woman, Grandma loved her husband like no one else in the world, and Grandpa had never recovered from losing the one he adored.

Would Fremont and I ever be that close? He wanted to discuss future plans while I worried about family, focused on making everything right. I must admit, I felt closest to him when we stopped to pray about our differences.

"No one has time to play canasta this morning." Mama set the big mixing bowl, measuring cups, and spoons into the sink. "Sorry, Dad."

"How about a movie? What was the name of that show we watched at the Hornbeck?" Grandpa leaned against the counter, slumping more than usual. His gait had weakened over the past few months, and his unsteadiness worried me.

"*The Hunchback of Notre Dame*." Mama's voice sounded irritable as if she'd already explained this a thousand times. "Blanche watched it over and over." Although Mama didn't have much money for frivolities, Blanche saved her nickels and would rather go to a movie than sip a root beer soda at Marmaduke's Drug Store.

Grandpa nodded. "Ah, that's right. That dog. That Frollo character. Reminded me of your nasty ex-husband, ah..." Grandpa's words ceased as he stared off into space. "What's his name again?"

"Malcolm." Mama spit out the word. "Malcolm Calvis Trimble the First."

"I'm glad you kicked him out." Grandpa's hatred of Papa was as apparent as Mama's. "He was about as good as a riled rattler."

"I didn't exactly kick him out. He found another woman."

"Well, good riddance, I say."

If Mama and Grandpa started complaining about how bad my papa acted, we'd be sitting in this kitchen all day.

Before I could change the subject to something more neutral, Mama said, "Now go on. Get out of the kitchen. Sibyl, will you help him?"

I took Grandpa's elbow, edging him toward the front door.

Grandpa pulled away from me. "I can walk by myself." He opened the door, grumbling, "That man had too many rules. I thought I was living back home in Michigan. Do you remember? He had no business telling me to sit up straight and keep my boots off the table. No business at all. No business at all."

He let himself down slowly into the porch swing next to where the children played, seeming frail, older than the Arbuckle Wilderness.

When I returned to help in the kitchen, the whole house smelled of chocolate. After we washed the dishes, Mama pulled the cake out of the oven and set it on the counter to cool before frosting.

"It's a nightmare living with Gramps. He isn't himself." Mama sighed as if the world had become a burden, too heavy for one person to bear alone. "He's getting senile. At nighttime, he can't remember where the bathroom is, so he pees everywhere. And during the daytime, he wanders off so much I have to watch him like a hawk. Just my luck to be the one to have to take care of him." Mama considered Grandpa another burden adding to the stress she already had.

"He seems fine to me, as contrary as ever. He can't be that much trouble." I didn't want to acknowledge Grandpa's decline, although I'd found him wandering around a few times. Did he have new health issues?

"Humph. That twenty dollars he gets every month from the state doesn't pay for the food he eats, much less a nursemaid."

I loved Grandpa, with his witty humor and fiddling western songs. An experienced carpenter, he had built the breakfast furniture in our Shawnee house, a table with two benches, the table I sat at, drinking coffee. He also helped build our house in Wewoka—the house awarded to Mama in the divorce settlement—along with the mortgage Papa put against it. The house she'd lost.

"It'd be better if he'd just pass away in his sleep."

"Mama! You don't mean that."

"Who are you to judge? I'm the one who gets up in the middle of the night to take him back to bed when he wanders off. You're not around. But don't worry about me. I can get along without my eldest daughter's help. Just go on with your life like I'm not here struggling with two kids, an old man, and four boarders, trying to make ends meet."

Had Mama just said that? My hand went to my mouth in disbelief at her words. What did my mother want from me? I stood quickly. "That isn't true, and you know it. I'd do anything to take care of Grandpa." My hackles rose and I started to protest more but stopped. I should come more often, help with extra laundry, bring over more meals. Drawn to meeting people's needs, I wanted to care for my family, to be there for them, and felt awful if I failed.

I called Margaret and Judson into the house and gave them a slice of the frosted, warm cake. Soon, traces of chocolate crumbs lined their mouths. I wrapped up a huge slice for Fremont.

"I'll come by with the children later and take Grandpa to the Ritz," I said as we walked out the door. I could afford the ten cents for a good double feature and newsreel with a cartoon thrown in.

"Don't bother. He wouldn't remember the show anyway. I can make do without your help."

I choked back the tears that threatened, hoping they'd wait until I got home.

I couldn't bear another crisis. If anyone needed help in my family at the moment, it was Grandpa. And I would help even if Fremont claimed I was trying to save the world. Family ties were as strong and binding as Dad's tow chain.

Chapter Thirty-Five

April 1941

Sibyl

Grandpa George Bennett left his home when he was twelve years old. One of a dozen kids, he heard family talk while growing up about being kin to the famous Benjamin Franklin. No one could convince him otherwise, and he threw the genealogy into almost every conversation he had.

Since the move to Mama's new house last year, he would take off, making unsupervised trips like going downtown to get a haircut even if he didn't have a quarter. Since he was a long-time customer at the Central Barbershop on Main, the barber would occasionally offer a free trim.

"How's Grandpa?"

"Not doing well. He's eating like a sparrow lately."

"How can I help?" Although I tried to assist with Grandpa's needs, my contribution was limited. I brought meals, played checkers with him, and took him to get monthly haircuts, but I didn't know what else to do.

One day, Mama thought he had been gone too long when the telephone rang. I happened to be visiting that day, so I answered it and recognized the deep voice of a neighbor who lived near our old bungalow on Beard Street. "Mrs. Trimble, I think it's your father sitting on my front steps. He looks lost."

"I'll send someone right away," I said, not bothering to inform her I was not Mrs. Trimble.

177

Frances left to get him and bring him home while Mama and I finished cleaning his bedroom and doing his laundry. We waited on the front porch and about thirty minutes later, Frances skipped into our view without him. His pace must have been as slow as sugar cane molasses because Frances had already hopped up the steps when he trailed in around the corner.

I walked down the sidewalk to meet him, straightened his wrinkled gray shirt, and helped him across the porch and into his bedroom. Exhausted, he lay back and closed his eyes while I took off his shoes. I returned to the front porch swing where Mama waited.

"I don't know what I'm going to do with him," Mama said, wringing her hands. "He's gotten worse."

"What do you mean?"

"He's confused. Ever since we moved, he gets out of the house and wanders back to the old place. Someone has to go fetch him and lead him home. He lays down his pipe—his *lit* pipe—and forgets about it."

"He'll get used to the move eventually."

"You don't understand. He doesn't know who some people are, and terrible cuss words —words I've never heard him use before—come out of his mouth."

"Cuss words? From Grandpa?" I shook my head helplessly. Maybe it was time to address Gramp's problems. The last time I visited, he lost his hat and failed to put on his shoes when he went outside. I didn't mention it, not wanting to alarm Mama more.

"I've tried every remedy I learned from Grandma Bennett—from potato water to peppermint tea—but nothing helps." Mama slowly pushed the swing back and forth, its chains complaining with rhythmic squeaks. "He's grown worse over the past few months. Last week he cursed Mrs. Goodpasture and her husband when they were visiting. In no uncertain terms, he told them to get out of our house. Any stranger who dares enter this place faces Grandpa's wrath." Mama paused. "At least he likes the boarders, although sometimes he mistakes Mrs. Peterson for his wife."

I snickered. "Can't Uncle Lewis help?"

Mama nodded. "He sends a little money every month, but when he manages to visit, Grandpa doesn't know him and asks him to leave the room. And it always takes several minutes to recognize Adah."

He didn't know his own son and daughter? It was worse than I'd realized.

Several folks in town cared for needy people in their houses. Mama visited three family homes and talked to folks who sat around fireplaces and had beds in the back room for the elderly. Mama had come home disheartened and stated she couldn't afford to pay someone to take care of Grandpa.

"He can't eat without vomiting," Mama said. "Something's seriously wrong."

"What do you mean? What's wrong?"

"He's out of his mind—forgetting to wash his face, wandering outside in his underwear. He sleeps all day and pees the bed at night, either because he can't get up or can't find the toilet."

Blanche slept in a second bed in his room, and I'd heard her complain. "I heard Mama in the middle of the night yelling at Grandpa, 'You little fool! Get back into bed.'"

Before Mama could explain more, Grandpa stumbled onto the front porch. "Mabel, can't you do anything?" he said, looking at his daughter. "I have this awful bellyache. Have you got any tonic?"

Mama looked distraught or irritated. I couldn't tell which. "Do you see what I put up with? It can't go on like this." She guided him back to his room.

Our once lively, funny, white-haired gramps had deteriorated into someone I hardly recognized. And it broke my heart.

***

Mama placed a cot in the dining room and let Grandpa Bennet sleep there. He'd grown weak and couldn't always get out of bed to walk to the kitchen. His failing health put stress on everyone, especially Mama.

When I arrived for a visit, Mama said he'd asked to see me.

I knelt beside him. "Hi, Gramps," I said softly.

"Hi, kid." His words came out mumbled, but when he looked at me, I could tell he recognized me. "I got bedsores, and these bellyaches are getting worse." He paused and took a deep breath.

"Do you want some soup? I can make it for you."

"Can't eat a thing."

"I know. Mama told me how sick you are," I said, but he had already closed his eyes. "I love you, Grandpa." I tiptoed out of the room.

"I don't know what else to do for him." Mama sat in the kitchen, rubbing the back of her neck.

She vocalized my thoughts. What could we do? How do you help an elderly relative when they're suffering so much? Fear of losing Grandpa pressed like a boulder on my chest but seeing him in pain equally distressed me.

"Maybe we should call Dr. Fortson," I said.

"We don't have money for the doctor," Mama snapped.

I understood Mama's sharp reply. Her concerns about money were legitimate, adding to her helpless feelings. However, after a few minutes, she relented and picked up the telephone.

Dr. Fortson, our family doctor since before Margaret was born, arrived that afternoon. He examined Grandpa and delivered an impossible diagnosis. "He needs to go to the hospital."

"I don't have a nickel to spare for a hospital," Mama said, her voice trembling. She looked at me pleadingly. "What about you and Fremont? Can you come up with some cash?"

Fremont and I hardly had enough funds to support our family. Our cigar box didn't hold nearly enough to cover a hospital bill. Biting my lip, I shook my head.

"What about your papa? Can you finagle some money out of him?"

That wasn't a possibility, given Papa's job loss. I pressed my lips together and shook my head again.

I heard Grandpa groan and went in to see him. I held his bony hand between my palms and cried. The situation seemed hopeless, and all we could do was sit and let time run its course. And pray. I did a lot of praying.

***

The following day I walked into Mama's house and noticed Grandpa in bed snoring loudly and breathing heavily. I shook his shoulder to wake him, but he didn't blink an eye nor budge.

Alarmed, I ran to get Mama from the back yard, where she was cutting roses for a bouquet.

"What happened to Grandpa? He won't wake up."

"Since we couldn't afford a hospital visit, Dr. Fortson gave him a dose of twilight sleep to sedate him. He hasn't woken since."

"Twilight sleep? The doctor must have given him too much. That can kill people."

"What was I supposed to do?" Mama wailed again. "If we'd only had the money, we could've sent him to the hospital." Over and over, she asked, "What was I supposed to do?"

I couldn't answer. Twilight shots, commonly given to old folks when there was no hope, were common in our society, but I didn't want it to be given to my sweet Grandpa. I wasn't ready for him to die. Two emotions tore at my heart—relief that he was not in pain and guilt that his death might have been hurried along.

I went back to Grandpa's bedside and heard him moan, like a soft gargle. Was it the death rattle? My stomach churned and my muscles tightened. I'd read about how they'd taken to euthanizing mentally disabled patients in Poland and about how they suspected old people were neglected or left to die in concentration camps. Hints came from Germany that Jews and the elderly were loaded into vans and gassed with carbon monoxide. Inhumane.

I understood Mama's decision, but I had strong reservations about such potent drugs. Morally, was it right? The shot might have done nothing more than relieve his pain, but I couldn't be certain. Regardless of the method or motive behind the act, was it murder if our doctor's injection caused Grandpa's death? Which was worse, to see a man writhe in pain or to help him escape his misery? Throughout the ages, how many people watched loved ones suffer and experienced this same dilemma? There seemed to be no end to the unanswerable questions.

I could never have agreed to what Mama allowed the doctor to do. All I could do was sit beside him and hold his hand, not knowing how long the vigil would be. Mama and I took turns, and tears came easily.

Three days later, on May 7, 1941, Grandpa Bennett passed away without ever regaining consciousness. I placed a black wreath on Mama's front door to signify a death in the family. Even if our loved ones lived a long time, they leave an empty spot.

Frances burst in from dance class. "What happened?" We'd tried to protect her from the inevitable.

I took her hand and led her to the sofa. Telling her about Grandpa's death upset me more than telling my own children. While Margaret and Judson had many people who loved them, Frances had so little love in her life.

***

Grief gripped icy fingers around my heart. Fremont hugged me as I sobbed the night of Grandpa's death. Throughout the entire ordeal, my husband had been my rock. Death struck fear in me, bringing back memories of Keith's death. Death, the enemy of old and young alike.

Mama didn't grieve as much as I did over Grandpa Bennett's death, but perhaps we all respond to loss in different ways. Maybe my mama saw his death as a blessing—a release from his pain and the work he created. She might not have been a saint, but she had taken care of Grandpa for years, and caring for him hadn't been easy. She had assumed the responsibility, and I loved her for that.

Blanche picked up Grandpa's old fiddle and went into her room and played by ear as he had taught her. Strains of *Arkansas Traveler* and *Old Joe Clark* floated in the air. When Grandpa played those old tunes, I had always wanted to dance. Hearing them now brought an ache to my heart.

Grandpa, George Orlando Bennett, was born May 23, 1855. He died sixteen days shy of his eighty-sixth birthday. He was buried in Sulphur,

Oklahoma, next to his sainted and beloved wife, Cordelia Harriett Clay Bennett.

Aunt Adah and her family came to the funeral, as did Uncle Lewis and his children. Cousin Bernard and his wife Elloween Peach were there. Mildred Bennett Kirkpatrick, another cousin, joined us. Fremont, Margaret, Judson, and I sat with the family, as did a slew of Grandpa's descendants, including Marjorie, Calvis and his wife, Blanche, and Frances.

Everyone dressed in their Sunday best. Men wore suits and women wore black dresses, gloves, and hats with veils or netting.

Papa didn't come, but that was just as well. Grandpa wouldn't have wanted him there.

Dr. Chesterfield Turner officiated the ceremony and gave a moving eulogy. I heard little of it except the words, "No one is promised tomorrow."

At the end of the short service, Bernard Bennett, Irving Bennett, Melvin Bennett, James Kirkpatrick, Calvis Trimble, and Fremont Pope—serving as pallbearers—solemnly carried Grandpa's wooden casket from the church.

Mama—in typical Mama fashion—leaned over and whispered, "They're the best-looking bunch of pallbearers I ever saw at a funeral."

The Sulphur First Baptist church members outdid themselves and produced mountains of food for the family meal. We visited with relatives we seldom saw, and stories of Grandpa abounded. He was certainly loved and had lived life to the fullest.

Could I say that? That I lived life to the fullest? I tried to follow God, to say the words he wanted, to go where he wanted, to teach where he wanted. Was that enough? I thought about Grandpa Bennett's life and all I didn't know about him. I wanted to ask him about his childhood, about his observations on life, about growing old and feeling alone. But the time for those questions had passed.

The morning after the funeral, Mama poured a little whiskey she had on hand over some hard candy and swigged it down. Grandpa always believed in drinking whiskey with rock candy before tackling a big job.

Then we began the task of cleaning the house and washing Grandpa's bedsheets and blankets which made me think of Emily Dickinson's poem, *The Bustle in a House,* about the morning after a death.

Family. So important to me, and I had lost another member.

Family creates such a tight bond.

Sometimes too tight.

Chapter Thirty-Six

May 1941

Fremont

After getting off work, I rushed home and burst through the front of our house, tossing my jacket into a corner, and throwing open the bedroom door. "Sibyl! You won't believe what happened!"

Her morning grogginess had not faded, but she managed to pull her eyelids halfway open. "What happened?"

I gave her my usual morning kiss on the cheek.

"I got a call from a car dealership in Ardmore. It's a great place. They have some of those spanking new Chevrolet Deluxe sedans I like."

"Ardmore? Why did they contact you?" she asked, sitting up and rubbing her eyes.

"Someone recommended me for a mechanic's job. I think it was that fellow whose jalopy broke down last week and I fixed it for him." I sat down in a chair and began to untie my work boots.

"What fellow? What jalopy?" Sibyl wrapped her robe around herself and pulled her hair back under a scarf. She stumbled into the kitchen and I followed, giving her a quick pat on the bottom.

I'd spent so much time working on different automobiles, I couldn't keep them straight. Well, I could, but Sibyl couldn't. "You know. That tin bucket I worked on last week. The one I said was held together with baling wire."

"The fellow who couldn't pay the full amount?" She placed a cup of coffee in front of me and began cooking hotcakes on the griddle. I enjoyed

185

watching my sleepy wife make a delicious breakfast in ten minutes. She set aside several pancakes for the children, who had not yet woken. After retrieving homemade syrup—sugar syrup like my mother made—from the pantry, she set a plate of food in front of me.

"Yeah, the guy didn't have much, but I might have a job—a mechanic's job!"

Standing at the kitchen sink holding a dirty skillet, Sibyl turned to me. "Day time job?"

I raised my eyebrows and nodded.

The pan landed in the sink with a clang. She rushed over to the table, dropped into a chair opposite me, and grabbed my hand. "We've been praying about what to do for so long, this must mean the Lord's ready for us to move. Maybe this is his answer. We could help in the church there."

"Could be. The fellow said their church needs workers."

"How long before you have to decide?"

"Two days or they give the job to someone else."

Two days. A big decision to make in two days.

Sibyl and I joined hands at the breakfast table. "Please, Lord, show us what to do. Let us know if this job is right for us."

Sibyl seconded my prayer, and we raised our heads and grinned at each other. God was leading. If we trusted and obeyed His direction, surely, he would guide us. After such a long wait, was He leading us away from Shawnee? Was it time?

The possibilities kept circling in my mind: more money for food, new clothes for the children, an electric refrigerator for Sibyl like the one advertised by Sears & Roebuck. A spanking new Chevrolet right off the line. No more worries about finances. My heart warmed to the thought that maybe God was leading us to a place to serve him—just like we wanted.

At last, I could provide without struggling and keep my promise to take care of Sibyl.

***

The next day, Sunday afternoon, Sibyl and I drove to Mrs. Trimble's house, Margaret, and Judson howling in the back seat like late-night coyotes, literally pretending to be wild animals. Now, where did they get that idea? Not from their fun-loving dad.

I opened the door for Sibyl and took Carol from her. The toddler grabbed my neck and held on tight. Our goal was to tell Sibyl's mother of my pending new job.

With Sibyl's pocketbook tucked under her arm and my best shirt starched, I felt good about moving and for the first time in months, felt happy to be alive on this joyful summer day.

We sat around Mrs. Trimble's table while she scooped cobbler into bowls and passed them out. When we couldn't wait any longer, we announced our good news.

She didn't share our excitement. "What're you thinking? Move all the way to Ardmore? That's ninety miles away!" Mrs. Trimble's voice sounded unusually stern. "You can't just up and leave!"

I had hoped Mrs. Trimble would be happy for us. "I'll have a better job, more pay," I explained, remembering the lack of money to help Grandpa.

"Money doesn't mean anything if you neglect your family. If you move, you won't be able to visit me when I need you, and Sibyl would be stuck at home with three kids and no family around. No. That is *not* a reasonable plan."

Sibyl raised her fork in the air to get her mother's attention. "Money isn't the only reason we want to move. We heard a church in Ardmore needs help."

Mrs. Trimble's lip curled. "What can *you* possibly do at the church?"

Was she belittling my capable wife?

"Fremont and I both know how to teach a Bible class, and Fremont's a good handyman. Why, he'd make an excellent deacon for a small congregation, helping out as he does at Calvary."

I stayed quiet and let Sibyl make our case, thinking she could convince Mrs. Trimble better than I could.

"Humph." Mrs. Trimble wagged her head back and forth. "You have no business going if you ask me. God doesn't need your help in Ardmore or anywhere else. He needs you to stay and take care of your family—or haven't you noticed our needs? You must be too busy doing church work."

Tension hung heavy in the air, and I couldn't speak. Not thirty minutes before, I'd been on top of the world, and now I felt like the world sat on my shoulders. Only Mrs. Trimble could cause such a switch in such a short time. Had we not been good enough to her? Supplied enough food? Helped her? Anger steeped from my insides. What did this woman want from us?

"Right now, you're needed here in Shawnee."

I stood from the table and took my plate to the sink. Disappointed, I glanced back at Sibyl, who looked more composed than I felt. Perhaps she believed God wanted us to stay and serve people at Calvary Church, take care of our families. Had Sibyl changed her mind about moving? Did she support me? I stared out the kitchen window, dejected.

***

Normally, discerning God's will was easy for me. I could get a clear picture of how to obey him and decide right from wrong, but this time my spirit felt cloudy—hazy. Confusion didn't come from God; therefore, maybe we should wait until the way was clear.

Perhaps Mrs. Trimble was right. Perhaps it wasn't the right time for us to leave, not when the family struggled so much.

I waffled. The more I considered not taking the job in Ardmore, the more I rebelled. Why should I listen to my cranky mother-in-law? Could we ever break away from her control and manipulation?

This was a good job offer. Better pay and another step out of poverty. We wouldn't be that far from family, maybe a hundred miles away. No. I couldn't pass up this opportunity. We needed to trust God's leading.

My arms ached to grab Sibyl and run out the door, but instead, I turned and faced Mrs. Trimble. "Ma'am, I understand your concern, but we have to go where God leads us, and if that means leaving Shawnee, then that's what we'll do."

Her jaw dropped.

I put my arm under Sibyl's elbow and guided her and the children to the Chevrolet. I drove down Main Street, and neither of us spoke as we passed Sears & Roebuck, the Shawnee fire station, Immanuel Baptist Church. Familiar sights in a familiar town.

"I wish your mother understood," I said.

A glance at Sibyl chewing her lip showed her face as downcast as a lost puppy. She mumbled, "If we left it up to her, we'd never go anywhere. Maybe we should forget about moving away."

Even I could see that her mother was trying to influence us, but something else seemed to be upsetting her. "What's wrong?"

She shrugged and stroked Carol's hair, who had fallen asleep on her lap. "I'm not sure, but maybe God has something better for us."

I stopped the Chevy in the front of our house, and Margaret and Judson jumped out. "Don't you see? This is the right thing to do, even without your mother's blessing. We have to lean on God." I took her hand in mine. "Are you with me?"

Sibyl's eyes were full of trust—trust in God, and trust in me. She whispered, "I'm with you."

Her trust made me queasy, and self-doubt ate at my gut. For me, protecting my wife meant protecting her from hurts, especially deep-seated hurts inflicted by her family. Sometimes I felt like a failure—no, this was a good decision.

I put my arm around her and pulled her close, gazing down at our child in her arms. "Remember when we pawned our Crossley radio every week to buy groceries? At least we don't have to do that anymore. God has helped us through everything."

All that thinking and praying and worrying. And then...

Heavens to Betsy. You just never know how the Lord will work. By the time I called the fellow about the job the next day, he had changed his mind. Found another worker who lived down the street. I guess Ardmore wasn't in God's plan, after all. We might never have another chance to move away.

My heart as heavy as a fallen oak tree.

Chapter Thirty-Seven

Mother Pope was right, I needed spiritual guidance to help me survive the complexities of life. Although we attended church and I read my Bible regularly, I hadn't gone back to the Women's Missionary Union. I decided to attend the WMU circle again as I did before Keith's death.

The next Tuesday morning, I pushed myself to prepare for the outing, looking forward to reconnecting with church friends but dreading the frivolity. Wearing a cotton shirt-waisted dress that fell just below my knees with matching gloves and a hat, carrying Carol, I walked down Farrall Street to Effie's house where the WMU ladies' circle met. Margaret and Judson were in their last week of school before summer break. The line of oak trees along the narrow lane shaded us most of the way.

As soon as I entered, Carol toddled off, racing toward people her age, connecting as easily as butter to bread. I, on the other hand, felt as awkward as oil to water.

I stood in the doorway as Effie rushed to me. After a loud hello, she lowered her voice so only I could hear her. "Relax. No one expects you to be the life of the party." She took the applesauce cake I balanced in my hands and led me into the other room. "If you begin to feel uncomfortable, nod, and I'll send you to the kitchen to cut the cake."

No wonder we were such close friends. I liked having someone who could understand my heartaches, sympathize with me, and give sound advice.

As we entered the living room, the women welcomed me back like a long-lost sister.

"So glad to see you."

"We missed you."

"Carol looks well."

Mrs. Pope gave a lesson on missionary work, and women began to share their thoughts. I looked around at this gathering of friends, these well-groomed housewives in starched clothes. I had missed this comradery, this connectedness. The small, homey living room was a haven where we could share daily struggles. As mothers and grandmothers, we sought good nourishment for our family. We mended clothes to last another season while nursing sick babies. We grieved. We got up and kept going. These women knew hardship as much as I did. This circle felt like a refuge where I could express my frustration and draw closer to God.

I didn't cry with these sweet lady friends as I did with my family.

Refreshed by the openness in the room, I revealed my heartaches and need to help others, quoting verses I had recently meditated on. Like Galatians 4:28 where we are called the children of promise. What exactly did that mean? What was the promise?

I kept my deepest thoughts to myself, but the sense of shared fellowship sparked hope that I could mend the relationship with my mother and siblings. And hope that God had a plan for my life. I was willing to follow him anywhere, but did that mean he wanted us to leave Shawnee, Oklahoma? Or wanted us to stay?

After the meeting ended, Mother Pope joined me where I was standing by the back window. She gave me her gentle smile and asked, "Will you teach the lesson next week?"

"Me? You want me to teach?" My voice rose in alarm. I looked around at the ladies in the room holding teacups and nibbling butter cookies. Godly women, sincere women. Anna. Viola. Effie. Opal already cleaning up, serving others. Even Fremont's dear cousin, Inez, whose mother had stayed home with Marvin. All of these were much more stable than I. They had all gone through crisis and come out stronger.

What could I teach these women?

"I won't be here next week because I'm visiting my sister Mary Florence in Cushing," Mother said. "I need someone to teach in my place, and I know you're capable. I've seen your spiritual insight through the years, and you study the Bible consistently."

"But you're a great teacher." I leaned closer and whispered, "I won't be able to teach as well as you." I took out my embroidered handkerchief and wiped my forehead. I had taught Sunday School for children, but never taught adults, never women who had been believers for years before I turned to God. How could I match Mother's wisdom? She and Dad were practically charter members of Calvary Baptist Church.

I heard the sweet voices of little ones playing together in the other room, the tinkle of the china teacups on saucers, and the hum of women's voices. I'd never expected this request.

Mother put her arm around my shoulder. "Oh, dearie, sometimes faith is the ability not to panic, to trust in the good Lord to lead you. Go home and think about it. I'll need to know by Sunday."

I must have looked askance because Mother held out her well-worn King James Bible, the one she'd received from her father on her twelfth birthday a few years before he died. She flipped it opened and read a verse from Deuteronomy 32:2. *Let my teaching fall like rain and my words descend like dew, like showers on new grass, like abundant rain on tender plants.* Sweetie, teaching can be difficult and time-consuming, but it's a worthwhile goal."

I'd have to collect pennies for mission work, promote serving others, and pray out loud. I thought about that—praying out loud. Meetings began and ended with prayer, and I'd never prayed in front of adults before, only children.

Was teaching what God wanted me to do? My mama would disapprove. She scolded that I spent too much time in religious work, as she called it. I took a deep breath, convincing myself that, since she would lecture me like a child, it would be best to keep my teaching hidden. God would understand. I wouldn't lie. I just wouldn't mention my activities to her.

My compassionate mother-in-law took the responsibility of visiting the needy seriously. The next day, she and I visited what appeared to be the poorest house in Pottawatomie County. They had soapboxes for furniture, a mangle and press to iron sheets for others, a broken mirror on the wall, and maybe a bed in the second room. That was it. That was all they had. No knick-knacks, no sofa, no electricity. No running water inside the house.

I didn't know how to help the woman, but Mother Pope knew what to do. She handed over a bag of freshly picked corn from her garden and a plate of tea cookies. She laughed as one child snuck in and grabbed a cookie. She held the woman's hand and listened to her story. She prayed with her. She cared in such a way that the woman was not offended. Mother whistled a joyful tune as we left the house.

In Aesop's words, "No act of kindness, no matter how small, is ever wasted."

I wanted to teach others about God's love the way Mother did. Could I?

***

The next few days, I wrangled with the Lord. "Why me? I can't teach. And, did you forget, Lord, teaching is not what I planned to do with my life? Please, help me."

In my early years, I wanted to protest, to speak out for the poor and deprived, promote justice. I wanted to do social work that would change the world. Wasn't that what I would do by sharing the good news of Jesus? Surely, it would be okay to teach one time.

Sunday came, and we drove to Mother Pope's for lunch. While cleaning the table afterward, I asked, "Do you really think I can teach?" Her opinion meant a lot.

"Remember when we visited a family with a baby in the Shawnee City Hospital? Within minutes after we arrived, the tiny soul died. I didn't know how to comfort them, but you did. You helped in a way I couldn't."

I recalled the overwhelming grief that had permeated the room. A grief that still haunted me.

"You have a heart for God and a great mind that will give nuggets of wisdom to the ladies as you do now. After losing Keith, you can understand their heartache. So absolutely, you can lead women. Lean on the Lord."

I looked into the eyes of my mentor, a godly woman who believed in me. "All right. Just this once."

She turned her face away, but not before I caught a knowing grin.

During the next two afternoons, I studied and read while the children slept.

I researched words, references, and library books. As always, when too much information entered my mind, I made lists. Lists of verses and points I wanted to make. I felt a spiritual awakening—not an explosion, but a calmness that settled in my soul.

***

The next Tuesday afternoon before the WMU meeting, my nerves felt like needles prickling my skin.

I took a deep breath and smoothed down my printed chiffon dress before I walked into Opal's front door with Carol in my arms, Margaret and Judson following, the school year over. Opal and Effie stood in the doorway chatting like magpies who hadn't seen each other in years.

"Good morning." I nodded and greeted them.

"Where's Mrs. Pope?" Opal asked, her usual friendly self grew silent, waiting for an answer.

"She's gone this week, so I'm teaching." I hesitated, afraid the ladies might be disappointed, or worse, offended that I had been chosen to lead.

Effie's eyes lit up. "Wonderful. I always thought you'd make a great teacher. You study more than anyone I know."

My heart bounced with gratitude. My best friend believed I could do this.

As the women gathered in a circle, I opened my Bible to begin. I introduced the topic and looked down at my notes, but illegible scribbles filled every space. I gulped and set the paper down. "Let's pray." I muttered a quick prayer and raised my eyes to the waiting faces. Could I remember the words I wanted to share?

Inexplicably, my breathing calmed, and the lessons I studied during the week flowed easily. I could even smile.

After the session, I realized I loved sharing about God's good news. I loved sharing missionary stories and answering questions and seeing the light in ladies' eyes as they understood. I loved teaching.

My ending prayer was as sincere as clear spring water, the Spirit washing over our group like rain.

At the end of our time, I passed around a bowl for donations. As a teacher, I should sacrifice, so I pulled two nickels from my pocketbook. I had no time to think about financial woes or the money we had been saving. I just tossed them in, enjoying the plunk in the bottom, and trusted God with all of it.

Effie's homemade chocolate chip pan cookies were the best I'd ever tasted, and I asked for the recipe to add to my collection. The ladies chitchatted before going separate ways.

I paused as I gathered my books and papers. Was the Lord calling me to share with others? To teach people who needed to hear the good news? My spirit fluttered inside me. He could be. He really could be. He could want us to stay in Shawnee and work at the church. Maybe we didn't need to leave town.

I was not an expert leader like Mother Pope, but teaching ladies created a desire to share the hope of Jesus—like a promise that God was leading me toward something useful and fulfilling. As I sensed God's presence, my heart felt fuller than it ever had. *Can you use me, Lord?*

My serious desire to make a difference was not a shallow change like my papa preached, but a deep-down, spiritual transformation brought about by trusting the Creator. Could God want me to teach in a different church, a different town, or state? Is that why I yearned to leave?

Did I have the faith to follow Him?

As I desperately worked toward influencing my mama and family, I could help other people. I hoped they would listen.

Yes, I'd love a chance to teach again—even if my mama never understood.

Chapter Thirty-Eight

June 1941

When Blanche finished training with the NYA, she needed a business course to get a decent job. She mentioned that need to Mama. In turn, Mama mentioned it to Aunt Adah, and Aunt Adah—a get-the-job-done kind of person—raced into Shawnee from Marietta to work out a plan. Aunt Adah finagled for Blanche to attend the Cheatham Business College in Shawnee, where I had gone after high school. In exchange for classes, Blanche would clean the teacher's house, which she would hate, but since she wanted to improve her situation, she would manage.

For school clothes, Blanche borrowed a few dresses from Marjorie. Also, Mama re-made a second-hand dress and sewed another one out of material samples, which cost pennies apiece.

When I showed up at Mama's house, she was sitting on her couch, hemming a skirt for Blanche while Blanche sat in a corner filing her nails.

"That stinking girl at Sears assumed I was soliciting when I wore one of Marjorie's dresses. Poppycock. Just because I looked so nice," said Blanche.

Mama mumbled with pins in her mouth, "You can meet a hundred men with one dollar if you have a fur coat. Just ask Gladys. That woman and her fur coat snatched up my husband like a bargain hunter at a fire sale." Mama held up the skirt to examine the hem.

After setting the skirt down, Mama gave Margaret and Judson a piece of peanut brittle from the candy jar nearby. Then she brushed Margaret's unruly hair out of her eyes. "How was your morning?" she said. "Looks like you've been playing. Have you come from the park?"

"We came from Opal's house," Margaret said. "We played with the kids while Mommy taught Bible with the ladies."

I groaned inside.

Mama leaned back and gave me a disapproving frown. "That's just wonderful. I thought you quit going to the church all the time."

I heaved out the heavy load in my heart. "You won't understand no matter how much I explain." I took a deep breath. "I'm substitute teaching the WMU class again next week."

"You're what?"

"Teaching. I've studied hard and read several books on missions. I'm the teacher when Mother Pope is away."

Mama reached out and picked up the skirt again. "I can't believe it. You have a husband who can't earn two nickels plus two children and a baby, and you want to spend your time teaching a church class? Since you have so much spare time on your hands, maybe you should keep a tidier house...or get a part-time job." Her voice rose. "I can't believe you're socializing. Religious activities are not that important."

My chest was ready to explode, and I said a quick prayer for patience. "I agree I should keep a cleaner house and take the kids to the carnival and give them tennis lessons. But teaching is more important than scrubbing the linoleum. My WMU friends want to learn about what's going on in the world." I paused, unsure how Mama would take my next comment. "And we need to spread the truth about Jesus."

Mama's sour face conveyed her disgust. "Nonsense. If you want something important to do, take care of your sisters and nephew. But you never want to help your family, do you? Here I am, an abandoned wife struggling to survive and my own daughter refuses to help me.

"How can you say that? I brought you a chicken casserole just yesterday. Did you forget?" I struggled to control my anger, my hot tears. But her mean-spirited words and inability to understand my feelings, hurt.

Mama went back to her sewing. "All I'm saying is you need to rearrange your priorities."

"Yeah," said Blanche, who had remained quiet. "Think about it. Rearrange your priorities."

"I do think about it." My voice sounded harsh and I knew it. "I visit Mama every few days, cook meals when she's out, and help mend your clothes. You don't understand."

"Waa. Waa. Do I hear whining?"

"Don't you care?" I asked.

"There's no need to get touchy. I'm just trying to help you. You seem to need help making good decisions. Your marriage started out all wrong, and it hasn't improved."

I exploded. "How dare you!"

I hurried the children from the back room, slammed the door, and walked out, sobbing on the way home. I tried so hard to be a loving Christian like Fremont and his parents. I wanted to grow spiritually, lean on the Lord to guide me, and become a godly woman.

But I'd lost my temper. Again.

Torn between wanting to throttle my family and wanting to point them to Jesus, I waffled between disgust and sadness. Pain and despair. One day, I feared, I would split in two.

What triggered my outburst? That was easy. Mama didn't understand me. Didn't accept me. Wanted to fit me into her mold.

But was she right? Did I spend too much time at church?

No, my family came first, and neither my children nor my husband was neglected. Although my housework might be. God understood I was serving others...and so did Fremont.

I felt a turn in my thoughts about leaving Shawnee. Could it be that the Lord was calling us away to take his message elsewhere? My family sure didn't seem interested.

Chapter Thirty-Nine

July 1941

Fremont

I arrived home from my night job early in the morning. My britches were crumpled, and my hair fell over my forehead like a pony's forelock. I gave my wild mane a quick comb-through with my fingers and kissed Sibyl on the check. Neither of us spoke while she prepared toast, bacon, and fried eggs for breakfast, setting aside extra for the children when they woke.

I wiped the last of the egg yolk from my plate with toast and left to shower and change clothes. As I pulled on a white T-shirt, Sibyl walked into the bedroom and shut the door behind her before sitting down on the edge of the bed.

"Do you ever dream?" she asked.

The question came out of the blue, but it didn't surprise me. My lady often asked unexpected questions.

"Dream? Like nightmares? Like the ones I had when we first married?" I'd had horrible nightmares about being a penniless drifter and unable to support my family, but they'd disappeared a few years ago.

"No, not like bad dreams." She tilted her head. "Like contemplating life. Doing something great in this world, something so magnificent and powerful that people can see God's love and be drastically changed."

I pulled down my clean T-shirt and sat beside her, my weight causing the soft mattress to dip and the box springs to squeak.

199

Sibyl's days were busier than mine, and, although the children were always around, I realized, that wasn't the same as having adult company. I tried to fill that gulf for her, but to be honest, I wasn't a great listener, much less, a talker. Although, usually, I didn't need to be.

She kept talking, her voice taking on a dream-like quality. "We've been planning to leave Shawnee and go wherever the Lord might guide us—to do any kind of work. Should we do more?"

"Honey, you're amazing, but you try too hard to please the Lord." I put my arm around her shoulder and squeezed. "Look at all the work you do. You take food to widows and sew dresses for the poor. Why, you even collect pennies for the hobos and work in the food line down at the church."

"That doesn't seem like much. Even singing to the old people isn't much since I'd sing to a ragamuffin if he'd listen."

I chuckled.

A crease formed between her brows, the one that always told me she was doing some heavy thinking.

"I'm serious. It seems even more important now to spread God's message to some faraway place. What if God calls us to Africa or Australia or…?"

"…or Hawaii? Now that's a good possibility."

She tilted her head at me, not amused.

What was I going to do with this sensitive dreamer? "Honey, did something happen for you to talk like this?"

"Maybe. Well, yes." Her shoulders sagged as she released a sigh. "Mama and I had another blow-up and Blanche got involved. In the middle of the fracas, I realized I don't want to be involved in their fights. Not as a participant, and not as an observer, and I sure don't want to be their referee." She grimaced. "But perhaps there's another reason to move. Maybe God is calling us to mission work somewhere."

Because of the family drama Sibyl dealt with, I would move tomorrow if we could. "Someday soon God will lead us away from here," I said. "I don't know when, could be months, but I do believe he has a plan."

She twisted her hands in her lap. "Nothing seems to satisfy my soul, not even spending time in prayer. I enjoy teaching but I can't take your mother's place. I thought my family right here in Shawnee would be open to God's goodness, and that He had a plan for us here. But I'm not sure it's my job."

"Well, in that case, I'd advise you to do the only thing you can for now. Keep on loving your family even when it seems impossible." I patted her leg.

"And then we'll leave? Follow Him wherever he leads?"

Sibyl had been restless since the day I met her, wanting to find a purpose greater than being a wife and mother. She waffled back and forth. Some days she spoke of moving away as if she couldn't wait and other days, she bemoaned leaving her family. Me? I would be content if she were content. "Honey, God will make it as clear as sunshine when he wants us to leave." I stood, and the bed groaned as it sprang back to normal.

She smiled at me. "Why can't I be as patient and peaceful as you?"

The statement caught me by surprise. My poor girl had no idea how much I struggled. Hawaii was sounding better and better all the time.

Sibyl

On July 8, 1941, Irene gave birth to our first niece, Marguerite Ruth Taylor. Mother Pope had counted the days to make sure the baby girl was born nine months after their wedding day. The baby had arrived on time—not too late and not too early—and looked healthy and happy. Irene looked happy, too. Marriage and children suited her well.

Shortly after Marguerite's birth, our friend John volunteered for the Army.

People from the south side of Shawnee joined our church fellowship. Young couples like the Browns, the Hills, the Meyers, and David and Frances Way started attending. I made many friends with ladies in our WMU circle. Throughout my childhood and young adult years, conflicts with my mother had often left my emotions as jumbled as a tangled skein of yarn. Bringing order and shape to that chaos, this group of loving people helped form me into a neatly wound ball that could eventually become something beautiful and useful to the Lord.

Our WMU circle grew so large that we needed to divide into two groups. We discussed beginning a class for younger women, and the ladies asked me to be the teacher. Me.

I wanted to spread the good news and change the world, but was this the right time? Margaret and Judson would be in school come autumn. I discussed the possibility with Fremont. What would happen if we suddenly moved to a different town? Was it right to take a class if we planned to leave soon?

Fremont was always so sensible. "Don't worry so much. You'll learn a lot and God will provide the next teacher if we move."

Eager to begin, I collected my study notes, surprised at how much information I had accumulated. Then I enlisted Mother's help and she came to my house carrying her big Bible. "Honey, you look as nervous as a cat up a tree, but I can't think of anyone else more qualified."

We studied the book of James and discussed his hope. In one of my favorite books, Edith Cavell, a British nurse, saved soldiers' lives no matter their nationality. I wanted to offer the same kind of hope.

At our first class, my friends Effie and Opal arrived early and entered the fellowship hall, where our first meeting would be held. Effie, short, plump, and motherly, led in her passel of kids. Opal Alexander, tall and somewhat eccentric, used a lorgnette for glasses and liked needlework, carrying a knitting basket with her.

"I'm looking forward to the lesson. Sibyl, your teaching always inspires me." Opal always helped me feel competent.

In a few minutes, several other ladies appeared in the doorway. "Come on in. So glad you're here," I said.

"Ah, I smell cinnamon." Effie gave hugs and directed the children where to go. Someone set an apple pie on the counter. At least, we'd have a good dessert after our lesson.

I kept the first meeting informal and listened to their interests and encouraged them to help plan mission work. Some wanted to begin a Sunbeam class for grade schoolgirls to teach the importance of missions. Others wanted to plan a fundraising for the needy.

Missions, to me, were vital to the flourishing of the church. Mission work, telling others about the Lord, could happen anywhere at any time.

***

A few weeks later while I was preparing for my next class, Mama dropped by. My head was lodged in a book—pen and paper on the table in front of me.

"Studying again?" Mama asked, disapproval in her voice. "What is it this time?" Her hair lay in perfect coils, and her dress was stiffly pressed.

I looked down at my wrinkled housedress and ran my fingers through my hair. "It's for my class."

"I thought you gave that up."

Mama with her litany of criticisms, stood with her arms crossed. *You're neglecting your children. You don't have time to sit around all day. Look at this messy house.*

I took a deep breath, exasperated, and hurriedly gathered a load of clothes. I dumped them into the washing machine, my heart pumping faster than if I'd run to Tecumseh and back.

My mother watched me racing around, looking at me closely. "You're having another baby, aren't you?"

My hands went to my stomach, protectively. "Yes. I didn't want to tell you yet. Fremont's excited." Why did my mother affect me this way? Yes, the dishes needed washing and the house picked up, but a spotless house wasn't the most important thing in life to me.

"You spend too much time at church as it is. Now you'll have to let someone else teach the ladies' class. Focus on this growing family of yours."

Before I lashed out at her in frustration, I closed my eyes and sent up a quick prayer. Then I lifted my head and gave my mother my most gracious smile.

"Yes, Mama, I could let someone else teach, but I don't want to. I'm learning so much by teaching. Do you believe God is real?"

Mama raised her eyebrows, "Don't be silly. We talked about this. Of course, God is real."

"If he's real, then it's important to tell everyone. This isn't a game."

Mama shook her head slowly as if she thought I was bonkers.

"You see, if God loves us enough to die in our place, then I have to tell people. We've all done wrong, and we all need forgiveness. He's the only one who can truly take our punishment."

Mama left with a dazed look on her face. She came to my house to intimidate me, but for once, I didn't feel frustrated. Simply sad.

I helped in the church office, visited newcomers, sang in the choir, but nothing felt as right as this teaching. I could envision mission work around the world, remembering how Jesus told us to teach all people. I pulled out the notes I'd written. The last page listed women's needs. Mother Pope had taught me an old Yiddish saying: If you pray for another, you'll be helped yourself.

I prayed for each of the ladies' concerns until I came to the bottom of the list.

My family I had written.

Oh, yes. My mama.

No words to my mother and siblings had been helpful, and I despaired they would ever forgive Papa or respond to God's love. Frances, with her tender heart, was the only one who listened, which encouraged me, but Mama and Papa and Blanche and Calvis? And Marjorie with her string of men?

When would God answer my prayers, and would we remain in Shawnee until they responded? In the quietness of that moment, the Lord answered. Not the answer I wanted or expected, but it reassured me that, no matter what, I could trust Him.

God whispered in my spirit, "Wait."

Chapter Forty

Fremont

Sibyl clomped around the house, insisting we needed an outing, and that she'd made plans to see the new flick *Gone with the Wind*. In reality, she—not I—was the one who needed the outing. And she'd neglected to tell me about the plans.

"I read the book and loved it," Sibyl said. "I think you'll like the movie."

"I can't go. I have to study my Bible lesson." I didn't have time to study at work, and it was already Saturday night. I taught a teenage boys' class on Sunday mornings, young men I had grown to love.

"Of course, you do. You're the level-headed one in the family."

I looked at her, puzzled. Commitment was not the same as level-headedness, but I didn't want to antagonize a pregnant wife, so I didn't reply.

When I was about sixteen years old, my family attended a nightly tent revival led by Brother Cherry, a favorite evangelist who led revivals and filled in at pulpits around the area. During the week of the meetings, my dad and I spent a day plowing and took a break to go fishing. Sitting beside me at the creek, Dad talked to me about being saved. Only he put it this way: "Your mother's been worried about you. Don't you think it's about time to go down front?" That was it. Dad didn't pressure or cajole. He simply gave me a nudge, and that was all it took. That very night I walked 'down front' to talk to Brother Cherry and gave my heart to Christ.

In the same way my dad had gently guided me, I wanted to teach my Sunday School class of boys to follow Jesus. I tried to explain to Sibyl. "If I can encourage one boy to follow the Lord's way, all the time I spend teaching will be worth it."

Sibyl nodded in agreement, and I'm sure she understood the importance to me.

The next weekend, *Gone with the Wind* was still playing at the theater. On Wednesday, Sibyl told me she wanted to attend, but again, I already had plans. I was almost afraid to tell her. "Honey, I can't go. You know I've been planning a campout for the boys. It's this weekend, and I don't want to let them down." The boys, fourteen through eighteen, were clean-faced, awkward, energetic young men. I loved them to no end. Attending a movie couldn't hold a candle to camping out.

I arranged to take the fellows to a spot behind my parents' house. My folks owned fifteen acres, and the densely wooded back half was a cross-timber section, difficult to walk through because of trees, underbrush, and overgrown shrubs and vines. The property backed up to a wilderness carved with gullies, their banks covered with dogwood, crepe myrtle, sumac, and scrub oaks. The timbers stretched north to the Pesthouse by the railroad tracks and south toward the Canadian River.

Thursday, I spent half a day cutting a pathway and clearing a site for the overnight campout. Sweat poured off my body as I worked. I had lived in the humid heat all my life, so for me, it wasn't unbearable—just downright miserable. At least the weather tended to cool off when the sun went down.

Friday afternoon I led the boys to the campsite, each of them carrying a bedroll and a canteen of water. They helped me hang a tarp before hiking to the other side of the creek. I didn't worry about them out in the woods, and their hollers told me they were having a whopping good time. That evening, I used a pocketknife to sharpen the ends of sticks so the boys could roast wieners for their supper. The next morning, I cooked a batch of bacon and scrambled eggs while they toasted bread over the fire.

I came home after camping, as happy and alive as I'd ever felt, singing Gene Autry's *Back in the Saddle Again*. I enjoyed being with my young students, and I like to think they enjoyed being with me. Being away from the stress of work and household responsibilities revitalized me. I placed a box of leftover food on the countertop and set the kerosene lantern on the table. "We had a mighty good time!" I told Sibyl.

Judson and Margaret came running up to me. "Daddy! Daddy!" I picked each one up and tossed them into the air, before taking Carol into my arms.

"Glad you survived it, dear."

I detected some coolness in Sibyl's voice but ignored it. "It was hilarious. We made a circle around the fire and told ghost stories. I told about the famous Lady Belle Star, the outlaw lady who was shot and died near Eufaula in 1889. Her murder was never solved, so I told the boys, the lady killer could still be out there."

Sibyl knit her eyebrows. "Don't tell those stories in front of Margaret and Judson."

I stepped toward her and lowered my voice. "The boys started moving closer and closer to the fire until they almost sat right on top of me."

Her mood must have been warming because she chuckled. "You didn't tell your favorite story about the Sacred Heart Cemetery, did you?"

"Of course, I did. That story is Oklahoma history, and those boys need to know it." I spoke in my spookiest voice. "For years people have reported shadowy apparitions, strange heavy breathing, and ghostly noises late at night." I raised my hands, wiggled my fingers, and gave an eerie "*whooo*." Then I laughed. "The boys were so frightened their eyes grew as round as saucers."

Sibyl joined me in my laughter. "Ah, Fremont. You shouldn't have."

"It could be true, couldn't it? After a few more ghost stories, I told them the tale about the handwriting on the wall. Remember that one in the Bible?"

"I remember." Sibyl began to wash the plates and glasses I brought in from the trip as I put away the leftover food.

"I told them God will do anything to get our attention. Life might bring some nasty blows, but we must trust he knows best. He *always* knows best. The boys asked more serious questions, and that's when I saw the good

Lord working in their lives." I felt a thrill go through me. "If I can help them know Jesus, won't that be something?"

I hoped Sibyl could see the joy on my face and how much I wanted to be a blessing to these boys.

Sibyl turned to me with a pleased smile. "You did good by going, and I'm proud of you." Her smile grew brighter. "Guess what? I made plans to go see *Gone with the Wind* with the Douglas' tonight."

I was worn to the nub, but I knew I dare not object. "All right. All right. We'll go."

She shook her finger at me. "And no excuses this time."

I laughed again. At that moment, going to the flick was fine with me. I didn't have a spare dime but felt like a million dollars. I'd been doing God's work, and Sibyl was proud of me.

Monday morning, I'd begin to ask around again for a daytime job that paid more. I would not be a deadbeat husband who could not protect and support his family.

Chapter Forty-One

August 1941

Sibyl

At the WMU meeting, I led the women in a new song, *When the Saint Go Marching In*, before we discussed our next project. I pulled out my paper and pencil to make a list, an inventory of the supply closet, items remaining from our summer Vacation Bible School. "What do we have?"

"We have memory cards and music sheets."

"Extra hand towels. We bought too many."

"There's a quart of paint left over."

"We still have string left from last year's VBS. The ones we used to make crosses."

"What can we do with it?"

"We could take everything to a church that needs help with their kids."

I smiled with delight. "Great idea!"

The ladies agreed, and their enthusiasm energized and uplifted me. These were good women. Like-minded women who sought ways to help others. Even if my family didn't understand my motives, this group of ladies did. My spiritual life had deepened through the last years as I interacted with godly people. I loved my WMU friends.

"What about taking this leftover material to Union Church?" I asked. "I'm certain they could use our old lesson books."

Silence. The Union Missionary Baptist Church on Farrell Avenue was located in the southeast quadrant of Shawnee—the segregated section, the poorest part of town, the "colored folks" area. "White" Christians didn't always live by their Christian principles.

"Lester, Mama's handyman from last year, works with Fremont as a janitor down at Norton's."

Still no response. It was highly frowned upon for a white lady to befriend a black person, even in my family. "I'll go myself first and visit Lester and his wife," I said, knowing white women—and white men for that matter—seldom drove down those alleys and visited the shambles and houses where Lester lived.

I hoped my mama wouldn't find out. She'd be horrified.

"Who'll go with me?" I looked around the room and saw fear. No one answered. They stared at the floor or their laps. Disappointment felt heavy on my shoulders because I thought I could count on these ladies.

"If you're sure this is a good idea, I'll go with you," said Effie, doubt on her otherwise peaceful face. "No need for you running around in that part of town alone."

"Thank you, Effie. That's brave of you." I said. "I appreciate it. Now, let's organize this closet."

***

When I phoned Pastor Fields at Union Church and inquired as to what he needed, he hesitated, maybe unsure if I was serious, before he said he'd been praying about help with the children. "If you could bring some sweets along with the crafts, we'd be mighty thankful. Not enough folks here to help with the Bible school we planned."

Eager to prepare refreshments for the children, my WMU circle and Mother Pope's circle baked so many batches of homemade cookies I didn't know who would eat them all. Crafts were stacked neatly into one box. Bible lessons into another. Yes, my ladies came through after all. The saints *were* marching in.

While Fremont helped load our Chevrolet, he offered to drive Effie and me, two pregnant women, to the church. I declined. It would cut into his sleep time, but I also wanted us to do this by ourselves. I think he was rather proud of Effie and me.

People stared at two white ladies driving down South Bell Street in the black district of southeast Shawnee, or maybe I imagined their stares. The black folks' housing area was blocked by railroads to the east and north and the Canadian River to the south. They could have expanded west, but the whites complained when they tried. Consequently, the black district was landlocked and unable to grow.

Prejudice still reigned in Pottawatomie County. Shawnee had plenty to prove it. Two water fountains at the back of Kresses' store were labeled "Coloreds" and "Whites." Sears and Anthony's stores had separate bathrooms. Black folk were declared equal but not treated equal—something I couldn't understand.

Oklahoma was home to over a hundred Klan klaverns, though I hoped none existed around Shawnee. Evidence showed that my father could have been involved in one.

Tuesday afternoon, I followed Lester's beat-up truck, not knowing what to expect because I'd never visited a colored folks' church before. He led us to a small clapboard building with a cross on top and introduced us to Pastor Fields, a sturdy man with a huge voice and a spirit as sweet as honey.

Effie and I unloaded cookies and Kool-Aid, crafts and lessons.

Pastor Fields treated us respectfully and expressed such gratitude for the children's lessons and refreshments, I almost cried. We'd done so little.

When I was younger, I would not have considered such a project. Oh, I attended political rallies with Papa and helped print fliers to change the law, but driving into the colored part of town, shaking hands with the pastor, and volunteering to help black children never would've entered my mind. Marriage, children, and God had affected me in good ways. The last few years of difficulties brought a peace to my heart that I couldn't explain.

When Mama found out through town gossip about our adventure, she screamed at me. "You did what? You traipsed through a dangerous part of town, unaware of what could happen? Not considering your children?"

Her words stabbed at my core. My heart was weighed down with questions, as heavy as this new baby. "Mama, I wish you'd seen the gratitude on their faces. They needed the help, and we were glad to provide it."

I shouldn't have been surprised at Mama's reaction, but in my zeal over the mission God had placed in my heart, I'd forgotten she was still an embittered, broken woman. She attempted to shame me, to convince me that my desire to serve God and those outside my family was selfish. I wondered if she'd ever understand the passion my heavenly father placed in me.

In the past, my goals had shifted as quickly as desert sand, but now they were taking solid shape. I could help poor children learn about God's love. I could be a missionary, taking a giant step toward becoming the woman God wanted me to be.

Would Fremont understand? Lately, he seemed content in his role in the church and community. Maybe that was all he wanted from life. Maybe he had forgotten about our plans to move.

What *was* God's plan? Could he possibly want us to stay in Shawnee and continue serving him there? If he asked us to move now, would we be willing?

Fremont

"They need a new deacon at Calvary," Sibyl blurted out at the supper table one night. "Mr. Smith left. He couldn't find a job, so he and his family packed up their jalopy and moved out to California."

"I heard about that." I glanced at her as I shoveled food into my mouth. "A good man. Too bad he couldn't find work around here. We're going to miss him."

"Your dad's been a deacon for years, always willing to do whatever needs to be done." Sibyl had mentioned the qualities of a deacon several times. It didn't require a college degree or special skills, just a willing heart to help out. "What would you do if they asked you to be a deacon?"

I looked askance at her, knowing her goal, and not wanting to give in. "I'm not my dad. I'll never be as good as he is, or as good as Mr. Smith. People look up to those fellows."

Sibyl reached across the table and took my hand. "You're not your dad or Mr. Smith, but you have a heart for the Lord, and you have a passion to serve. Just look at the wonderful job you've done teaching the young men's class." She gave my hand a light squeeze before letting it go. "You'd make an excellent deacon."

My eyebrows lifted. If chosen to be a deacon, would that mean we were stuck in Shawnee? What about our dreams? What about my promise to get my wife away from her demanding family? Hopefully, before this next baby arrived. The position wasn't a paying job, only a way of serving folks in our community, but why was Sibyl pursuing this? She answered like she could read my mind.

"It will give you confidence. Not that you need confidence, but you can be a great influence. Learn how a church is run in case you need it later."

Even if the appointment was only temporary until we left town, it was a serious step. One that might become permanent if we chose to stay in the area. Hopefully, the difficult decision wouldn't materialize.

That didn't happen.

***

A few weeks later, several churchmen approached me after the service, asking me to consider the deacon role. "We see the same qualities in you that your father possesses: dependability, trustworthiness, and honesty. Most important, we see you as God-fearing and able to hear his voice when he calls."

My mouth could have caught a dozen flies. I was flabbergasted, but more than that, I was honored. Humbled.

Even though yearning to move away, I agreed to the selection process. The deacons asked Sibyl and me questions about our beliefs and how we applied them to raising our children. I was amazed that the church would even consider me for such an important office. Would they still consider me when I told them about our plans to relocate, to leave the church?

They did.

Calvary Baptist Church approved me, Fremont Frederick Pope, as a deacon. The night they ordained me, the other deacons joined me at the front of the church and laid hands on me, blessing my future work, wherever it might be. I felt pleased, humbled, and honored all at the same time.

Sibyl understood. "I'm proud of you, Fremont. And you look tall and handsome in your Sunday suit." She placed her hand on my shoulder and planted a kiss on my cheek. I could feel my face glowing.

After the ceremony, Sibyl stood beside me and my heart swelled with pride and gratitude. I glanced around for Mother and Dad. They looked like they could float up to heaven right then, proud as peaches. A long line of folks shook my hand and hugged Sibyl and the kids.

I looked at my wife, her eyes misty, and she smiled. I wished her family could have been there, especially her mama. I wanted their family to know she'd married a good man, one who would seek to please God no matter where we lived, and lead my family wherever the Lord wanted us to go.

No matter if that was California, Hawaii, or the North Pole.

Or Shawnee.

Chapter Forty-Two

September 1941

Sibyl

With the hot summer over and fall beginning, we decided to take a little money from our savings box and return to our favorite beach. Galveston. We drove all day and set up camp in the evening. This time there were five of us—me, Fremont, and our three children. Thank goodness Blanche and Irene weren't with us.

After putting up the tent, we slipped into our bathing suits. My body filling out with baby, but I hoped I looked good in my one-piece wool swimsuit with the cap to match. Maybe Fremont would notice. He did.

"Honey, even after having four children, you have the figure of a fashion model. You're more beautiful every day."

I couldn't believe Fremont, with his broad shoulders and handsome face, still found me attractive, and that even after eight years of marriage, Fremont's words could make my heart flutter.

"Mommy, can I feed the seagulls?" Judson held out his hand, and I put breadcrumbs in his sandy palm and watched him walk toward the water.

The seagulls swarmed around him, and he screamed, running away from the greedy scavengers, and latching onto my leg. I touched the top of his head. "You're okay. The seagulls are just hungry."

I looked around and he was gone again, hopping through the water. Margaret joined him, and I followed with Carol. We splashed each other, made footprints, and wrote words in the wet sand that washed away before we could finish.

A few minutes later, I started itching. "Oh, something's stinging me." I wiggled, feeling like a swarm of ants were crawling over me. I ran to our campsite, rushed into the tent, and climbed out of my bathing suit. I dried myself off and got back into my clothes.

Fremont stuck his head in the tent, the kids right behind him. "We're all itching." He scratched at his legs. The kids were scratching, and I still itched after taking off the bathing suit.

"What is it? What's making us itch?"

Fremont held up my swimsuit, his wet hair falling into his eyes. "Sea lice."

"Sea lice?"

At the nearby shower area, I stripped everyone and rinsed them with fresh water. Then I took our bathing suits as well as Carol's baby blanket to the local laundry. That sad-looking pink cotton blanket ended torn, but Carol didn't mind. She snatched the clean cloth and hugged it to her chest.

The next morning, ready for beach time again, we drove to a different sandy location. Margaret and Judson ran ahead of Fremont into the deeper water while I sat on a towel watching Carol dig in the sand, her wet hair hanging down over her cute, plump little shoulders. We had the beach to ourselves, and I relaxed.

Fremont showed the older kids how to jump the big waves coming in. They laughed and dashed around as I kept a close eye on them. I loved to watch our happy, joyful clan. Fremont, holding the hands of both children, waded out to where the water was chest high on Judson.

Suddenly, Margaret started screaming, yelling louder than an angry seagull.

I jumped to my feet.

Fremont let go of Judson and the boy sank. He began flailing his arms to keep his head above water. As I watched, Margaret and Fremont thrashed about.

I raced to the water's edge, yelling. "What's wrong? Is it a shark?"

Fremont kept splashing about as if something in the water was pulling him down. Margaret's head went under, and I couldn't see her until Fremont pulled her up.

I ran into the waves to rescue Judson, leaving Carol on the beach. Practically dragging him to the shore, I saw several blue Portuguese man-of-wars floating around, their clear, long, stringy tentacles spread around like floating ropes. One man-of-war had his tentacles lassoed around Margaret.

Fremont kicked at the monster and carried a screaming Margaret to shore, where he laid her on a blanket. I ran to them and saw her left leg from the ankle to the knee was covered with the animals' string-like tentacles, wrapping Margaret's leg almost completely.

She thrashed about in pain as I knelt beside her, feeling helpless. She was in so much pain that her eyes rolled back, and she shook and frothed at the mouth.

Fremont had a tentacle wrapped around his leg, too, but nothing like the one on Margaret.

My hands shook. What could I do?

Within minutes, a Coast Guard patrol who must have been nearby, arrived and rushed over. "It looks like she ran into a big one," he said as he rubbed sand on Margaret's leg. When the tentacles came loose, there was such a line of wounds, the entire leg was one huge blister. He retrieved a large box of baking soda from his first aid kit and sprinkled it on Margaret's leg, and then wrapped her leg in a wet bath towel.

I pulled Margaret onto my lap. "Will she be all right?" I shrieked the words at the guard.

"A sting this bad can be serious. She needs to stay calm. If she starts having chest pain or difficulty breathing, take her to the hospital."

"Does this happen often?"

"We've had several people stung recently." His face was grim. "Nothing this bad."

Everywhere a tentacle had contacted Margaret's skin, a blister appeared. When we unwrapped her leg that evening, her injuries looked like second-degree burns.

Margaret moaned all night. As I sat beside her, tears rolled down my face. I thought of Keith and asked the question I'd asked over and over. Why did children have to suffer?

By morning, Margaret's pain had lessened, and she dozed. She got up later and I fed her breakfast, and then Fremont gave her an aspirin, reapplied baking soda, and wrapped her leg again.

Fremont

Since it was impossible to return to the beach, and Margaret seemed better, we took a ferry excursion around the bay and watched as the waves rose higher and higher. Unusually choppy waves, I thought, and quite nippy, but I thoroughly enjoyed being out on the gulf water. Even though it was summertime, the children took a chill. Sibyl hadn't packed warm clothes, so we wrapped bath towels around them to keep warm.

After the ferry trip, I drove to a seaside carnival, where we walked around, awed by the sideshows and roller coasters and bumper cars. The Ferris Wheel brought out the childishness in me, even though I'd had little sleep the night before. Even Sibyl participated, jumping on the carousel with Carol and going through the mirror maze with us.

Judson, the enthusiastic live wire, ran around me, pointing at every sight, wanting to ride every ride twice. The rest of us, exhausted after all of our misadventures, followed him until Margaret, her leg bothering her, sat on a bench, and leaned back.

"Do you think she's okay?" I asked Sibyl. "She looks really tired."

Sibyl sat beside the girl and handed her the soda pop I'd purchased. "She needs to rest." She wrapped her arm around Margaret's shoulder. "We could all use a nice, long nap." Sibyl look worn out too, her face glowing pink from the sun, and her hair falling in wild curls about her face.

While they rested, I carried little Carol on my shoulders to the sea wall built after the devastating 1900 hurricane. Steadying Blanche's black Brownie box camera in my hands, I snapped a picture of my cute toddler before returning to Margaret and Sibyl.

"Where's Judson?" Sibyl asked.

I swung around in a circle. No Judson! I'd taken my eyes off of him for only two seconds. I rushed through the circus grounds, searching for the tow-headed boy in a light blue shirt. He was gone. Completely disappeared.

Oh, dear God, please, I prayed. *Where is he?*

Already on edge from the weekend's trials, Sibyl's face streaked with tears when I returned without him.

Where could the boy be? Of course, the worst scenarios came to mind, but I didn't share them with Sibyl. Instead, I ran to get a policeman, who began to search with us. We retraced our steps and wound through the carnival rides and food booths, asking vendors if they had seen a seven-year-old boy.

The policeman finally suggested, "Go back to your car. Maybe he found his way there."

The smooth, round top of the '26 Chevrolet touring car came into view, the doors closed, nothing disturbed. As I rounded the corner, I saw Judson sitting on the running board, swinging his feet through the sand as if nothing mattered. I ran to him, picked him in my arms, and squeezed hard, ignoring his attempt to squirm loose.

What a vacation. I looked at Sibyl and rolled my eyes. "Let's go home. We don't have to stay any longer."

She nodded. "I don't think I'll ever enjoy the sea again."

A week later, we read about the storm that hit Galveston the day after we left. It was the worst in years, breaching the sea wall where I had taken Carol's picture. The cyclone traveled up from the Gulf of Mexico and headed straight for the place we'd camped. The agitated waters had stirred the sea life, and there'd been many reports of marine life attacking swimmers.

We had missed the hurricane by a day. Maybe the good Lord had been watching over us, after all. Maybe he knew we needed it.

***

When we returned to Oklahoma, Calvis announced that his timid young wife, Evie, was pregnant.

Since this would be the young woman's first pregnancy, my sweet wife was determined to help and encourage her along the way. Sibyl had a knack for helping people, and if she couldn't encourage her, no one could.

Sibyl's mama, on a rampage again, let us know that having another baby was foolish as running off with a circus clown. "If you can't take care of your children on a simple vacation, how do you expect to care for another one?"

Maybe we shouldn't have told her about our adventures.

As always, Mama managed to raise Sibyl's self-doubt. Maybe she was right. Maybe we'd been foolish to want a large family.

How could I even think that?

Chapter Forty-Three

October 1941

Sibyl

Charlie Chaplin, my hero after watching *The Great Dictator*, played in the silent movie that dramatized Hitler and Mussolini. Political and funny, the film showed each tyrant looking out for himself, unconcerned with the people under them. People did that, didn't they? Maybe not to Chaplin's comical extent, but my family certainly seemed to focus on proving who was best, on taking care of their needs above others.

I had the latest *Shawnee Morning News* in my hand when Papa called on Monday morning and said, "I need your help."

Papa had never needed my help before.

"My teeth are killing me," he groaned. "The dentist is going to pull them all out."

"Pull all your teeth out at once? That seems drastic."

"I don't care. I want them gone. Gone, I say. This pain is unbearable."

"How can I help?"

"I need you to take me to the dentist."

I thought Gladys should do that, but maybe she couldn't get off work. Perhaps Papa thought he had my sympathy since no other family member would be willing to help him. I guess he did have my sympathy.

"They said I shouldn't drive myself home, so I'll give you money for gasoline to take me Wednesday morning and bring me back."

I agreed to pick up him two days later at his house in Midwest City.

Fremont, as good a mechanic as you can get, checked our Chevrolet thoroughly and filled it with gasoline. He examined the tires but could do nothing about their threadbare condition. "Be careful, honey. I'm glad you're able to help your papa." My husband's attitude toward Papa had improved lately, which made me think maybe my prayers were working.

Wednesday morning, Papa was a grouch, but then, who would be in a good mood with teeth hurting so bad you wanted them all pulled out? He climbed into the passenger side of the car and began grumbling before I started the engine.

"Not been a good week. Officer Marks has me spitting nails."

"Marks?"

"A former banking friend. That scoundrel offered me a thousand dollars to influence the judge—to quash Barnett's indictment."

I remembered the name Marks in the *Ada Evening News*. Some officials had overheard conversations between Papa and Marks, claiming Marks had offered Papa a bribe. The Commissioner Barnett case, it seemed, would go on forever.

I kept my eyes on the road, not daring to ask the pertinent question. Did Papa take the bribe?

"Marks and Barnett are thick as thieves, and they're ganging up on me. And to answer the question I see in your face, no, I never took a bribe. The authorities arrested Marks."

I sat in the waiting room as Papa got his teeth pulled, thinking over our conversation. Papa had been more involved in the bank scandal than I'd wanted to believe. But he did turn down the bribe.

So, there was still hope for Papa?

When he came out of the dentist's office, he swayed and reached for my shoulder to steady himself. When had my papa grown so old? Always a strong and in-charge person, now he appeared weak and frail. I helped him to the car, finding it strange that my once robust father was having to lean on me.

In a reflective mood and woozy from the operation, he said, "You're taking care of me like my big sister, Eulia, did."

"You had a big sister? I never knew that. What happened to her?"

"She got sick—pneumonia. Our family was so poor, we couldn't afford a doctor." Papa held his hand to his jaw.

"What happened?"

"She died. Eleven years old. I was eight. I try not to think of her. She's buried in Bowie by my parents."

"Maybe we can visit her grave some time. It isn't that far."

He shook his head and grimaced. "Nope. I never want to go back."

Had Papa been so hurt from his sister's death that he focused on having enough money for doctor bills? Did he relate money to survival? Maybe his sister's death drove him to prioritize wealth, because something in his past had certainly affected him.

There was no more conversation on the way back to Midwest City. I guided him into his house, where he slumped on the sofa and nodded off to sleep. His face looked stately but pale and wrinkled and old, and I realized I still loved my Papa no matter what he had done. It didn't matter if he were a good guy or not, I would treat him with kindness even though it might take a long time before he softened to the Lord's call.

I stayed with Papa until Gladys returned home. As she rushed around and took over his care, she shooed me away. Papa was not my responsibility. He had a wife.

Chapter Forty-Four

Fremont

My best friend sat opposite me at the card table, shuffling dominoes. Sibyl and I regularly got together with Effie and Doug for a meal and games, and this rainy night they hosted at their house on South Market Street.

Doug and I had challenged Sibyl and Effie. The play was in full motion and went around the table several times with points earned on either side. The girls were beating us pretty badly, and only a few tiles remained.

Doug directed frustration at his wife. "Come on, Effie, we don't have all night. Play something."

Effie raised her eyebrows at her husband, "Don't rush me, dear." She laid down a four-two tile for fifteen points. "There you go, smarty pants. Just give me time." Effie, a fun-loving, happy-go-lucky soul, was the opposite of Sibyl, who enjoyed abstract talk and deep discussions. Doug was more serious like Sibyl, but when he and I got together, we joked to high heaven. The couple balanced Sibyl and me, bringing an ease to our get-togethers.

Doug played next but added no points. Sibyl scored ten.

My turn.

Sibyl, better at games than I was, would know which dominoes had been played. I couldn't remember what we had for supper yesterday, so I concentrated on adding points and hoped my partner had a lucky tile because I sure didn't.

I looked around the room before I played. The kids' noise, which had been at the level of a thrashing machine, had gone silent, and all we could hear was the rain pattering on the roof. The youngsters lay on blankets on the floor, sleeping in a heap like a pile of puppies—legs, arms, and tussled hair mixed together. With both Effie and Sibyl pregnant again, two more offspring would be added to the litter and, with both families growing like this, we'd soon field a baseball team.

I laid down my best choice, and Effie jumped in quick with a pointer. By the time Sibyl played again, it was an easy win for the girls. She jumped in her seat. "We did it again, Effie. Beat those fellows by a landslide."

"Lands, how do you gals get such good hands?" I faked a frown before I broke into a smile. I really didn't mind losing.

"Skill, my boy, pure skill," Effie said, looking pleased.

"More like pure luck," Doug protested. "The stars shine on you like always, darling." He lovingly pinched her cheek and shuffled the tiles on the table for the next hand. "But the game isn't over yet. We still have a chance to whip you good."

I selected seven dominoes from the scrambled tiles.

"How's your job?" Doug asked. "Any change?"

"Nah. They've been letting people go right and left. Lester's last day was Friday. Don't know what he's going to do." I worried about each of my buddies even while concerned about losing my job.

"How about Little Joe," Doug asked, "the midget who jokes with everyone? He's worked there since time began."

I tried to concentrate on dominoes rather than the grim information we were discussing. "Not looking good for him." My knee bounced under the table.

"Heard you might be looking for another job, too."

I nodded. "Not a dadgum job to be found in the entire state. Unless something opens up, I'm stuck at Norton's." I didn't mention that my pay had been drastically cut.

"Yeah. I heard the Pontiac place is not doing too bad, but who wants to work on a Pontiac? Have you thought about leaving Oklahoma? Finding work somewhere else?"

Sibyl and I exchanged glances. "Thought about it a time or two," I said as Effie scored.

Doug laid down a double four, adding to fourteen—worth nothing. "Sorry partner, no points this time."

Sibyl made points again.

My turn, and Doug, who leaned back in his chair, was still chattering. "You've mentioned moving away from Shawnee several times lately. I heard about an ammunitions plant in Colorado that's hiring. Chuck Mills told me he's going."

"I don't know much about Colorado, but I thought about moving to California," I said. "The economy might be better out there."

Sibyl frowned at me, wariness in her eyes. "You aren't leaving for California, are you?" She and I hadn't talked about moving in weeks.

I'd predicted the girls would win out the night. They did.

Dominos was a good diversion for Sibyl, her worries magnified with this new baby she carried. Her mama criticized her for having too many children, for working too much at the church, for helping the black children, and for talking with Papa. According to Mrs. Trimble, Sibyl couldn't do anything right.

A naturally happy man, I didn't struggle with life questions as Sibyl did but enjoyed the good moments as they came. This would have been one of them if Doug hadn't brought up work.

We ended the evening by eating slices of Effie's applesauce cake. After rounding up the children and loading them into the back seat of the Chevy, we drove home. Mud puddles from the drenching rain shone in the beams of the headlights, and the talk about jobs weighed heavily on me. My thoughts went back to my promise to Sibyl—the promise to provide for her needs and take care of her.

Once as clear and pure as rain, that promise now seemed as muddied as the water in those brown puddles. But blazes, it sure seemed time for a change.

Chapter Forty-Five

Sibyl

My fear of war worsened when forty-two Pottawatomie County men were drafted into the Army. They had lunch—paid for by Uncle Sam—at the City Café before catching a train to Oklahoma City for their physicals. A newspaper tidbit.

The same day the men left, a four-year-old boy got trapped in a burning house and died. I could smell the smoke from our house and cringed at the thought of a broken-hearted mother sobbing through the night. Fires always made me tremble.

My theology became more confused the more I struggled to understand such events. I had so many questions that seemed unanswerable. Why did men fight wars? Why did children have to die? Why did tragedies not always bring families closer?

The only person I could confide in was Mother Pope.

On Saturday, I pushed Carol's black buggy toward Mother's house on Tennessee, Judson and Margaret bouncing behind me. October is a rather unpredictable month in Oklahoma weather-wise, but that day didn't feel terribly cold since we had bundled up.

On arriving at the Popes', I took Carol from the buggy and parked it on the porch before sending Judson to the bedroom to play with his beloved trucks. Mother Pope was making an outfit for Margaret from one of her dresses and wanted to pin the hem. "Come here, Margaret. Stand on this footstool." Mother helped Margaret up and knelt in front of her while I sat on the paisley love seat with Carol. The child took in the world around her before closing her eyes to sleep.

As I told Mother about the boy's death and the draftees, she listened, emitting grunts of shock and sadness as I talked. She didn't know the deceased child's family, but she did know two of the boys who'd left for the war. "I can only pray for them and reflect on a God who makes everything right in the end."

"My mama believes differently about God than you do. She says supporting family is more important than anything else."

"What do you mean?" Mother removed the pins from her mouth and sat back on her heels.

"Mama doesn't think I should spend so much time at church and hates that I teach WMU."

Mother's eyes widened as she pushed pins into the corn pincushion. I think Mother Pope sometimes found Mama as confusing as I did.

"Family *is* important, but there's more to Christianity than taking care of loved ones." Mother Pope turned Margaret around to pin the back of the flowered dress. Mother's everyday dresses were made from printed feed sacks, which also made sturdy dresses for little girls. "We have to put God first and place our family in his hands."

"You and Dad don't have much to worry about."

"God's been good to us, but our lives haven't always been without trials. After all, until the good Lord returns, nothing is perfect. So day by day, we've had to trust God to take care of us."

Questions seeped through my mind in a constant flow. "How can I trust him more?" My efforts weighed heavier than a mill full of grain, ready to burst.

"Stand still, child." Mother mumbled as she pinned, and Margaret did as she asked, or tried to, anyway.

"How can I know God's talking to me?" I asked before acknowledging my greatest fear. "Sometimes I think he's pushing us to move away and then I worry that he is. What will happen to my family?" My question hung in the air for several moments. "I mean, how do I know what God wants me to do?"

I placed my hand on my belly and saw Mother watch me. I wondered if she would see my worry.

Mother smiled like she could read my mind. "A joy. A baby always brings joy." She took the garment off Margaret and carried it to the wooden ironing board in the kitchen. I quickly dressed the child and sent her to the other room with Judson.

I followed Mother and stood before her, unable to express my frustration.

The Popes had a wood-burning stove and two old-fashioned flat irons. Mother set one iron on the cookstove to heat while she used the other one, and when one cooled, she'd switch them out. She never confused the two irons, as efficient and confident as a honeybee making honey.

I finally spoke. "My lifelong dream to help others seems futile. Keeping my children bathed, the dishes washed, and the dust from collecting on the furniture takes all my time. I love teaching, but…with another child…."

Mother stopped ironing the dress and straightened up. She set the heavy iron back onto the stove. "Oh, sweetie, our heavenly Father knows you and your concerns. He isn't worried about you doing everything right. It's like this…" She paused and pressed her index finger to her lips. "If Margaret didn't listen—let's say she falls into the mud in her good dress—would you scold her for that?"

I chuckled, remembering the incident. "Of course not. No mother would be upset—at least for long."

"Think about that. God isn't disappointed or surprised when life doesn't go the way you plan. He doesn't expect everything to be perfect and, gal, he won't turn his back on you. He's your spiritual Father. Trust him and your fears will fade away." She shook her finger at me in a motherly way. "Remember, He'll *never* stop loving you."

"How do I trust Him more?"

Mother looked intently at me. "Open your Bible tonight, dear, and read Philippians 3:15."

"Oh. I have that verse memorized. *Let us therefore, as many as be perfect, be thus minded: and if in anything ye be otherwise minded, God shall reveal even this unto you.*" To me, that verse meant that in his time, God would reveal what he wanted me to know. My connection to him wasn't based on my feelings, and if God's plan for me was to pursue mission work, to teach Sunday School, and share my faith with others, he would guide me—even through giving birth to another child.

My mind cleared, and I thought about God's loving guidance, feeling more hopeful than since I found out I was pregnant again.

"All of us have questions, child," said Mother. "No one knows the future, so we trust God today. Instead of worrying, keep reading your Bible. Pray. And make yourself available. Eventually, God will let you know what he wants you to do."

Gratefulness filled me. God had sent Mother to help me when I had questions.

On my walk home, I considered our conversation. Truly, I didn't want to offend my mama. I loved her. However, I also wanted to be led by God and do what he asked of me. I'd keep that thought in mind as I talked to Fremont.

The more I thought about the future, the more anxious I got. What unexpected things did God have in store?

"Be available," Mother had said. *Be available.*

Excellent advice. My mama might be a puzzle to me, but God had given me a wise and wonderful mother-in-law.

Chapter Forty-Six

While living in Lawton, Marjorie met a fellow named Ed Wynns. She called me on the telephone to tell me about him. "I met a swell dude, sis. He enlisted in the army earlier this year. Ain't that something?"

"Hold on. Tell me more about this fellow," I said, by now, knowing Marjorie's taste in men was questionable at best.

"He likes the dance places in Lawton. Of course, what doll-dizzy, military fellow doesn't? Lawton has the best bars around. They're not as hotsy-totsy as the old Blue Bird, but still mighty good. Ed's a real fun guy and loves to bogey as much as I do. Dancing fools, we call each other. Count Basie, Yip Yarborough, we love them all. And Frank Sinatra! Oh, sis, he's the up and coming."

Marjorie's non-stop chatter continued. I wound the telephone cord around my fingers as I waited for a chance to break in and ask questions.

"He stared at me across the table and his first words were, 'What a dilly!' meaning me, I guess. Then I snapped back at him, 'What's tickin', chicken?' Isn't that hilarious? Ed's a private, even though he's had four years of college. He's a smart dude. He's stationed in Wichita Falls at Sheppard Field, and he's come up to Lawton every night since we met to go dancing with me. He's a real hoot, sis. You'll like him."

My dear, crazy sister. There wasn't a hop near the military base that Marjorie had missed. She was always out having a good time—or looking to find a man. She loved dancing, and with shapely legs and a bubbly smile, she never lacked a partner.

"Ed likes the way I tango and said I have good moves." She laughed as if life were just one grand party after another. "We jitterbug better than Judy Garland and Fred Astaire. Dearie, both of us love it."

"You seem enamored, that's for sure."

"Oh, sweetie, I've met the man of my dreams. We've had three formal dates to fancy café's, and I'm in love, love, love. We're slap-happy and even talking about getting married."

"Married! How long have you known him?"

"I met him ten days ago, but don't worry. I know a top dog when I see one. His folks live in Snyder, and he and his mother are close. His father works for a granite company making tombstones." Marjorie's voice lowered into a whisper. "Sis, he makes a lot of dough—a fortune!" She sounded as excited as she did the time we found a silver dollar under a tree stump. "I think Larry and I will be set for life."

I looked toward my front porch. Larry sat on the wooden slats looking as dejected as a lost puppy. "What did he say when you told him you have a son?"

"Oh, he'll love Larry," she said breezily. "Everyone loves Larry."

I lowered my voice. "Have you told him about…you know."

"I have." Marjorie's voice fell too.

"And..."

"He said he didn't care about the miscarriage."

Marjorie had always referred to her abortion as a miscarriage, perhaps because it was easier for her to digest. She continued to speak quietly. "I've never told you the rest of that story. I was living with Papa when I had the surgery, and Gladys's woman doctor from Germany cut my tubes."

I reeled from this information. "But that means..." I placed my hand on my baby belly. I'd suspected Marjorie was unable to have more children but had never known the cause. "How did Ed take that news?"

"Ed's a strange bird. Wherever he is, he always takes an hour nap after lunch." She snickered. "So, Ed just nodded like it didn't matter and trotted off home for his afternoon nap."

All I could do was pray Marjorie made a better choice this time for a mate.

Ed and Marjorie married a little later after knowing each other for twenty-one days. A few days after that, he received military orders to transfer to Panama City, Florida.

The U.S. landed in Iceland. The Nazi bombers blasted Britain, and the Pacific situation was dark because of Japanese demands. War was teasing our family, and I hoped my sister had not just married someone in its crosshairs.

***

Marjorie brought her new husband home to meet the family the next weekend. She wore a new dirndl-type dress, red lipstick, and hair waved to perfection, prancing about on heels as high as a mountain.

Ed Wynns wore a fedora when he walked into Mama's house. Mimicking Bogie standing on the airstrip, Ed had his trench coat cinched around his waist and his fedora pulled low over his sullen eyes. In a dramatic voice, he said, "Here's looking at you, kid."

The whole group broke into laughter.

Ed had a fun and engaging personality, and his performance endeared him to the family. He made a good first impression. Ed knelt in front of Larry and held out his hand to shake. "Hey, do you think you can put up with me being a part of your family? I promise to take care of you and your mom the best I can."

Larry stared at him. This little imp had become Fremont's buddy, but living with females all his life, he needed a man to look up to—a father figure. Larry shook Ed's hand as if they were making a pact. I wanted to believe I could trust Ed to take good care of Larry and Marjorie.

"Mama dear, you won't have to take care of Larry anymore." Marjorie beamed like she had given Mama a birthday present.

Mama's eyes widened. "What do you mean? Are you taking him with you to Florida?"

"Not yet. Ed's parents are excited to have a grandson and offered to watch him in Snyder while we get settled. We have to find a place to live first and all that."

Blanche stepped toward Larry. "You can't send him to strangers. We can keep him here."

"He'll be fine. Ed's mother loves kids." Marjorie gave a dismissive wave of her hand.

Mama's thoughts had moved on. "Maybe now you can give Larry a brother or sister. One more kid would be enough."

Marjorie nor I could never tell Mama the truth of why Marjorie couldn't have more children. That would stay our secret.

Marjorie and Ed left the next day to drive to Florida, probably laughing and singing the whole way. If I had to guess, they'd probably stop to dance at a dozen joints as they journeyed. I caught myself envying the opportunity to leave Shawnee.

A few weeks later, Larry left Ed Wynn's family and traveled to Pensacola on a bus by himself. Marjorie wrote Mama to say Larry had arrived safely. However, he was so hungry on the trip he ate all the aspirin he was delivering to Marjorie. Apparently, not enough food was sent with him.

They set up housekeeping, and Ed became the daddy Larry always wanted. My heart rested knowing Marjorie had a chance at happiness. I hoped Ed didn't have to go overseas any time soon.

Chapter Forty-Seven

November 1941

Fremont

The town of Shawnee had several car dealerships, but the largest ones were the Ford place on West Main, and my workplace, the Norton Motor Sales, which sold and serviced Chevrolets. Located at North Union, it sat half a block north of Main across the street from the bus station and the Gaskill Funeral Home. Every time I drove to work, I was reminded of Keith's funeral and the heartbreak of that day.

One evening I arrived five minutes late for work, and Sam Norton stood by the garage doors waiting for me. He slapped me on the back. "That pretty wife making you late?"

Sam Norton and his brother Mead owned the company. Members of the Masonic Lodge and Lions Club, they were bigshots around town. Sam and I had a bantering relationship that had lasted for years. Even though the business employed around thirty people, Sam needed someone he trusted to stand guard at night because they'd had several break-ins in the past.

He opened the garage door. "Can you still drive that wrecker parked in the back? The one you drove a few years ago?"

"I could drive a pit bull if it would carry me. Why're you asking?" I had driven only a few times until a permanent driver was found.

"We let the driver go. What say you drive that wrecker if you get a phone call from the police. They're needing help at night. Of course, there's extra pay when you go on a call."

"Sure thing." I knew Sibyl would be happy with the extra money to add to the Havana box, even if she wasn't sure she wanted to move just yet.

"Be sure and lock up if you have to leave."

We shook hands, and Sam stepped through the front door into the semi-darkness. I pulled the heavy door closed behind him and looked around. All seemed safe and quiet. A wrecker driver did little except haul damaged cars back to the shop, so that would be easy.

Norton's handled major repairs done by trained mechanics. The place had six car stalls on each side where the mechanics did wheel alignments and tire rotations and other jobs, which I helped with. Off to the right stood a parts shop with windows along the front. Upstairs had a storage room, where workers entered from inside.

When a customer brought their car in, we opened the big garage doors. Then an attendant—usually Little Joe, who had to stand up behind the wheel to reach the pedals—drove the vehicle to the bay.

The shiny new vehicles lining the showroom were the latest models and started at six hundred dollars and went up from there. Mostly Chevrolets and Cadillacs. At nights I'd ogle those gorgeous jewels with smooth curves and shiny chrome. I knew the make and model of every car on the lot and despaired of ever owning a four-passenger roadster, a suburban carryall, a town car, or especially a beautiful four-door sports sedan shipped directly from Detroit.

Thankfully, the good Lord provided my family a decent automobile. My '26 Chevrolet touring vehicle could take us wherever we needed to go. But someday…someday, I'd have a different job and more pay and extra funds to purchase a spanking new set of wheels. Yes, siree.

Doug liked the curves on the new '40 Ford Deluxe, but I wouldn't have a Ford, not even if Governor Phillips gave it to me. I was a Chevrolet man through and through.

My nights could be lonely. I worked by myself, the only one in the garage where a solitary streetlight lit the outside parking lot. Most of the time, I didn't mind because the quietness could be soothing after a day of family crises.

I liked my night job. It could be boring, and although I didn't want to do this for the rest of my life, it gave me time to pray and study for the next week's Bible lesson. The steady work and regular pay it provided kept us afloat, but I yearned for a better job to give Sibyl the life she deserved. Next time I had a day off, I'd call other car dealerships to see if they had an opening.

I couldn't depend on money from the wrecker job because I wouldn't need to drive it often—hopefully. Lord forbid a serious accident should happen on my watch.

***

That evening at Norton's began normally enough. Quiet, except for a few dogs howling over by the Rock Island Railroad Station. Once a mutt got started, the others joined in like a chorus of yodelers. At midnight, I walked the place, checked doors and windows, and peered outside, seeing nothing.

I went back to my chair and sat, nearly nodding off to sleep. Maybe not *nearly*. The telephone rang loudly enough to wake a corpse. I jerked and ran over to pick it up, still trying to get my bearings.

"This Norton's?" A piercing voice came from the other end of the line.

"Sure is."

"Got an emergency east of town. Bad accident. Can you come out?" The voice, which belonged to a police officer, gave the exact location, which I jotted down.

"I'll be there in a jiffy."

I pushed my hat on my head, grabbed the keys, and opened the back door. The wrecker started in an instant. I rehearsed the directions in my head and sped off, taking fifteen minutes to find the place. Near the Rock Creek Bridge on Highway 270, four miles east of Shawnee.

When I arrived, I jumped out of the wrecker. "What happened?"

A policeman came up to me. "Looks like the driver lost control. Smells like he had a tad too much bootleg."

Lights from two patrol cars flashed, circling the scene.

A '36 Ford Coupe lay on its side in a ditch, the front-end smashed in halfway to the windshield. A '36 Plymouth lay upside down on the pavement nearby.

I looked around for the driver and saw a body lying on the ground, bloodied, and torn. My heart beat wildly against my ribs.

The last time I'd seen a body like that was way back in November of '37 when I rode along with a fellow who drove a wrecker. Accidents don't give you notice. That horrifying experience still haunted me.

This accident in November of '41 would also stay etched in my mind forever. Two cars traveling at high speeds had collided. The Ford's speedometer was jammed at seventy-one miles per hour. As more police cars pulled in around the scene, their revolving lights flashed on broken bodies lying on the ground. My stomach clenched at the devastation, the carnage, that surrounded me.

I ran to a nearby ditch and threw up. I rose and walked to the man lying on the pavement. His body broken. His face still. His eyes lifeless. There was nothing I could do. I ran to another person, and another. A girl torn. An arm lost. A child lying in the ditch.

I saw a young teen lying on the ground alone and squatted beside him. I held his hand and begged the Lord for mercy until he died. A medic tapped me on the shoulder, and I backed away, stopping in the middle of the tragedy, dazed. More police cars and ambulances from around the county began to arrive and the chaos swelled.

Seven people died in the crash. Two children.

I hauled the crunched Plymouth back to the shop, my body numb, my eyes leaking rivers of tears, and my hands shaking.

I had to find another job. I had to. I was no medical person nor police officer, and never would be. No matter how badly we needed the extra cash, I could not drive a wrecker anymore. My heart couldn't take another night like that one.

Chapter Forty-Eight

Fremont

The next morning when I arrived home, I helped Sibyl get the children ready for school. When all was quiet, I walked into our room and sat on the side of the bed, resting my elbows on my knees, and cradling my head in my hands. I hadn't told Sibyl about the car crash because I couldn't talk about it yet. I had flashbacks of that horrifying scene.

She sat beside me, her arms around her baby stomach. "Is something wrong? You look like you're praying."

"Just asking the Lord to help us," I said. "Asking for strength."

"It's about that bad accident last night, isn't it?" Sibyl must have heard it on the radio. "You were there?"

"It was the worst thing I've ever experienced. I keep seeing those people in front of my face. The children. The boy who died while I watched. How could God let that happen?"

She sat quietly for a moment before speaking. "The news said one of the Jackson boys died. It must have been awful." She put her arm around my shoulder, and we sat still for a long time with our heads touching each other, contemplating, remembering, praying.

Sobs broke my prayers. "I can't do it, honey. Some people may be cut out for it, but I just can't do this job."

"Do you want to talk to your dad or the pastor about it? It might help."

"Maybe. And I'm serious about finding another job. There just aren't many opportunities around Shawnee."

"You want to move?

239

I nodded, unsure how to explain my certainty, the peace about what I needed to do.

"Don't make a decision because of last night. You're still in shock."

My motivation for moving wasn't the same as Sibyl's, but I didn't consider it any less important. I wanted to find a job where I could take good care of my family—provide for their needs and keep them safe. Above all, I wanted to keep my promise to move Sibyl away from family stress. That would be in her best interest, and if, in that process, she could fulfill her dreams, so much the better.

The accident had pushed me from the edge and sealed my decision, but I still needed to convince Sibyl. I took her hand in mine. "Honey, it's time to move."

"How do you *know* God wants this change right now?"

"He hasn't spoken in a big, loud voice, but he's been nudging us for a long time. Well, more like pushing us, but definitely preparing us for a move."

Sibyl released a sigh. "But life could be a lot worse somewhere else."

"Yes. It could," I said. "But it could be a lot better, too. Staying here has risks. The car business is tough right now, and they've already cut my pay. I may get laid off like everyone else, and then what would we do?" The words boosted my confidence.

I looked into Sibyl's eyes and saw confusion and uncertainty. She had been pulled back and forth by her family long enough. My role was to reassure her it was a good plan. "I want to find a better job for you and the kids." My breathing slowed. "Whatever the future holds, we don't have to be afraid. The Lord promises to go before us and prepare a place. He's been preparing us for several years now."

Sibyl gazed at her lap. "I said I'd go wherever God leads us, but...it's scary."

"Sure, it's scary," I said. "We'll be leaving family and friends, and in the middle of all that change, we'll have a new baby to care for." I caressed her hand. "But don't overanalyze. Just trust. I heard they need help with churches in other states, and all the Bible lessons you've studied could be put to good use."

Sibyl sat quietly, still staring at her lap.

Realizing the enormity of this decision, I said, "Why don't I go out west and check out a place first? I can take a bus, and, when I find a job, I'll telephone you, and then you and the children can join me."

"I don't know."

"Just trust me and we'll see what happens. If I can't find a job in a month, I'll come back."

The plan seemed reasonable, and Sibyl didn't argue. My heart raced with anticipation, and I sent up a short prayer of thanks—and a long prayer for all the families who'd lost loved ones the night before.

***

I had worked as a night guard at Norton Motor Sales for a lifetime, or so it seemed after almost five years. The once-booming automobile industry had slacked off, and many of my friends who'd been laid off in the late thirties were still looking for work. Fortunately, I still had my job, but I didn't know for how long.

My dad had worn many different hats throughout his lifetime: farmer, carpenter, mill worker, custodian. He'd also worked at the highway department and as a cobbler. He'd worked at the Shawnee Mill, and side-by-side he and I helped build the Shawnee Lake Dam as part of a PWA crew. My father, Willie Ollie Pope, didn't mind doing whatever it took to support his family.

I loved being around automobiles at Norton's, but the hard fact was that we needed more income, and like my father, I needed to put provision above job satisfaction.

"I know you don't like California, but what if I can find a good job there?" I asked her a day or two later, knowing she had never wanted to move to the west coast. As for me, having worked there when I rode a youth, I'd always wanted to return. "I'm sure I can get better pay."

Sibyl drew her mouth into a pout of disapproval. "How about a different state? All the news from the west coast is horrible. Why don't you go to New Mexico or Colorado instead? There might be good jobs there?"

My heart was set on California, where years before I'd seen green pastures, mountains, the ocean, and—most importantly—great opportunities. I could no longer stand the strain of near poverty and my shaky job status. "What do you say, honey?" I asked.

"Shouldn't we pray about this again?"

"We've prayed and prayed. It's time to make a decision."

Sibyl's big brown eyes caught mine. "All right. If you want to go, you're a free man."

I raised my eyebrows. "I'm a free man?"

"Well, as long as you remember you have a wife and children, you're free." Sibyl smiled.

I drew a deep breath. "Well, then. I guess I'll be leaving this weekend."

"This weekend?" Sibyl was no longer smiling.

The quietness was deafening. When Sibyl was the quietest, her mind was the busiest. Was she doubting? Retreating into fear? "Honey, this is the time for us to make our move. I can feel it."

I gave my notice at work, and Sam Norton told me I would have a job if I decided to come back. The following Saturday morning, despite Sibyl's reluctance, I counted out half of the money in our cigar box and packed a light bag.

When I kissed Sibyl good-bye, she clung to me. "I love you," I said. "Don't ever forget that, and I'll call as soon as I can."

It was early dawn when I left for the Santa Fe Train Station, and I would be far away from home within two or three days. Despite my brave front, I was nervous—not about traveling but about leaving Sibyl. She was six months pregnant and vulnerable, and we'd never been apart before. I wasn't sure how she'd handle everyday crises.

I needed to find a good place for my family—a place where I could provide what we needed, away from discord. Where we could experience life on our own with God as our guide, and a place where Sibyl and I could serve others in peace.

Chapter Forty-Nine

I heard nothing from Fremont for a week. Not a stinking word. I'd heard stories about other husbands who took off looking for work and had abandoned their wives and families. I worried that could happen to me. Other times, I worried Fremont might have fallen into trouble or gone missing or lying hurt somewhere and I'd never see him again. Once or twice, I attended his funeral in my mind. Buried him. I'll admit I was a world champion worrier, but I couldn't help myself.

I paced the floor. I stomped. I prayed. I sobbed.

The absolute worst thing I did was complain to Mama. She let me know in no uncertain terms that my worries were justified. Men did that. They left you just like Papa had left her. She believed men were unstable, undependable, and could not be trusted with a task as simple as throwing out the bathwater.

Mama came close to convincing me she'd been right all along.

I was considering going after Fremont to drag him back home when he called.

"I'm in Colorado!"

"I thought you were going to California?" Euphoric he was alive, I forgot to scold him for the agony he'd caused.

"I'm in Denver," he said. "The morning I left, I met some fellows at the train station headed to Colorado. They talked me into traveling with them and then going on to California if I couldn't find work."

Fremont practically yelled into the telephone due to a bad connection. "When I got to Colorado, I ran into Chuck Mills, that fellow from Shawnee. What were the odds of that? Chuck suggested I apply for a job at his workplace, a newly opened ammunition plant, and guess what? I got the job!"

Giddy with happiness, I let lose a whoop. Fremont was safe, he had a job ... and he hadn't abandoned me!

Fremont

I described my new job to Sibyl, probably giving her way more information than she needed, but I wanted her to share my enthusiasm.

With war preparations setting up in case the U.S. got pulled in, the Denver Ordinance Plant contracted with Remington, a subsidiary of DuPont, to make ammunition.

Spread out on the flat plains near Denver, the Remington Plant was known for the high quality and accuracy of its ammunition, particularly its Springfield rifle ammunition known as M2 Ball, highly prized by the U.S. Army. One plant made incendiary bullets used to set buildings on fire. Maybe I shouldn't have mentioned that to Sibyl. The details both scared and intrigued me, but I'm not sure she cared about the details.

"I'm so glad to hear your voice," she said, laughing and crying into the phone. "I was worried to pieces."

I went on to explain how I worked as a mechanic for the plant—walking through the three buildings fixing breakdowns. I was confident I could handle the job, given my experience and engineering-type mind. Plus, I'd be helping the war efforts.

"And guess what else. I found a house," I yelled through the receiver of the wall phone. "It's small, but it's the best I could do. The location's great—it's in a housing area near my work."

"Exactly how small?"

"Two bedrooms. Another couple lives in the basement." I paused, and when I spoke again, my voice cracked. "Can you leave tomorrow?"

"Tomorrow?" Sibyl's voice rose.

I jerked the handset away from my ear. As I waited for her answer, I paced as far as the telephone cord would allow me. The request for her to move tomorrow was absurd, but what I wanted was reassurance she would not back out or procrastinate. I missed her greatly.

"At least give me a week," she said. "There's a lot to take care of."

My heart leaped with joy. I had my answer. She was coming soon.

"December the sixth?" I asked. "I'm off that weekend, and I can meet you."

"All right. All right. I'll leave early Saturday."

I lowered my voice to an apologetic tone. "I forgot to mention I have to work nights at first. Everyone starts on the night shift."

"Makes sense." A few beats passed before she spoke again, her voice cautious. "We'll manage. It isn't like you haven't been working nights for years."

We said our good-byes and hung up. I was crazy with excitement that my family would soon be joining me, although a bit of worry gnawed at my happiness. Sibyl didn't like being alone at night, and I wasn't sure how she'd react in a strange city. I'd heard the disappointment in her voice about the night job, and she had only five days to pack up everything we owned and move. Would she make it? Or would she put it off?

Sibyl

"You have three children, you're six months pregnant, you have practically no money, and you merely *hope* Fremont's job will work out. How will you survive?" Mama stood by the front door as I was leaving her house.

As usual, Mama didn't keep her opinions to herself, and her objections to our move didn't bode well for the favor I was about to ask. Nevertheless, I steeled myself and came right out with it. "I understand your concern, but we'll be all right. However, it's a long drive—"

"You bet it's a long drive. You're just asking for trouble. Driving alone with all those kids in the back seat, yelling and hungry and irritable. Carol will need bottles and her diapers changed. This is the worst idea you've ever had."

The nerves I'd steeled seconds ago were turning to mush. I wished Mama understood and didn't doubt our plans. Maybe I should put off moving until after Christmas—or after this baby was born. Even if Mama didn't approve, I *would* be leaving sometime. However, a little support would be helpful.

I braced myself a second time, leaning against the door to hold myself up. "I know, Mama. Driving alone is an awful idea. That's why I'm asking you to go with me."

Mama jerked as if something had startled her, and then her face gave the slightest of softening. "Moving so quickly is ridiculous," she said, not willing to completely give in. "But, since you're so desperate, yes, I'll go with you."

"You only need to go halfway. Fremont will meet us in Garden City, and then you can jump on a bus and come right back to Oklahoma.

Mama nodded. "The bus ride will be just fine, but you'll have to pay for it."

What could go wrong if God were with us?

Chapter Forty-Nine

Mama came to see me the next day. She seemed almost happy about a new baby as she helped me retrieve the leather steamer trunk tucked in the back of my closet. I hadn't looked in the trunk since placing Keith's baby items inside after he died.

As I lifted the lid, an aroma filled the room. Not a musty scent, but a nostalgic waft of memories. I blinked back tears, sad, even as I thought of the good times I'd had with my son. I thanked God for him.

I sank to the floor beside the trunk and sorted through tiny clothes, baby blankets, and pictures. I picked up a suit jacket Keith wore on Sundays and held it to my chest. "Mama, do you remember Keith wearing this little suit?"

She nodded.

I refolded the suit and put it aside, then pulled out the tiny white shoes—buttoned ones—that every one of my babies had worn. Now, our newest family member would wear them.

I packed the kid's summer clothes and my non-maternity outfits on top and then stored it in Mama's attic. She promised it would remain there until I returned to Oklahoma. Would she ever accept that we were moving without her approval?

"I hope Fremont's prediction of a boy is right. Won't he look darling in this?" I placed my arms around my huge belly. "I can't wait to hold him."

Mama sat on a chair nearby, and a thoughtful look crossed her face. "At least you want this baby," she said softly. "My mother never wanted me."

I frowned, not understanding. "But every mother wants her baby."

"Not so. When I was around seven, I was standing in the hallway when I heard Mother and Daddy arguing. I pushed myself up against the wall so they couldn't see me, and distinctly heard Mother say she had never wanted another child. Never wanted a third baby."

I stopped sorting clothes. How awful for a child to hear. I seldom saw this side of my mama. Reflective. Vulnerable. Hurt.

Mama pressed her lips together before she spoke again. "I'm sure my mother eventually fell in love with me. How could she not? I was such a plucky kid—full of mischief." Her voice carried a false cheeriness as if trying to convince herself those words were true, and then she eyed my huge body. "You might be having twins."

"Oh, please don't say that. I can handle only one infant at a time." I took a deep breath and smiled. "But we'll welcome whatever God sees fit to send."

"Twins do run in our family, you know. I gave birth to twins after Frances was born."

I sat up and gaped at her. "You never mentioned you had twins." What other secrets did I not know about my family?

"I got pregnant in '29. We were living in Tulsa, and I already had five lively children." Mama leaned back in the chair and wiped her eyes. "Your papa was traveling a lot with work and didn't want another child, much less twins. But I really wanted those babies." Her eyes had a faraway look like her thoughts were lost in the past. "I miscarried at five months, but I never told anyone."

I placed my hand on Mama's knee and felt a rare closeness with her. She seemed so much softer than I'd ever seen her. Her hurt must've gone deeper than she'd let on.

Why, after birthing five children herself, had she been so against me having another baby? Maybe she'd been afraid I would lose another child, or that I'd reject my next one like she was rejected. Or that it was too much work.

"The pain of losing a baby cuts more deeply than a knife wound," Mama said. "I've never completely recovered from the loss, and your Papa never understood." Her lips squeezed together. "He never wanted the twins, like I was not wanted when I was born."

Had Mama felt her babies were rejected like she had been rejected as a child? Had that feeling always been with her? Had it hardened her heart?

At that moment, I connected with my mother in a way I never had before. We weren't just mother and daughter; we were two women who'd lost pieces of ourselves and coped with that loss as best we could. We both wanted to be loved.

Why, then, had she not understood me when Keith died?

It came to me that when I'd lost Keith, I'd had Fremont and his family to share my grief and comfort me. Mama'd had no such support. Keeping her miscarriage a secret from everyone but Papa, who didn't care, she'd held all her grief and hurt inside and borne it alone. Perhaps, in the following years, that pent-up sadness and rejection had turned to bitterness—the only emotion she let others see.

Could all of Mama's and my differences be resolved? Probably not soon, but at least whenever my mother criticized me, I could accept it better. I'd know the unkindness was coming from a broken woman, a sour woman who was dealing with her pain in the only way she knew how.

"Oh, Mama. God wants you. He loves you." I heaved my vast body from the floor and went to Mama, and even though my big belly made it awkward, I enfolded her in my arms. Love for her gushed out and I hoped it would make a path for when Fremont and I left town.

***

I sorted our belongings, deciding what to take, what to dispose of, what to put in storage, and what to ship by train later.

Effie came over bringing boxes, old newspapers, and willing hands. We were dressed almost identically—in dungarees and oversize shirts—and we both had our hair pulled back in kerchiefs. What would I do in Colorado without my best friend? The idea saddened me, and I pushed away the thought.

We worked like spinning tops all afternoon, and although I needed to rest due to my pregnancy, I didn't have time for dilly-dallying.

Mother Pope opened the front door without knocking. Our house looked like a tornado had touched down with every drawer and cabinet door open and all the contents littered across the floor.

She handed me a sack of vegetables from her root cellar—potatoes, onion, and carrots. "Thought you might be able to use these. Not that you can't find food in Colorado, but this'll get you through."

I hugged her and, ignoring my dusty clothes, she hugged me back.

"Would you mind taking the kids home with you?" I asked. "Until I can get this place packed and cleaned up?"

"Mind? Of course not, child. I'd love to have the kiddos for a few days. Been hankering to see them."

"Also, please take the food in the icebox. It won't keep." I heard my voice coming out rushed and breathy. Recalling Mama's words, the thought of uprooting my family had thrown me into a panic. What if we were wrong? What if this was not God's plan, but mine...or Fremont's?

Mother Pope—my earthly source of peace—put her hand on my shoulder. "Don't be afraid of the future, dear. God has prepared a place for you, don't you know?" She quoted one of her favorite Bible verses: *"Cast all your care upon him, because he careth for you."*

Tears filled my eyes. What would I do without this tower of love and support nearby?

Mother searched my face, her gaze full of understanding. "You're going to be fine. We can be in touch by letter, and I'll call occasionally. And you'll have not just my prayers, but many in the church will be lifting you up." Her hug felt settling, and her words sounded like the confirmation I'd sought.

Was moving to Colorado, right? We'd prayed and agreed to follow God wherever he might lead. I'd talked to Mother and my friend Effie about it, godly women I trusted to give sound advice. I looked back on the Bible studies that had helped me grow, and specifically at the verse I'd read recently, Isaiah 48:15. *I, even I, have spoken; yes, I have called him. I will bring him, and he will succeed in his mission.*

I trusted Fremont. For the last few years, I'd watched him pray, read the Bible, teach young people. If God was leading him to Timbuktoo, I'd follow.

I took a deep breath, and a peaceful calm enveloped me. I wanted this move. I wanted to share ideas and tell others about God. There were people to help, classes to teach, and churches to encourage.

***

I put an ad in the Shawnee Morning News the next day and began to sell furniture.

Larger items sold a piece at a time, and I got pittance for them. What furniture we couldn't sell, or I wanted to keep, Fremont's dad hauled over to his old shed to be retrieved when we returned or shipped to us later. I took a note pad and listed everything I sold, how much it sold for, and what was left. Then I listed what we'd stored and where.

With everything sorted and sold or packed, exhausted, I went to gather the children from the Popes, taking the dog with me. Dad Pope had agreed to keep the mutt while we were gone.

"Why did you bring Patches?" Judson asked, hugging the dog around the neck.

"We can't take him with us, dear. It's too cold in Colorado, and we don't have anywhere to keep him."

Judson started wailing. "We can't leave Patches. We can't. He'll miss us." Patches whined as if she'd never been left at the Pope's before.

"I'm sorry, son. Really I am."

Grandpa Pope picked up the brown and white terrier and took him to the backyard along with his food and water bowl and then attached a rope to the dog's leash. Judson followed, crying for his pet. I followed Judson and he turned and buried his face in my dress. I put my arm around my boy and, squatting down, wiped away his tears. "Grandpa will take good care of him."

After urging the kids to the car, I drove to Mama's house, where we would stay the night and leave the next morning.

I dropped off the kids and then met Dad Pope at the filling station. He checked the oil and tires and filled our Chevrolet with gasoline. His last words before seeing me off were: "Don't worry about Patches. He'll be fine. Now, keep my boy happy and tell him to keep on trudging down the path God laid out for him."

Instead of going directly back to Mama's house, I drove to the Fairview Cemetery, driving through the massive gate to the back. I knelt in front of the stone that marked Keith's grave, picturing Fremont standing at this very spot, sobbing for his son.

I gently dusted dirt and leaves from the top of the tombstone and ran my palm over the words and dates. Who would tend this little grave now? Our family wouldn't be here next spring to see the trees turn green or the irises bloom. I took a deep breath and wiped my eyes. Someday, we'd come back. Someday.

With tears streaming, I kissed my fingertips and lightly touched them to the marker before driving to Mama's.

Chapter Fifty

December 1941

I woke early Saturday morning, December the sixth, minutes before the clock bellowed five o'clock. I wanted to be on the road by six and still had last-minute preparations. The car was almost loaded, and I checked off items on my list: water, bottles, diapers, food.

I had a separate list for trip expenses down to the penny. I would also keep a mileage list. In my pocketbook, I had the list of the furniture and household belongings I'd sold or stored. If lists were any indicator of how a trip would go, this one should be a roaring success.

Mama stirred in her room and popped her head out into the hallway, hissing her displeasure once again. "What are you thinking, leaving like this? It's foolhardy to follow a poor man who can't buy beans. You can't spend your life trying to please a man. You should change your mind and unpack your bags right now."

I stood in the hallway with my back straight and my feet firmly planted. "Mama. You know how I feel. I'm going whether you approve or not."

"No family up there to help you out." Mama shook her head as she stuffed tissues into her pocketbook. "I don't like it and I did my duty by warning you."

I rolled my eyes—not where Mama could see, mind you—before I entered my bedroom for one last inspection. Mama was packing glasses when I went into the kitchen.

"Did you get the biscuits and sausages I laid out for breakfast?" I asked as I rummaged through a drawer for another pencil.

"They're already in the car, dear. I wouldn't forget something as essential as breakfast. I wouldn't want to listen to complaining children all morning."

I was too concerned about the trip to get offended.

"Diapers, baby bottles..." I checked items off my list. "Now, what about water? We'll need water."

"Don't worry. I'll wedge a milk bottle full of water between the biscuits and my pocketbook. We'll be fine. After all, we're not driving to China."

I walked outside carrying the last suitcase. My skin tingled, whether from excitement or from the crisp December air, I couldn't say. Maybe both. I was moving away from Shawnee—something I'd always wanted to do.

When I checked the mail one last time, the car title had finally come, and I stuck it in my pocketbook. We could now purchase a Colorado car tag when we got there.

I rushed back inside and shook Margaret awake. The child's blue eyes immediately popped open. "Shh..." I said. "Be quiet now and don't wake the baby." Margaret dressed by herself.

Judson, a seven-year-old sound sleeper, grumbled when I woke him and led him toward the Chevy, his grogginess making him wobble. Both children crawled into the back seat, where I had placed items in the floorboard raising it to seat level. Blankets and pillows lay across the long back seat.

I gathered eighteen-month-old Carol into my arms and tiptoed to the car. Margaret and Judson sat quiet and wide-eyed, waiting for the journey to begin. I laid Carol, still sleeping, between them. She had her thumb in her mouth and clutched the pink baby receiving blanket she couldn't live without.

Now. Now we could leave. I went back and looked through the house one last time and spied Margaret's shoes halfway hidden under Mama's sofa. I definitely could not forget Margaret's only pair of shoes. "Heavens, that child must have walked outside in her stocking feet."

On the front stoop, I stopped and gazed down the familiar street. "Goodbye, Shawnee," I whispered. The future looked like an adventure, the anticipation of a long trip not deterring my optimism. I was as excited as a toddler with a piece of chocolate.

This was mine and Fremont's chance, a chance to make a difference in the world. To get ahead, to move away from our hometown where everyone knew about my parent's divorce and how my banker father left mama for another woman. Our family's disgrace paraded in front of the whole town in court and splashed across the newspapers. Papa's legal difficulties. How my sister and I had to get married because we'd gotten pregnant. How could I have been so naïve?

But despite the poverty and disgrace, life had gone on, and would now improve with Fremont's new job. What excited me most was taking the Word of God out into the world. I heard there were not many good churches in Denver, and I determined to begin a Women's Missionary Union, teaching young women the truths I'd learned, my folder of WMU lessons packed securely in the trunk. Fremont could teach young boys like he did at Cavalry Church. We would show my family that living for God was a better way. Life would improve now that the economy looked up and the dust had settled from the last decade.

"Aren't you going to say good-bye?" Blanche's voice startled me, and I swung around.

"I didn't want to wake you," I said. "We said our farewells last night."

"You seem a bit eager to leave your mother and sisters behind. Hope we don't starve to death while you're gone." Blanche's words erupted as if they couldn't be contained any longer. Her bitterness reflected Mama's.

"I'm sure you'll survive. The good Lord will take care of you."

"No thanks to you, I must say."

I kissed her cheek and walked away.

Suddenly, I felt sad. I would miss the barbeque at Van's Pigs Stand, the Hamburger King, where the best hamburgers in the south could be found, and Owl's Drug store, where we bought icy root beer sodas. I'd miss our church. Our friends. Our community. No matter what we'd gone through, it was a caring town, and I would miss the good people who lived there. The town's people had come together to help us through many hardships, not the least of which was the loss of baby Keith.

And then, I wanted to jump over the bare treetops in exhilaration. Always full of energy, I would drive the motorcar ten thousand miles if necessary, despite my protruding, uncomfortable stomach.

Mama climbed into her side of the car, and I started the engine. I drove out of the sleeping town, leaving friends and family and church and neighbors.

The baby moved inside me as a reminder. A boy, if Fremont's predictions were right, this child would be different. He would be born in Colorado—if only we could get there.

Chapter Fifty-One

Sibyl

Mama and I talked as we traveled. Something about being stuck together in the Chevrolet brought an unusual intimacy. I nodded as she chattered, keeping my eyes on the road. As expected, she eventually came around to speaking of Papa, and since I couldn't walk away, I had to listen.

"Your appalling Papa. That no-good rat of a man never treated me like he cared. He's the most self-centered person I've ever met. Doesn't give a whap about anyone but himself. I hope he rots in hell."

I gasped at her words, remembering calling Papa to tell him goodbye and his acceptance of our move. "But Papa loved you at one time, or he wouldn't have married you. Right?"

"Nope. He married me for all the wrong reasons. Never seemed to like me. Pushed me away as my mother did. Of course, my mother didn't want me either. No one's ever wanted me." Her voice grew distant, sad. "I grew up on my own. I've had to work through that. Had to survive by clawing my way toward sanity."

Hearing Mama's feelings of rejection had helped me commiserate with her hurt—hurt that incited her hatred and anger toward Papa—anger that had turned on me on many occasions. She dealt with her misery by being harsh. Anger could hide a mountain of heartache.

As the oldest child, I'd experienced the same feelings of rejection, the feeling of not being wanted, of being the underdog. But, sadly, Mama didn't have the Lord to help her recover.

"God sees your hurt," I said, hoping she would listen. "He'll never reject you. Just ask him, and he'll tell you how much he loves you." The only way my mama's heart could be completely healed was to accept God's overwhelming love. "He's helped me many times."

"Not me. He doesn't care about me." Her heart seemed to have hardened over the years as she erected barriers to pain. Could anyone get through?

The children fussed, the winds grew worse, and I had to focus on driving. Mama's soul-baring session ended, and I was concentrating on keeping the car on the road when Mama spoke again. "You know this is a foolish endeavor, traipsing across the country with three children and one on the way."

So much for our intimacy and closeness. One thing I could say for Mama: she was relentless.

"We're trying to follow what the Lord wants. Fremont and I think this is what we should do."

"Lordy, Lordy. You're so wrong. God wouldn't ask you to do this. You just wait. This'll be the death of you all. Miserable, I say, you'll be miserable."

I prayed she was wrong.

"You never listen to me. You've always been a stubborn and thoughtless daughter, not considering others at all. Leaving your mama to the dogs."

What could I say to that sinister remark? How in heaven's name did God expect me to deal with such a difficult person, especially one so close to me?

Forgiveness.

And choices.

I had a choice. I could hold onto the knife of rejection lodged in my soul, becoming bitter like she was, or I could forgive her and stay vulnerable, enduring pain even if she never changed. It would be easy to ignore my mother, send her back to Oklahoma, and never speak to her again, but I couldn't. Even though, honestly, our relationship would probably never be easy, living in Colorado would certainly help.

***

When we reached the Oklahoma panhandle, I drove very slowly in the terrific winds. Tense from my shoulders being hunched over the steering wheel, I watched thousands of tumbleweeds blow across the prairie, hundreds crossing the road in front of us. The huge round balls of thistle—three or four feet across—bounced off the hood, crashed against the windshield, and got stuck on the car's front bumper. More than once, I pulled off the road to yank the prickly weeds off the radiator.

But I kept going.

We reached Garden City, Kansas, halfway to Denver, about one o'clock the same day. Soon after we arrived, Fremont stepped off the bus to meet us, and I practically jumped into his arms, I was so glad to see him.

Mama caught a bus back to Shawnee, shaking her head and claiming disaster would strike our family before a year was over. Fremont and I ignored her doomsday prophecies and decided to drive all night so we could arrive in Denver early Sunday.

Around three in the morning, both Fremont and I grew sleepy. We stopped for a nap, and a winter storm began to drop heavy blankets of snow. When we woke, the vehicle had become covered and was so cold it wouldn't start. We hadn't put in antifreeze because we couldn't afford it, so Fremont took off his coat and draped it over the radiator. The car warmed up, and we went on our way again.

This was my first trip north of Oklahoma, and I looked forward to seeing the Rocky Mountains. As the sun came up, I woke the children and together we *oohed* and *ahhed* at the rugged peaks looming in the distance.

As we got close to Denver, Fremont pulled into a gas station and spoke to the bundled-up attendant putting fuel in our car. I got out to stretch my legs and take the children to the toilet inside. Road-weary, I carried Carol while Judson and Margaret traipsed behind me. Fremont brought up the rear.

When we stepped into the gas station, warm air greeted us. "Have you heard about Pearl Harbor?" a man said as the door closed behind us. "The Japanese bombed the naval base in Hawaii."

I swung around and faced Fremont, and we looked at each other in disbelief.

Japan bombed the U.S.? We didn't have a radio in the car and had heard nothing.

We rushed over to where several people crowded around a wooden console radio sat in the corner.

A static-laden voice announced, "We interrupt this program to bring you a special news bulletin: The Japanese have attacked the U.S. naval base in Hawaii by air."

Pearl Harbor had been attacked!

This attack was major—catastrophic.

The room felt heavy with fear. Everyone stood with their mouths open, each person lost in his or her thoughts. How could this have happened? Would the U.S. enter the war? Would other American cities be bombed? Were we safe? Alarm etched a mark on my soul, a dark blot that marred our move.

We hurried back to our car, eager to get to Denver, but silent as the children slept.

We finally reached our new quarters, a quaint two-bedroom furnished rental with neighbors living in the basement. Throughout bed preparations, baths for everyone, and a quick meal, we remained solemn—even the children. Exhausted. Mute as mummies.

Was this the disaster Mama predicted?

***

The next morning after we unloaded the Chevrolet, we set up our Crosley radio to listen to the news report. "Japanese aircraft in two waves launched from six aircraft carriers. Four U.S. Navy battleships were sunk, and four others were damaged. The Japanese also sank or damaged three cruisers, three destroyers, an anti-aircraft training ship, and one minelayer. Many U.S. aircraft were destroyed, thousands killed and wounded."

I went through the day with my heart in my throat.

The next day, the United States declared war on Japan. I bought a special edition newspaper with a giant black headline: *Japanese bombers attack Pearl Harbor.*

I set up house, numb from the news. The small house was located in Arvada, a suburb of Denver, and Fremont had paid $37.50 for a month's rent.

The house had a large furnace, a lovely kitchen and breakfast patio, a dining room, a living room, two bedrooms, and a bath. No rugs or carpets lay on the floor even though the temperature was twenty-five degrees below zero and the snow was two feet deep outside. I made sure the children wore socks whenever they were out of bed.

News of war blasted from the front page of every paper Fremont brought home. All of America clamored for news. Mama called and said Harrell Mattox, a boy who graduated with Blanche had died at the Pearl Harbor attack. Our country had been divided about the war before the strike, and many had thought we should stay out of the controversy. No one objected to getting involved now. My heart stood as still as a sentry…waiting, wondering about the future. Would Fremont be drafted?

We discussed news of the war only after the children went to sleep. In a new place, far away from friends and family, they were already dealing with enough uncertainty.

The furnace was large, and fuel was limited. We started running short on coal, and I was afraid we'd run out completely before we could get an order delivered. Winter in Colorado was much colder than winter in Oklahoma, and the holiday season might delay deliveries.

Fremont calmed me down and worked out an arrangement with a friend. We had coal delivered the next day. As always, Fremont knew what to do in a crisis.

Chapter Fifty-Two

Fremont

Two harried weeks went by. Christmas of '41 would be our first holiday away from family, and Sibyl kept me as busy as one of Santa's elves.

I didn't want to get the children out in the freezing weather, so I drove into the Rocky Mountains through knee-deep snow by myself looking for a perfectly shaped spruce. I found a five-footer and tied it to the roof of the Chevy. When I got home, I lugged it into the house. Proud of my choice, I set it up in the dining room near the kitchen.

The children and Sibyl jumped in circles over the tree, then decorated it, and danced around it like little pixie dolls. That night Sibyl and I wrapped the few toys we'd purchased. Actually, she wrapped, and I watched her wrap.

On Christmas morning, the children, in as good of spirits as Sibyl and me, laughed and ran around like banshees. High pitched squeals of downright joy.

"Look, Mommy! I got a truck!" Judson drove it all around the apartment, up the table legs, across the back of the sofa, and over my feet. I'd never seen him so excited about a toy.

Margaret got a new Dick and Jane Reader and coloring book and crayons, which would keep her busy for hours. Carol received two rattles and a warm sweater.

Sibyl prepared a meal that would have made my mother proud. Roasted chicken and mashed potatoes along with her first try at a tart apple pie. I did a lot of bragging on the tasty pie, which meant I could finagle another piece.

Sibyl's mother had been flat wrong. Moving to Colorado had been the right call. Our life would be perfect once we settled into a routine, found a church home, and began meeting neighbors.

The day after Christmas as I was getting ready to leave for work, Sibyl reached into our cigar box, our savings, and pulled out the fifteen one-dollar bills tucked inside. She handed the money to me.

"You keep it here," I said, already bundled and ready to drive to the night job.

"I don't need it." Sibyl stuffed the money into my pocket. "Keep it in case you get stranded or, I don't know, have a flat tire. Besides, look at me. I'm expecting a baby in two months. I won't be going anywhere."

I kissed her good-bye.

I wish I had stayed home that night.

Sibyl

A few hours after going to bed, I jerked from sleep and sat up straight. My eyes popped open. Something was wrong.

Smoke! I smelled smoke.

My feet hit the cold, wooden floor. My worst fear.

"Margaret!" I yelled as I lumbered out of bed, my swollen belly making me slow. If only Fremont was here. He would know what to do.

I dashed through the living room toward the kitchen. Smoke billowed around me, and I ran to the children's bedroom. "Wake up!"

Margaret sat up rubbing her eyes. "Mommy, I smell something." She looked at me puzzled. "What's wrong?"

"Go get the baby! Now! There's a fire!" Carol slept in a crib in our bedroom.

I went to Judson's bed and shook him. Always a hard sleeper, he groaned and turned away from me. I pulled him to the side of the bed, and my heart pounded as I hurriedly put his coat on over his pajamas. He was so groggy he could barely help. I couldn't find either of the children's shoes or socks, but I couldn't waste time looking for them.

Heat and smoke crept toward us like a stalking predator.

Margaret rushed back from our bedroom carrying Carol wrapped in a blanket. The baby didn't whimper but looked around wide-eyed. I grabbed Carol and directed Margaret to put on her jacket.

We stepped back into the living room, and I snatched up my pocketbook. I looked to the left toward the kitchen. Reddish gold flames soared from the boiler that heated the building. The blaze lashed out in rage.

The decorated tree caught my attention. Christmas was only yesterday.

"I want my truck," pleaded Judson, pulling at my hand, but the front door was to the right.

"We have to get out!" I yelled over the crackling and hissing of the fire. "Hurry! Go toward the front door."

With sparks flying around her, Margaret hesitated. Frightened by the awful scene, she balked, stopped short. My heart pounded and I let go of Judson's hand and began leading them all toward the front door, looking over my shoulder to make sure they followed.

Then I saw Judson headed toward the Christmas tree, toward his toy truck. Instead of away from the blazing fire, he was stumbling toward it! All I could see was a silhouette of him against the blinding smoke.

"Margaret! Take Carol!" I thrust the child into Margaret's arms and ran to snatch the back of Judson's coat, pulling him toward me just before he would have disappeared into the blaze. I grabbed his shoulder as the Christmas tree burst into flames, and pushed him, along with Margaret and Carol, out to the snow-covered porch.

"Go over by that fence." I pointed. "Hurry. I have to wake up the Wilsons!"

"My truck!" cried Judson. "I want my truck!"

"Make sure Judson doesn't run off!" I threw the words back over my shoulder. Margaret, still holding Carol, was responsible enough to watch her brother.

Breathing heavily from the exertion, I wobbled around the house toward a back door, holding my belly.

I banged on the small windows of the basement and yelled, "Fire! Fire! You have to get out!" No one answered. I walked down the two narrow steps leading to the apartment entrance and twisted the door handle. It was locked. I could feel the scorch of heat on my bare feet and held up my nightgown. I took a deep breath and muttered, "Jesus, help us."

I banged again.

I was turning to leave when the door cracked open and our neighbor Raymond peeked through. "What's the commotion?"

"Fire! You have to get out!" I screamed.

The door opened wider, and Mary, carrying an infant, appeared behind her husband. Her mouth widened in shock as Raymond swept up a second child into his arms. The couple gathered coats by the door.

I turned around to go back up the narrows steps I'd just walked down. Flames engulfed the back of the house threatening to overtake me. I tried to run, but my gown bunched around my heavy body. Loose hair fell about my shoulders. Ice on the sidewalk sent a shock through my scorched feet.

As I flew back to the front steps, I heard a loud boom behind me. The kitchen and dining room floor collapsed into the basement.

My children. Where were my children?

I saw Margaret near the driveway holding Carol. She was shivering in the cold and almost blue, the baby's blanket a bright spot on the ground.

Judson. "Where's Judson?"

"He ran off, Mommy." Margaret cried, terror twisting her face.

"No!" I screamed. Would he dare return to the house for his toy? Why had I left them alone? I could not bear to lose another child. I spun in circles looking for signs of Judson.

"He went that way." Margaret pointed and started to walk toward the house in the direction indicated.

"Margaret, stay there! I'll find him." I ran off screaming, "Judson! Judson!"

Fremont

My last job of the night was to stack boxes of ammunition produced during the previous day. I always got home tired and sleepy, worried about feeding and clothing my family. Now, with another child on the way, my responsibility weighed even heavier.

The last hour of the work night always seemed the slowest, knowing I'd have to drive home eight miles without a heater in the car. Colorado winters were more intense than Oklahoma's, and with the wind, this could become the coldest night we'd ever experienced. I shivered uncontrollably.

I drove onto Maple Street just before seven o'clock a.m.

And stopped.

Firetrucks surrounded the building. Lights flashed. Busy firemen sprayed water with hoses. A fire? In our building?

I jumped out of the car. Where were my wife and kids?

I ran toward the house—black smoke billowed from windows. "Sibyl! Sibyl!" No, God, please, no. Don't let anything happen to Sibyl or the children. I dashed around the yard yelling at the firefighters, "Where's my wife? Where's my family?"

Chapter Fifty-Three

I rounded the corner of the house looking for Judson. He was standing alone, gazing at the flames. I grabbed him up in my arms. Tears streaked down our cheeks as we stood and watched the glaring inferno and golden embers blowing about, before running back to Margaret and Carol.

"My new truck," he whimpered. "My new truck."

There was a fire station across the street, and I hoped they would hurry to put out the fire, but the firemen merely stood, staring at the burning building, watching the flames. Why were they not helping?

As sirens screamed in the distance, I pulled the children to me. Their bodies shivered in the bitter cold. None of us wore shoes. I couldn't stand here in the cold and let the little ones freeze, but where could we go?

The Wilsons stood beside us, holding their babies, as forlorn as we were. Together, we watched as flames engulfed our homes and all our belongings.

The firetrucks from far away arrived and sprayed the cabin with water as we watched helplessly. They apologized for the station across the road. The firemen had been powerless, couldn't even bring us a cup of water. We were not in their territory.

"We can't stay here," said Mary Wilson. "My parents live down the street. Come with us." She motioned for me to follow. I had no other choice.

I shivered as we walked through the deep snow, my feet nearly frozen. I carried Carol and didn't want to think of the children's cold, bare feet, but they didn't complain.

Almost two blocks away and through an alley, we came to a house with a blue door. Mary banged on it several times before her father opened it slightly. When he saw his daughter, he swung the door open wide. "What in blazes is going on? What's wrong?"

"We had a fire," Mary said.

"Wilma! Wilma! Come quick!" The elderly man yelled to his wife as he took his grandbaby from Mary's arms. "Bring some blankets!"

I pushed Margaret and Judson into the house, handing Carol to Margaret. "I have to go back."

"You can't go back, dear," Wilma said as she came into the room bringing a load of blankets. "You're in no shape, and there's nothing you can do." She draped a coat over Margaret.

I rubbed my hands together and stepped into the warm kitchen. The kind lady wrapped a quilt around my shoulders before she stuffed my feet into house shoes.

"I need to call Fremont."

The older man took me to the hallway, where their black telephone sat on an end table. I dreaded giving this news to Fremont. It would be a massive blow. I dialed the number to the plant but no one answered.

"I'll go check on the house." Mary's father hurriedly put on an overcoat and hat.

"Would you put a note on the front door? Fremont won't know where we are."

I scribbled on a piece of paper Wilma handed me. "Come down Murray Street to the house with the blue door." Then I dropped into a chair and hugged my pregnant belly, waiting for Fremont to clock out and come home.

Fremont

The heat of the fire scorched my skin as I ran around the yard screaming. Then I turned, and there was Sibyl.

She came around the street corner, a red quilt around her shoulders, soot over her face, and her hair disheveled. She looked frantic, as if not sure what to do or where to go. Then she saw me and ran in my direction, a quilt flapping behind her. Relief flooded me like summer rain.

I ran toward her. Tears streaked down her face, and she grabbed my shirt.

"Sibyl!" I breathed her name into the air and pulled her to me in a bear hug, her belly squished between us. "Where are the children? Are they okay?"

"They're at the Wilsons' parents' house. I knew you'd be home soon, so I came to get you."

We stood holding onto one another before I asked. "You're sure? Everyone's safe?"

Sibyl's words stumbled out. "Yes. Yes. We're safe."

While we stood there, everyone left—the firetrucks, the neighbors, the gawkers. The silence felt uncanny, the dark, scorched building a shrine against the white snow. In the stillness and cold, Sibyl and I stood alone observing the wreckage of our lives.

Burned walls stood against the clear morning sky, the back half of the house almost gone, the roof caved in. Snow packed around the house looked as if a hundred people had stomped it down.

Still in shock, the quilt surrounded Sibyl like an Indian squaw, and her hair hung in straggles around her face. "What are we going to do?" she asked.

I pulled her close. "I don't know, honey. I don't know."

***

That day, after a hearty breakfast at the Wilsons', Sibyl and I left the kids and trucked over to the burned-out house to see if we could salvage anything. The area was icy from the firemen's attempt to put out the fire.

Inches of new snow covered the ground, more than we ever had in Oklahoma. Piles of soot and ash lay in patches under the white layer, but the front wall stood. How, I didn't know.

Sibyl stared at the disaster. "Why did this happen? Why?"

"That isn't the best question to ask. None of us know why."

"We almost lost Judson! What if I hadn't turned around and seen him in time? He could have died!"

"He didn't, Sibyl. We didn't lose what's most important." I put my hand on her back to calm her down. "We'll make it. You'll see. The Lord'll take care of us."

No one had been injured. All the items we had packed and hauled up to Colorado didn't matter as long as we were unharmed. We still had the fifteen dollars Sibyl had given me the day before and the car title Sibyl had tucked into her pocketbook.

Mother Pope must have been praying. The good Lord had known what would happen.

We donned gloves and sorted through the debris, starting in the kitchen.

Sibyl squealed when I found one of her new Wearever skillets from a set of pans, still useable. I walked through our destroyed bedrooms and found Margaret's socks frozen to the ground. Firemen had hosed down the house, and everything had turned to ice. None of the Christmas toys survived. The baby's cradle and family photos were ash. Not even my work clothes escaped the flames.

We didn't stay long. We took the few blackened items home and washed them, but the smoky smell did not go away. It would stay with us permanently.

Chapter Fifty-Four

We spent the next few days with the Wilsons, and then an anonymous person paid for a week at a hotel. We purchased a small supply of groceries, but payday was still days away, and no store would give a stranger credit.

I wanted to cry, and I feared I'd go into labor from the stress.

I held my tears in check until the landlord came by and accused us of putting too much coal in the furnace. That was when I bawled. I was relieved when we found out it had been an electrical fire and we were not to blame.

The Red Cross brought food supplies and a large box of clothing. A godsend to be sure, even though I don't know how they found us. From the bottom of the box, Judson pulled out a suede Davey Crocket jacket with cowboy fringe along the edges. Matching boots lay beside it, with a slit to put a knife in. He plopped an aviator cap with flaps on his head and pranced around like a proud frontiersman, the happiest of any of us. He never asked for his truck again.

Fremont was constant. I was a mess.

I dreaded calling my mama, but I had to.

Before I could say anything, Mama asked, "What's wrong? What happened?"

"You won't believe it."

"Sibyl, don't beat around the bush. Just tell me."

"We had a fire—"

"I knew it. I knew this move to Colorado was a bad idea. You should never have gone. You need to come back to Oklahoma this instant." I listened to her scolding. I didn't know how my mother could irritate me so much when she was a thousand miles away. When she took a breath, I interrupted.

"Everyone is all right." Not that she'd asked. "God protected us. I know he was watching over us."

"God, petunia," Mama spat. "You were just lucky, that's all. You might not be so lucky next time, and you're so far away from home. You need to move back."

Was Mama right? Had this move been the Lord's will? Had we moved to Colorado to prove something or had we followed our path instead of his? Doubts gnawed at me. Did God lead us here?

Fremont

I paced the small hotel room where Sibyl and I and the children were crammed. Much had happened within the last month. We were exhausted.

Not that I didn't want a new tyke in the family—I did—but a baby couldn't have been due at a more inconvenient time.

Carol sat in front of Sibyl on the floor, a washcloth tied around her neck like a bib. Her bibs had been torched in the fire along with every stitch of clothing the children owned.

Sibyl made no effort to hide her disappointment. She waved the baby spoon back and forth through the air. "It feels like this is the end of everything. Our dreams, just like our possessions, are a pile of ashes."

I slumped against the wall, wishing I had more encouragement to offer my wife. My initial shock from the fire had given way to worry about survival. I rested my forehead in my hand, covering my eyes. Life had thrown a grenade in our midst, and we were reeling in the aftermath of the explosion. I looked at Margaret and Judson sitting quietly in a corner, taking in every word Sibyl and I spoke and absorbing our despair. Then I looked at Sibyl. And baby Carol. And at Margaret and Judson again. They were healthy. They were whole. They were alive. Like he'd delivered Shadrach, Meshack, and Abednego in the Bible, the Lord had delivered my family from a flaming pit.

We would not be defeated.

The tiny room confined me as I paced two steps forward and two steps back, contemplating how I'd tell Sibyl what I'd decided. On the tenth time around, I turned toward the spot where she was still sitting on the floor. I stood erect—towering over her—and crossed my arms over my chest. "We can't tuck our tails between our legs and skulk back into Oklahoma," I announced.

Sibyl opened her mouth, but before she could speak, I jumped in. "I've found a new apartment and—"

"We *can't* stay here!" she shouted. "In case you haven't noticed, we have nothing to put in a new apartment. We'll have to start from scratch. Purchase toiletries and pots and pans." Still holding the baby spoon, she used it to emphasize each item as she continued her list. "Sheets, pillows, towels, not to mention clothing—shoes and coats and gloves and…" Her hand dropped to her side.

I was trying to control my temper, but my voice rose. "We *can* do it. A little at a time, and we'll have help. The fellows at work said they'd pitch in." I held out my hands, pleading. "My mother always said home is where the heart is. With hard work and a little help, our home *can* be here."

Sibyl's face twisted into a scowl. "And what will we eat in the meantime? We can hardly afford baby food."

I stared at my wife, seeing fear behind her fierce determination. "Is this what you want, Sibyl?" I asked softly. "To give up on our dreams?"

Tears spilled over the rims of her eyes. "I don't know what I want," she said, swiping at the tears with the heels of her palms. "Maybe Mama's right. Maybe the timing is all wrong. We can come back to Colorado later, After the baby's born—after we get our lives together."

I motioned for Margaret to take the spoon away from Sibyl and feed Carol. When she did, I took Sibyl's hand and pulled her up to face me. "I'm not going back to Oklahoma," I said as gently as I could. I'd promised

273

long ago to take care of her, and I could do that better in Colorado than in Shawnee.

She jerked her head up, and her eyes met mine. "What do you mean, you're not going back?"

"I'm staying here. I'm not going back to Shawnee. You and the kids can go back if you like and stay with your mama, but I'm not leaving." I saw the alarm in Sibyl's wide-open eyes, but I stuck to my decision. "God led us here and I have a good job. I can send money back to you."

Her eyes narrowed into something closer to rage than anger. She pushed herself away from me. "You would abandon us to stay in Colorado? You would send us back home without you?"

I knew shouts from me would only escalate the situation, so I called on all my resolve to keep my voice steady. "Don't you remember our discussions? How we believed God would show us the way? Sibyl, what are you afraid of?" I lowered my voice and repeated. "What are you afraid of?"

Sibyl stood rigid as a flagpole, her arms at her sides and her hands balled into fists. Her chest rose and fell with long breaths, and then she melted into my arms. "I'm not sure God led us to Colorado." She sobbed as tears flowed down her cheeks. "I was at first, but was this his plan? For us to lose everything in a fire—even my Bible? Maybe this is his way of telling us we were supposed to stay in Oklahoma."

"Or maybe," I said, stroking her hair, "this is his way of seeing how willing we are to trust him and follow his will. Remember how we were certain God wanted us to move? Don't doubt him now."

As I held Sibyl against me, I felt our baby kick inside her and became aware of the children clinging to my leg. The enormity of my responsibility to care for, provide love, and protect this precious clan of people hit me with such force I almost crumbled to my knees.

This was no time to lean on my own understanding or rely on my own strength. Conversation with God was essential. As I prayed, I remembered how he'd brought us through poverty, the loss of a child, family strife, sickness, and now fire. I could depend on him to bring us through this current storm.

Chapter Fifty-Five

Sibyl

Mother Pope heard the news of the fire from Mama. She called, and I blubbered about losing everything, even the Bible I'd carried since my teen years.

"I'm so sorry about the fire, dear, and so glad everyone got out okay. We'll be praying for you. Dad sends his love."

My soul warmed after being cold for days, and I hardly heard her next words.

She explained that the WMU class wanted to help. They were furiously knitting gloves and scarves and would be sending a care package. Mother's friend, Mrs. Stapp, was sending baby bottles. Effie would send baby clothes, and Anna would send linens and tea towels. Knowing how cold it was in Colorado, she would also send jackets.

I cried at the news. Here I was, the one who always wanted to help others, now needing help myself. I felt humbled.

Fremont smiled when I told him about the coming supplies. We sat shoulder to shoulder on the hotel's deck steps, watching the children play in the snow, gazing at the majestic mountains in the distance. "Look at how God has helped us through the years," he said. "Remember when Margaret and Judson got sick at the same time? They're running around like jackrabbits now, aren't they? And Carol, healed from diphtheria when she was just a tiny tot."

275

I looked at him as if he were proclaiming good news from the mountain top. Perhaps he was.

He continued to recount the times God had protected and cared for us. "And we didn't have to spend the night in the cemetery that one night, did we?" He chuckled. "Although we came mighty close. And Margaret recovered quickly after that man-o-war attack. The Coast Guard fellow being there at just the right time was no coincidence."

"And the storm," I added. "We avoided that hurricane in the nick of time."

"And God saved us from the fire."

We both shook our heads in amazement, recalling the many incidents where God had brought us through. Nothing less than miracles.

For a while, we sat still, listening to the call of hawks and mountain jays.

Fremont broke the quiet. "Remember my promise?"

I tilted my head. "What promise?"

"I always said I said I'd protect you and take care of you. Take you anywhere in the world where we'd be safe. Well, here we are. On a great big adventure—following our hearts—and following God's plan."

The first package we received had a return address of Mrs. Eva Pope, Shawnee, Oklahoma. I opened it and touched the worn cover of Mother Pope's Bible. Sweet memories floated through the fragile pages as I thumbed through it. Memories of her waking in the morning and reading the word, of her quoting the underlined passages. A note fell out with Mother's handwriting on it: *Dear, you can withstand anything with the Lord's help. Send this back when you get a new one.*

I bawled.

Fremont had been right. For now, God wanted us in Colorado. We'd be fine.

***

Fremont got his paycheck, and we hunted for an affordable place to live. We toured a nice apartment in Golden, a small town at the foot of the Rockies. The apartment was one of four in a huge two-story house that had been remodeled into rental space. We paid a month's rent of thirty-eight dollars for a downstairs two-bedroom unit. Located on the highway going toward Look Out Mountain—where Buffalo Bill Cody was buried—it was nicer than any place we'd ever lived and had more room than our Shawnee house.

I loved the area immediately, and Fremont did, too. "Chuck Mills and his family live in a little house behind ours. We'll have good neighbors."

"We need to find a church here." I thought it important to find one as soon as possible.

"But where? I haven't seen many churches for miles around."

"There's that big, monster church downtown just off Main Street. I imagine they believe pretty much the same as we do."

The Sunday morning after we moved into the apartment, I was readying the children for church when Fremont came bustling in from his night job, a gust of wind in his wake. He'd been up all night, but I begged him to stay awake a while longer and go with us. We walked to the church on Twelfth and Jackson Streets, to attend the services.

After the pastor preached, he led a long prayer to remember the families of the men lost at Pearl Harbor, brave men, family men, good men. Then the congregation sang *Standing on the Promises*. God's promises. The hymn—one I'd sung many times in Shawnee—comforted me and made me feel welcomed. God had made us many promises, and we could depend upon them because he never failed. I recalled Nahum 1:7. *The Lord is good, a stronghold in the day of trouble, and he knoweth them that trust in him.*

I had a choice. I did not want to become hardened like my mother, unable to trust and bitter at the world. I wanted to love others without being held back by pain. I wanted to trust God's promises.

The words to the last hymn, *Let Me Hide Myself in Thee*, were equally comforting. How many times had I stood with a church choir, wearing a similar robe, and sung that special song myself? The words meant so much more now than they ever had in the past.

***

Mama refused to send our leather trunk, claiming it would cost too much, claiming it would be a waste because we'd be moving back to Shawnee soon.

A week later, a knock came, and I opened the front door. "Mrs. Pope?" I noticed a delivery truck parked in front of our building.

And then I saw a steamer trunk sitting on the porch—the one Fremont's parents had given us as a wedding present. The seemingly bottomless one that held so many secrets. My hand flew to my mouth.

Mama didn't want to send it, yet here it was.

Fremont dragged the heavy box into the living room.

I loosened the brass clasps cautiously, as if all my past experiences and emotions would escape like a genie from a bottle.

A note lay on top of the contents: *Dear Sibyl, although I disagree with your decision to stay in Colorado, I have to admit you are brave to follow your heart. Please call me when your baby is born. I'll come if I can. Love, Mama.*

Our belongings lay inside: children's clothes, shoes, and keepsakes. Thank goodness, after the baby's birth, I would have something to wear. I shuffled through layers of clothing to find Keith's cup. Hugging it to my chest, I closed my eyes. A memento of our baby's life had come to Colorado.

Fremont knelt beside me, and I handed the cup to him. As he grasped it in both hands, tears filled his eyes.

I continued to unpack the trunk and reflect on the woman who'd sent it.

Mama had been wrong many times. I understood Papa had hurt her deeply, but she was wrong to hold onto her hate and not forgive him. She was wrong to criticize our choice to have a large family. Margaret, Judson, and Carol had brought life and love and happiness into our lives. This new baby, soon to be born, would be no different. He'd bring us immeasurable delight.

Mama was also wrong to resent our work in the church. She was wrong about our move to Colorado, wrong about many decisions she made regarding my sisters. She'd been wrong about so many things, but I loved her dearly and prayed for her nightly. I would no longer let her bitterness cloud my life.

The next day, I went to a neighbor's house to use their phone and called her. "Mama, it's me."

"Is everything okay?" Worry laced her words. We seldom made phone calls except in emergencies.

"Thank you for sending the trunk. It means a lot."

"Can't leave you up there with nothing, now can I? And remember to call me when the baby comes. Take care of yourself and the kids." Mother didn't speak outright proclamations of love, but small shreds of evidence revealed God working in her life, and that brought me gladness.

I reflected on my journey. The fire brought a new focus to spiritual matters, and trials taught me to lean more on the Lord. In the past, I'd listened to so many voices instead of God's, not always trusting him to direct my steps. Now, I could look back and see how God had protected me and my family, how he always provided what we needed, and how he prepared us, leading us on the right path at the right time. I could trust Him to lead us in the future.

Before Fremont left for work that evening, I walked with him to the porch steps of our new apartment. We stood silently for a moment admiring the majestic Colorado mountains in the distance. I reached for his hand and drew him toward me. As he leaned down to kiss me, his promise to take care of me, to protect me, and to work to pursue God's plan for our lives filled me with hope.

He threw his head back and looked into my eyes. We smiled at one another, a smile full of peace and love and joy—and promises kept.

That was what we smiled about.

Author's Notes

Margaret Akin Pope is the inspiration behind this book. She not only had the vision, but she holds all the memories. I have never known a godlier and more brilliant woman.

Certain people's names have been changed to protect them.

I interviewed many family members and friends and incorporated known wedding dates, births, and deaths, in an attempt to stick to confirmed facts. Most of the information is taken from family history. For years, I sat on the floor and heard my relatives tell stories of the cement barrels in Earlsboro, camping on Mr. Pope's land, and getting stuck in the muddy ruts on Tennessee. They would laugh together, embellishing tales along the way.

Sibyl Trimble Pope taught Women's Missionary Union for years, as did her mother-in-law, Eva Pope. Her assistance to the black community was documented a few years after this time period in a newspaper article. The Pope family was a steady, spiritual influence in Sibyl's life.

As indicated in Malcolm Trimble's convoluted book, *Our Awakening Social Conscience-The Emerging Kingdom of God,* he believed in a future universal utopia. His words were taken from that book. The legal battles involving him were based on articles and legal documents collected, which I condensed. The stack of papers is thick, and I probably haven't found them all. I found a picture of Malcolm's father in front of his grocery store in Texas, *W. S. Trimble Groceries.*

Mable Bennett Trimble was actually loved by her family even though her bitterness about the divorce was evident. And although she never fully recovered, the Lord softened her spirit.

Mable with her daughter Blanche Trimble wrote *Nothing but the Truth, Autobiography of Mable Trimble,* and self-published it in 1982. Much information is taken from their book. Blanche also left numerous writings. When I went through Blanche's house after she passed away, I found over 125 awesome drawings and paintings tucked into various nooks and crannies. She worked for the NYA for a while, and had quite a colorful, if ill-mannered, character. To learn more about her life, see www.blanchtrimble.wordpress.com.

The 1939 Shawnee graduation yearbook information was correct, Blanche and Irene's class standing easily verifiable. Sammy's story is true according to family lore although his name has been lost.

The Douglas family stayed good friends with the Popes throughout their lifetime. Doug and Fremont were friends as single men before marrying, while Effie and Sibyl became best friends afterward. Many of the Douglas' family remain in the Shawnee area.

The information about Keith is based on facts. Margaret still has the Skippy cup and other items Sibyl kept. The button-up baby shoes worn by all the children have been bronzed. The family once got locked in the Fairview Cemetery where Fremont often grieved in front of Keith's grave. The story Mrs. Pope told about Keith and the Billy goat was true, as were most all the other anecdotes in this book.

The Galveston vacations actually happened, not every word spoken of course, but the essence of the trips as told by Margaret, her scars from the man-o-war sting still visible.

Frances Trimble, three days older than the astronaut Gordon Cooper, attended Jefferson Elementary the same time he did. The dancing lessons from Mrs. Tapp and the performance stories are from her.

Information about George Orlando Bennett and other relatives were taken from obituaries, family stories, notes, and genealogy sites.

Marjorie and Ed Wynns married on December 10, 1941, three days after Pearl Harbor was bombed but I moved the date up for this story. They moved to a base in Florida soon afterward.

Fremont Pope's job description in Colorado is as accurate as possible, and he clearly described viewing the '37 and the '41 car accidents, the details remembered many years later. Newspaper articles confirmed the wrecks, although the dates have been changed.

Sibyl's move to Colorado took place on December 7, 1941, Pearl Harbor Day, an unusual coincidence. I'm not sure how they reacted when they heard about it, but she met Fremont halfway and they were traveling the day the tragedy happened. The fire where the Pope's almost lost their son occurred a few weeks after Christmas, a definite crisis in their lives.

May your faith be as strong as Sibyl and Fremont's.

You are loved,
Kathryn Spurgeon

Other Sources of Information

Public Documents

Calvary Baptist Church Minutes, Shawnee, Oklahoma
Pottawatomie County Historical Society, Shawnee, Oklahoma City,
Shawnee News Star, Microfiche Newspapers from 1932-1935
Shawnee Public Library archives

Books

- Calvary Baptist Church, *60th Anniversary Celebration*, 1920-1980, published by Calvary Baptist Church, S. Market and Farrall, Shawnee, Oklahoma, 1980
- Chronicles of Oklahoma. *Fifty Years Ago in Shawnee and Pottawatomie County* by Ernestine Gravley.
- Gaskin, J.M., *Baptist Women in Oklahoma*, Messenger Press 1985
- *Shawnee, 1895-1930*, Forgotten Hub of Central Oklahoma, reprinted by permission for the Historical Society of Pottawatomie County.
- Trimble, Mabel and Blanche, *Nothing But the Truth*, Autobiography of Mabel Bennett Trimble, Self-published 1982.
- Trimble, Malcome C. Sr., *Our Awakening Social Conscience-The Emerging Kingdom of God*, Vantage Press, 1958.
- Yarbrough, Slayden, The Lengthening Shadow: A centennial history, heritage and hope of the First Baptist Church, Shawnee, *Oklahoma 1892 – 1992*, published by First Baptist Church, Shawnee, Oklahoma, 1992

Thank you!

A good book is not written without help from many, many people. Editors and reviewers are invaluable assets to any author. Special thanks to Robin Patchen, DeeDee Chumley. Kellie Stanley, Jenna Kattrick, and Ben Williams. They are the best.

Thank you to Ken Landry with the Pottawatomie County Museum, Shawnee, who had several important observations. For example, at the time of this book, Sears was located on Main Street where the public library is now, and The Hamburger King was at 412 East Main until they moved following a fire to 322 East Main.

Thank you to historians Ann McDonald, and Mary Ruth Hatley Sadler. You are amazing.

And thanks to the many others who gave advise, opinions, and encouraged me, especially members of our home church, Henderson Hills Baptist Church, and the many friends and readers who inspired me to finish. Without you, I might never have completed this book.

Especial thanks to my mother, Margaret Pope Akin, the great storyteller of years gone by. Her detailed memory amazes me, while the love of my family motivates me.

It has been an honor to write my grandparents story and share their faith. I hope I did the tale justice. God bless you all.

The Promise Series Books
by Kathryn Spurgeon

A Promise to Break
A Promise Child
Fremont's Promise
A Promise of Home

Reviews

I'd love to hear from you! You can contact me on Facebook, Goodreads, Pinterest, or my website. It would mean a lot to hear your feedback. If you liked this book, I would appreciate an honest review on the following sites:

<u>Amazon</u>
<u>Bookbubs</u>
<u>Goodreads</u>
<u>www.kathrynspurgeon.com</u>

A Promise to Break
Faith, Loss and Hope
in the 1930s

Book 1

Kathryn Spurgeon
with Margaret Pope Akin

Sibyl Trimble promises her father to be part of a socialist political movement to change the world. From a wealthy banking family in Shawnee, Oklahoma, she is comfortable with fashionable clothes, cruising in a new Chrysler, and dancing at the local speakeasy. Even the Depression cannot put a damper on her comfortable lifestyle. By 1932, the timing to fulfill the promise to her father seems right.

When she meets **Fremont Pope**, a handsome, blue-eyed, down-on-his-luck hobo, her life is turned upside down. The more she gets to know him, the more she learns about her world, her purpose, and God. Her love for him opens her eyes to a different way of life than she has ever known.

Based on a true story, this novel follows Sibyl through difficult choices. She must dig deep within herself to find the strength to face her upbringing and determine which, if any, of her past beliefs can be salvaged. She must decide which is most important, love or duty.

https://kathrynspurgeon.com/book/a-promise-to-break-2/

The Promise Child
Faith, Loss and Hope in the 1930s

Book 2

Kathryn Spurgeon
with Margaret Pope Akin

Sibyl Trimble, a young wealthy woman, gives up everything to marry a poor man. She worries about her destitute mother and siblings. With two children of her own, she struggles to keep food on her table, and love alive in her heart —for her family, her husband, and for God. She does her best to listen to God, even in the bleakest times when her father advises her to quit.

Fremont Pope comes from the wrong side of town. As the Depression rips through his hometown of Shawnee, Oklahoma, it leaves dying stores, repossessed farms, and countless men and women out of work.

Based on a true story, Sibyl and Fremont want to make the world a better place. Changes come—a new baby, a new job with the PWA, and a promise of a bright future. Will that be enough?

Many people have already headed west to save their families. Will Sibyl and Fremont abandon Oklahoma and their hopes and dreams, for the promises in California? Or will they find a way to make it work in Shawnee?

https://kathrynspurgeon.com/book/a-promise-child-2/

The Promise of Home
A WW2 Drama

Book 4

Kathryn Spurgeon
With Margaret Pope Akin

With WW2 brewing, **Fremont Pope** finds a job working at an ammunitions plant in Colorado. **Sibyl** looks forward to leaving her hometown. She's taught ladies for years and yearns to share her knowledge of God's word.

Fremont, while a deacon in Oklahoma, taught young men. Now most of those fellows have left for the war. Will any of them return?

When the large Colorado church they attend has no need of their benevolent services, they are devastated. Should they leave Colorado?

Maybe they should return to Oklahoma. Or look for a different city or state where they might be useful.

Mother Pope wants them to move back home while Fremont's boss offers a promotion to stay.

Where is God leading them? Will it take another disaster for them to find their way?

www.ingramcontent.com/pod-product-compliance
Lightning Source LLC
Chambersburg PA
CBHW052029240626
47153CB00006B/2017